HATTRICK

# HAT TRICK

S.R. CLARK

TILLY RIDGE

# *COPYRIGHT*



ISBN: 979-8-9907261-6-1

Edited by Sadie with Dot The I Edit

Book Cover and Formatting Images by S.R. Clark Designs

Formatting by Tilly Ridge

First edition 2025

# CONTENTS

# AUTHORS NOTE

Welcome to the world of Palm University! It is a fictional college based in Pensacola, Florida. We hope you enjoy The Palm University Panthers. And if you're coming here from either of our previous books, be warned, this is a full-on rom-com.

This book was written after the name, image, and likeness (NIL) rule for the NCAA was put into place. It does vary state by state, but for the fictional purposes of this story, Palm University in Florida participates in NIL for its collegiate players.

# CONTENT WARNINGS

Alcohol use

Sex while under the influence of alcohol

Mentions of parent death (off page)

Characters being scared of commitment

Side character talks of unplanned pregnancy, a horrific
baby daddy/sperm donor, and single motherhood.
There is also mention of postpartum and healing from
an emergency c-section of the side character.

Bondage

Degradation

Praise

Double vaginal penetration

Anal

Use of toys

Cum clean up

Physical violence (the two main male characters)

Anxiety attack

Pregnancy in Extended Epilogue

# DEDICATION

*For the women who are learning to embrace their softness while remaining strong, who love themselves as much as they love others, and who will stand tall and kick down anything in their way while still being afraid… this one's for you.*
*Be strong. Be courageous. Be resilient.*
*And for being such a good girl… here's a hockey player sandwich.*

-S.R. Clark

*For the ones that went right into your "adult job" while everyone else was having fun in college…*

*I hope you can see a little of yourself in Liliana.*

-Tilly Ridge

# PLAYLIST

As you read, you will find footnotes throughout the book. The footnotes will indicate which song is playing at the time of specific scenes. You can play the song until the next footnote indicates a song change or until the chapter ends. The playlist is linked below.

Jawbreaker - mgk
Right Now - PARTYNEXTDOOR
Bottled Up - Daniel Di Angelo
Like What (Freestyle) - Cardi B
Back to Back (feat. Future, Southside) - Nardo Wick, Future, Southside
Let Me Clear My Throat (Live) - DJ Kool
Animals - Nickelback
If I Ain't Got You - Alicia Keys
Lovesucker - Haiden Henderson

Friends- Chase Atlantic

Forbidden Fruit (feat. Kendrick Lamar) - J. Cole, Kendrick Lamar

Pink Pony Club - Chappel Roan

THE WITHDRAWALS - Kae

Salt Shaker - Ying Yang Twins

fake love don't last (feat. iann dior) - mgk, iann dior

Gimme More-Britney Spears

New Rules - Dua Lipa

So What - P!nk

Build Me Up Buttercup - The Foundations

Kerosene - Miranda Lambert

Holy Smokes - Bailey Zimmerman

Kiss Land - The Weeknd

305 - Jordan Adetunji, Bryson Tiller

Cannibal - Ke$ha

New To Country - Bailey Zimmerman

Iris - MGK and Julia Wolf

Muse - Isabel LaRosa

WHY - Jon Bellion & Luke Combs

REACTION - Xavier Mayne

Tidal Wave - Chase Atlantic

Glass House - Sad Version - mgk, Naomi Wild

Nothing Without You - The Weeknd

Gunpowder & Lead - Miranda Lambert

Kerosene - Vanish

No Friendship - Daniel Di Angelo

# CHAPTER 1
# LABIA WALL

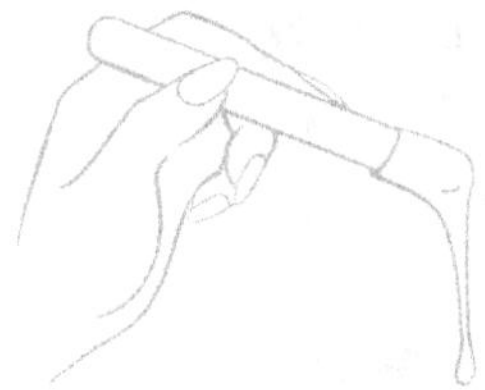

**LILIANA**

"Clay… a private boat to a private island is a little extreme, don't you think?" I'm holding my phone to my ear with my shoulder while I finish folding my towels as my future brother-in-law huffs and puffs on the other end. "You know Rocky gets motion sickness. Plus, don't even get me started on how he would react to you spending money on something so ostentatious." I don't mention the fact that I still consider it a miracle that Rocky is even letting a tropical wedding in Turks and Caicos slide. But, we all know he'd do just about anything for Clay.

"Fine," Clay huffs dramatically.

"You two keep this up and you'll be getting a therapy invoice from me," I mock in a serious tone.

"Send them." I can hear his smirk through the phone. "Oh yeah, before I forget, who do you want to bring as your plus one?"

"I've told you both over and over, I don't need a plus one. Between it being a destination wedding and my maid-of-honor duties, I am not going to have the time to entertain anyone besides you two bridezillas." As true as that might be, it also may be because Emerson Baker will be there with the rest of the crew since his older brother Jackson, is Clay's best man. And let's just say, Emerson and I are… *familiar.*

*Who couldn't use a good fuck buddy on vacation?*

"OH! What about one of the twins?!"

"You cannot be serious. Are the twins even of age, Clay?"

"Yes! They're eighteen! You could rein in that cougar title." The line goes silent for a moment. "I'm winking. You just can't see it."

"Okay, that's enough out of you today." I may be Rocky's maid-of-honor, but I swear Clay calls me more than he does Jackson. But I love him nonetheless. However, I can wholeheartedly say I *never* want to do this shit again—not even for my own wedding.

*If I ever decide to get married, the courthouse better watch out.*

[1] After saying my goodbyes to Clay, but not before I assure him I will arrive in Turks and Caicos on time on Thursday as planned, I hurry through wiping down my suite for my end-of-shift deep clean. I am beyond ready for this day to end and for my vacation to begin. But as fast as I'm going, I still make sure to sanitize all of my facial tools, the table, and every other surface my clients

---

1. Jawbreaker - mgk

may have touched. I may only rent this suite but it's still my pride and joy. I've been an esthetician here in Pensacola for about a year and a half, and the space is finally starting to feel like mine. I painted the walls a deep forest green and hung funky gold decor wherever I could. Last week, I was able to install a light fixture I've had my eye on for months. But what truly makes it mine is the labia wall.

*Yes. Labia wall.*

A fellow local small business owner makes custom wall stickers. And since one of my main services is body waxing, I reached out to her to see if she could make it for me. My god, did she fucking deliver. I'm entirely obsessed with it. The main concern I find vagina owners have in common is their worry that theirs is "weird looking."

*These are their words, not mine.*

So, I just point to the wall and explain that they are all different. That I've never seen the same shape or size on two different people. And, whatever theirs may look like is completely normal.

All my clients love it. If anything, it never fails to make them laugh… even the men.

I smile to myself as I move about my suite. And I can't help but think, just like I do every other day—I have the chance to work with my clients—that I'm so grateful that I'm here.

Rocky, my older brother, convinced me to move to Pensacola once he and Clay finally made it official. I was working at a dead-end body waxing chain back home and was utterly miserable. Once Rocky put the idea in my head, it continued to fester. Then, Clay moved into Rocky's apartment, which just so happens to be above Clay's favorite artisanal bakery supply shop —whatever that is—meaning Clay's fancy apartment on the other side of town was empty. Instead of renting it out to a random person, he was all too eager to offer it to me as a rental. So, I pulled the trigger and moved in. Then I found this rental suite to run my esthetician business, and the rest is history.

They had every friend of theirs book any and every service they could. For months, the entirety of the men's volleyball team had the best-looking skin on campus. Now, a good amount of the school's athletes come to see me, and most have stuck with me as loyal clients. I will forever be thankful that I made the move and will always be in debt to my brother and future brother-in-law.

Not only is my business thriving, but I'm slowly living out the college years I never got the chance to have, without having to be in college. All of their friends have been so welcoming—especially Emerson.

And with Emerson comes Dominic. They're best friends, and I wanted nothing more than to stay away from their friendship, but before I knew it, I was fucking around with both of them. All three of us see different people. I'm fine with it, and I know they're fine with it. As long as everyone is being safe, it's not an issue for me. We don't talk about our other relation-ships. Period. End of discussion. But… the part I find myself wrestling with often is that they know one another, yet neither one of them knows the other knows me.

As guilty as I feel about it sometimes, I've never been able to own up to it.

I'm having fun, and nobody is getting hurt.

For the first time in as long as I can remember, my life feels exactly how I want it to.

I don't want anything to come between that.

# CHAPTER 2
# PROMISES, PROMISES

## EMERSON

"Ready?" I ask Dom.

Standing from the locker room bench, he grabs his duffle and throws it over his shoulder. "Ready, Freddy."

[1] Smiling, I shake my head as the two of us walk out of the locker room because no matter how many times I've told him it's lame as fuck for him to use the term "ready, Freddy," I hear him say it at least once a day. That, along with at least a dozen other terms I also frequently hear come out of my fifty-year-old father's mouth. As a matter of fact, Dominic Foster and Dawson Baker like to act like they're best friends forever whenever they're around one another. My dad is obsessed with the man, not that I can blame him. Dom has that effect on people. The best way I can describe his person-

---

1.  Right Now - PARTYNEXTDOOR

is like an overly excited five-year-old at his first monster truck show, mixed with the love and affection you'd get from a golden retriever, mixed with a man who has the protective instincts of Jack Reacher.

Dominic Foster doesn't have a mean bone in his body, but he will not hesitate to put someone's head through a wall if they fuck with the people he cares about.

I'm not even exaggerating. I've seen him do it.

"Ahh fuck," Dom groans as he sidesteps a little while we're walking down the hallway.

"You good?"

"Yeah, it's just my hip. It's been bugging me since our game on Tuesday. And that last full spread I did during practice might have been a little overboard." Dominic is our team's starting goalie. At six-foot-six and a whopping 258 pounds of pure muscle, the man is built like a brick shithouse, but his flexibility compares to some of the girls I've seen on the gymnastics team. But, that comes with the job. As a goalie, not only does he need to take up space, but he's got to be quick on his feet. He's got to know where the puck is heading before the other team's forwards even do. And when he doesn't, he needs to be able to react in a way that'll stop the puck. And unfortunately for his hips, that sometimes means full splits.

Every time he's in pain, I can't help but feel guilty. Because if I did my job better as a defenseman, Dom wouldn't have to push himself so hard... and so far. "You wanna stop by and see the trainer before we head out?"

He shakes his head. "Nah, I'm good. Nothing I haven't dealt with before. Just needs a little extra rest over the weekend." Dom pushes open the double doors to the parking lot as he side-eyes me with a mischievous smirk on his face. "You could get down there and kiss it all better if you'd like, though."

I raise a brow. "You expect me to get down on my knees in the middle of a school parking lot?" Dom shrugs, and I snort a laugh. Once we reach his Bronco, he opens the back door and throws his duffle inside. My house is just a couple of blocks away, so I usually walk to campus, but Dom lives in an apartment further from school, so he normally drives. After Jackson married Theo and moved out, Dominic and I briefly threw around the idea of him moving into my house since I—well, my parents actually, but that's neither here nor there—own it. But decided that, because of our current situation, it's best we keep that part of our lives separate.

Oh yeah, in case you didn't pick up on it yet, Dominic and I are best friends, but we also fuck. Frequently. Now, before you get too excited, that's all it is. Just fucking. Neither he nor I are in a spot where we're looking for a serious relationship. And we are both perfectly content with the way things are. So content, that each of us also sees different people. The only rule is we don't discuss our other partners with one another, and we don't hide the fact that we're seeing other people from each other... or the other people.

*Oh, and practice safe sex, because we're not animals.*

Dom looks at the ground in front of his feet, then back up to me, wiggling his brows playfully. "I'll tell you what, when I get back on Monday, on the floor in front of you is the first place I'll be."

He sighs so heavily, I swear people across campus could probably hear it. "Ugh. I forgot you were going to be gone all weekend."

"Jealous?" I ask with a wide smile.

"You know I'm jealous, asshole. It's fucking Turks and Caicos." My older brother Jackson's best friend Clay is getting married this weekend. It's a relatively small wedding, but because Jax is Clay's best man and we're like a second family for Clay, the entire Baker family was invited. It's safe to say, I am beyond excited to spend a weekend on a tropical island sipping Coronas with lime.

Not to mention the raven-haired beauty I'm going to get to sneak away with all weekend.

I feel like I should mention… the other person I'm seeing… Well, it's Liliana Campos. Clay's soon-to-be sister-in-law. Younger sister of Rockwell Campos. When I tell you this woman keeps me on my fucking toes, I mean it. I genuinely mean it when I say that just thinking about her too long gets me fucking hard.

Fuck, focus Emerson.

"Why don't you go out with your other friend this weekend?"

Dom rolls his eyes. "She's going to be gone all weekend too, apparently. I guess I'll actually have to rest for real this time. You all suck."

I can't help but laugh at his petulant pouting. Fisting

the front of his shirt I pull him to me, bringing his face close enough to mine that my lips ghost his. "I'll make it up to you, I promise."

His signature beaming smile resumes its usual place, and his deep brown eyes twinkle. "I'm gonna hold you to it."

I quickly kiss him, not wanting to get too caught up in something we can't finish. Because, as much as I hate to admit it, that's the effect he has on me. Slowly, I walk backward in the direction of my house. "Counting on it," I reply with a wink.

Dom pulls his bottom lip between his teeth before shaking his head and climbing into his Bronco. I can hear his groan of pain over the sound of the engine, so I yell, "Ice and ibuprofen!"

Rolling down his window, he sticks out his middle finger, and I laugh as he peels out of the parking lot.

# CHAPTER 3
# CHA CHA SLIDE, ANYONE?

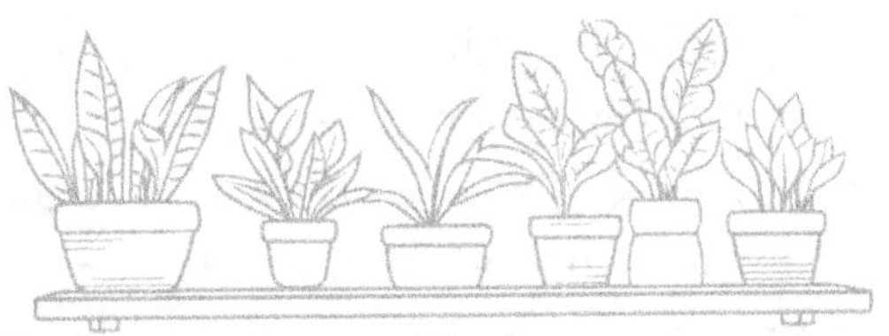

## DOMINIC

"I let my hand roam up her thigh. Doing my best to memorize every whimper that falls from her lips. I can't believe she's fucking mine. She is like a dream I never could have imagined—"

*Fuck. Well, that wasn't right.*

Hitting a couple of keys on my keyboard, I delete the last audio clip. *Again.* I've been trying to record this script since I got home from practice, and I can't quite seem to get it the fuck together.

I arguably have the coolest job among all of my friends. Even though, right now, I want to throw my computer through the wall. One of the perks of having a super deep and sultry voice, coupled with an almost-degree in audio engineering… I make one hell of an erotic audio narrator. It's a relatively new thing since the apps are just now really starting to gain popularity, but once I realized I could do it, I dove in headfirst. All it took was one audio submission to one of the more popular apps, and three days later, they had me producing my first clip.

I'm not ashamed of it either. I think it's really fucking cool. My friends like to give me shit, but I know they're secretly all a little jealous about the extra attention I've gotten around campus since I've started.

It also helps a little that a year and a half into this gig, my schooling is now fully paid for, and I am living more comfortably than most people my age.

But, even super sexy voice actors have bad days on the job, and today is just one of those days. So, in the spirit of persevering, I clear my throat and take a drink of water. However, just as I'm about to hit record, Emerson's face pops up on my phone screen with an incoming video call.

[1] Putting my headphones around my neck, I answer his call. "Aren't you supposed to be packing?"

"I—wait. Why does your voice sound like that?"

"Like what?" I ask and clear my throat once more.

"Like it does after we—oh I see. The headphones. The acoustic panels. Were you recording an audio?" Emerson sing-songs. "Are we about to get a new piece from Dom The Don?" His eyebrows wiggle playfully.

I can't help but laugh. "I was until you interrupted me."

"What can I say… I missed you."

"You just saw me two hours ago." He's being uncharacteristically playful. Something's up.

------

1.  Bottled Up - Daniel Di Angelo

"That and I have a once-in-a-lifetime opportunity for you." Consider my interest piqued. I raise a brow at him, waiting for him to continue. "The twins have the flu."

"Okaaaaay. And?"

He sighs dramatically. "Dominic. *The twins have the flu.*"

"Why does that concern—oh shit. Does that mean they're—"

A wide smile spreads across Emerson's face as he nods aggressively. "Oh yeah. They're staying with Grandma and Grandpa. Which means there's a shiny spot on an all-expenses-paid vacation just for you."

I stand abruptly from my seat. "Are you serious? I get to go to Turks and Caicos?"

"Flight leaves bright and early Friday morning, good buddy."

"Oh my god. I love you so much right now, you have no idea. You don't even have to give me a blowie anymore. I'll give *you* as many as you want. Oh shit. I can give you unlimited blowies on a tropical island! This is the best day EVER!"

"Alright, now you need to take it down a notch."

Completely forgetting the audio, I throw my headphones off and start stomping around my room, grabbing my suitcase from under my bed, and digging my summer clothes back out from the depths of my closet, all while Emerson watches from where I have him propped up on my desk. "Nope. Never. Hope you're ready to get your world rocked in Turks and Caicos, Emmy. Ohmygod, wait until you see my wedding dance moves. You're going to be so impressed." I spin and point my finger at the phone. "World. Rocked. Emerson Baker."

Emerson just laughs and rolls his eyes. "I'm going to let the Emmy go because I know you're excited. We're leaving tomorrow night and spending the night at the hotel by the airport since our flight leaves so early Friday morning. My parents should be arriving in Pensacola from Montana tomorrow around six, so we can all get dinner before we check in at the hotel. Sound good?"

"Sounds so fucking good. Wait until Mr. Baker gets a look at my moves. Oh! Do you think he'll do the Dougie with me?" Emerson looks at me deadpan. "Yeah, you're right. He seems more like a Cha Cha Slide kind of guy. Doesn't matter. I'll dance to anything. I'm so excited!"

A bright smile beams at me through my phone. "I'll see you tomorrow then?"

I snap with both hands and give him double-finger guns. "See you tomorrow, good buddy!"

His laugh floats through my bedroom before he hangs up. I stand in the middle of my room for a moment before sending both fists in the air. "Turks and Caicos, baby!"

# CHAPTER 4
# MIMOSAS, BUT NOT BOTTOMLESS

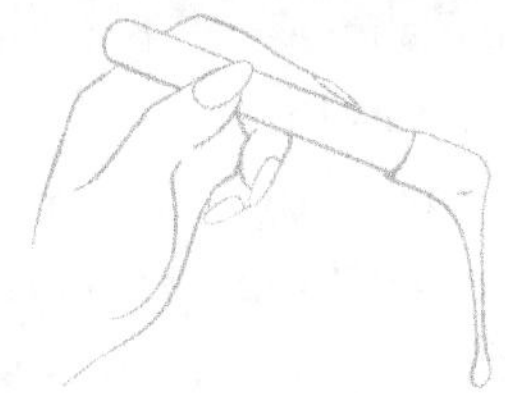

## LILIANA

The lovely waitress sets a champagne glass filled to the brim with a mimosa in front of me, and all I can do is sigh while sitting back and enjoying the glorious view. My family decided to meet for breakfast at the resort's restaurant before the day's wedding prep starts. It's Friday, meaning we only have today until my brother gets to marry the love of his life.

[1] So, there is no getting sloshed from mimosas at eight in the morning, regardless of how much it's calling to me. I have too much to do today to prep for this wedding.

*Yeah, I'm rolling my eyes too.*

Taking a sip, I pull up the to-do list that's on my phone and mentally start to prioritize what needs to get finished first while I wait for the rest of the Camposes to

---

1. Like What (Freestyle) - Cardi B

get down here. I'm about halfway through when Rocky's voice breaks my eyes away from my screen. "Mom, you cannot get that drunk before the wedding! It's barely after eight; Jager bombs are *not* happening."

*Ahhh, music to my ears.*

Cassandra Campos loves herself some Jager. I don't want to paint my momma as an alcoholic—it's only at events—but she'll order the whole bar a round if that means folks will take shots with her. She's always been the life of the party, and I love it for her. But what I love the most is my dad right there alongside her, supporting her, and matching her energy, always. They may be my parents, but their love is something I will always look up to, and I will never settle for anything less.

Standing up from my seat to greet them, I roll my eyes at Rocky. "One shot won't have her hungover, Rocky. Now that I think of it, why don't you take one, too, it might calm you down a smidge." I raise my hand up and pinch my thumb and forefinger together, leaving the smallest space between them.

A second later, Clay is sprinting toward me and wrapping me up in a giant hug, as if he didn't see me yesterday on the *private jet* he had booked for our flight here. Yeah, you heard that right. Rocky was so far up Clay's ass about spending money on a private jet, he could probably see out of his mouth. And yet, my brother somehow managed to lean back in his seat and sleep almost the whole flight here.

"Thank you for everything you've done and are

doing for us and our wedding. You're the best sister I could've asked for," he whispers, tears lining his eyes.

Goddammit. Now I'm gonna cry. "I wouldn't do any of this for anyone besides you two." I give him a wobbly smile, really trying to hold back my tears.

"Can we have four Jager bombs, please?" My mom's voice distracts us from our feel-good moment as she asks the waitress, and the pissed-off look on Rocky's face is enough to push away the tears and has me snorting a laugh instead. Clay gives my mom a wink, and she shrugs her shoulders with a smile on her face. Meanwhile, Dad just stands there shaking his head, knowing good and well that Mom's going to do what Mom's going to do.

We all finally take our seats, and my dad asks me, "What's on the to-do list today, Ladybug?" He's called me Ladybug since I was too young to remember.

"Oh you know, just bossing people around, making sure everyone is doing what they need to be. Which happens to be one of my favorite activities." I've always loved planning things, organizing, and leading people, but I could never deal with being in charge of people daily. This is why I have my own business but no employees. "Is Poppy ready to walk down the aisle? Where is she anyway?" Clay and Rocky have the sweetest little Saint Bernard puppy. They got her a couple of months ago, and she is both the fluffiest and cutest thing I've ever seen in my entire life. Everyone is obsessed with her, and she knows it. They've also been working with her to walk down the aisle to them.

"Our little princess is snoozing away up in our

room, but she's been doing so good! We're worried about the sand distracting her, but I think she's going to do great." When Rocky talks about her, his whole face lights up.

This wedding is kid-free, but puppies? Not even a question.

Clay counters. "Rocky's being hard on her. She's done great anytime we've practiced."

"Because you come in after the thirtieth time when she's gotten all of her energy out."

My dad chuckles as he says, "You two already sound like an old married couple."

"We do not," they answer in unison before grinning at one another and kissing.

"Gross, no making out in the restaurant!" I'll never grow out of wanting to tease my older brother.

When the waitress returns with four shots, my mom holds her shot glass up. Everyone else does the same, and I raise my champagne glass. "Here's to you, and here's to me! If by chance you don't agree... Fuck you! Here's to me!"

We all whisper-yell, "Fuck 'em!" Clinking our glasses together, I chug the rest of my mimosa. As we all sit around talking, I look at my parents on one side of me, then Clay and Rocky on the other. Suddenly, it hits me harder than it ever has.

I want this.

I want the love.

I want the passion.

Above all, I want a partner with whom I can share

everything, who my parents love, and who will be accepted into my family without question.

It steals my breath, because I have never wanted any of this. My parents raised me to learn to love myself above all, and I do—wholeheartedly—but my mind floats back to Emerson. I've never been more content in my career and my friendships, but I feel like something is missing in me.

And it doesn't stop at Emerson either; Dom is there, filling the back of my mind as well.

I wish they could both be here, but they still don't know about one another, and my brother's wedding sure as shit isn't the place to hash all of that out.

"When are the rest of the Bakers supposed to get here?" I ask, trying to keep my question sounding casual.

Clay is quick to answer, "They should be here some-time this afternoon. Why? Do you need them to help with something? Jax and Theo are just hanging out by the pool if you need them. He hasn't done enough, has he? Hold on, I can add you to the group chat!"

"No! No group chat." The last one he added me to, I had to remove myself because every time I opened my phone over three hundred messages were waiting for me. Pointing my finger at Clay, I narrow my eyes. "You are never allowed to add me to a group chat again."

"I wish I could get out of the group chat," Rocky mumbles. Clay's mouth drops open in shock, and the whole table breaks out in laughter.

# CHAPTER 5
# UNDER THE ISLAND SUN

**EMERSON**

The moment we step off the small plane onto the tarmac, the most perfect tropical breeze sweeps across my face. And as we stand there underneath the hot sun, I can't even find it in me to care that beads of sweat are already rolling down my back. I'm in fucking Turks and Caicos, baby.

Grunting, Dom picks my parents' suitcases off the luggage ramp. "Here ya go, Mr. and Mrs. B."

Mom blushes like she always does when Dominic does anything remotely nice for her, and Dad claps him on the shoulder. "Would you please stop with the 'Mr. and Mrs.'? *Dawson and Catherine*, Dom. Please."

"Sure thing, Mr. and Mrs. B," he replies with a smile.

"Brown noser," I mumble under my breath, and he chuckles.

"Somebody is just jealous because they're not mommy's favorite when I'm around."

Dominic continues to laugh as the four of us walk through the small airport and out to the pickup lane. "Keep it up and you'll get no vacation sex all week- end," I say, quiet enough for only him to hear. He just keeps laughing. "That's fine. You just keep laughing. You think she's obsessed with you, just wait until you see her with—"

"There she is! The most beautiful woman on the island."

"Theo," I finish as I spot him hanging his head out of their rental car. My older brother, Jackson, puts their car in park and the two of them climb out, immediately sweeping my parents up in hugs. As Theo squeezes my mom dramatically, I watch in amusement as the pink on her cheeks deepens. And when I look back at Dom he looks as if someone stole his birthday.

"Well, what the hell?" he whines.

"Yeah. You've got nothing on that one." Now I'm the one chuckling. It is true, though. Ever since my brother Jackson for real married Theo back in March— it's an incredibly long story—Momma Catherine has been absolutely smitten with the guy. But I suspect it simply has something to do with the fact that she sees how annoyingly happy he makes Jax.

Now that I think of it… is that why she likes Dom so much?

We have never explicitly told my parents about the ins and outs of our *relationship*, but we've never really hidden the fact that we're more than friends either. And my parents aren't stupid. As a matter of fact… they're some of the smartest people I know. Regardless, they have never poked or prodded. They simply let me and Dom be, well, me and Dom.

Jax spots Dominic standing slack-jawed next to me and asks me, "What's his deal?"

"He's mystified by the fact that someone can flirt with Mom better than he can."

Jax tips his head back in laughter as he puts his arm around Dom's sagging shoulders. "Cheer up, buttercup. Wait until you see yours and Emerson's room."

That perks him back up. "We're sharing a room?"

"Well, yeah. I mean, he was supposed to share it with Tweedle Dee and Tweedle Dumb, but since they're sick, the other bed's all yours."

Dom raises his brows playfully. "Oh, we won't need the other bed for what I have in—"

Jax clamps his hand over Dom's mouth. "Yeah. Don't need to hear it. Just remember your room is between ours and Mom and Dad's. So for the love of god, keep it down." Jax pins me with a death glare, and I mimic a zipping motion over my lips. "Thank you," he sighs dramatically.

The six of us put all of our luggage in the back of Jax and Theo's rental and pile in. It's a Suburban, but none of us are exactly small people, even Mom stands at five-foot-nine, so it's a tight squeeze. However, the drive from the small airport to the resort is only about fifteen minutes, and with Jax driving like he's on the set of *Fast and Furious*, we make it there in about ten. And like something out of my favorite rom-coms—I know, don't judge me—the moment we step out of the van, we're greeted by a member of the resort staff with a tray of what look like very tasty frozen drinks.

"Piña Colada, anyone?" he asks.

Dom claps him on the shoulder. "What's your name, my man?"

"Aadan, sir."

"Aadan." Dom grabs a piña colada off the tray and takes a giant sip. "You and I are going to be good friends. I can tell already." The rest of us reach for our drinks as another member of the staff unloads the trunk and places our bags onto a luggage cart, and another hands Jax a valet slip. But before my mom can grab the last one, Dom snatches it up and hands it to her. "Here you go, Mrs. B." Then he gives Theo the side-eye.

Theo doesn't even notice. Nor does he care.

It's hilarious.

"Alright." Jax claps his hands together. "Theo is going to take you guys to your room. I have some things I need to go do in the meantime."

"Are the grooms busting your balls today?" my dad asks.

Jax huffs an exhausted laugh. "Try the groom's sister."

A chuckle rumbles in Dad's chest. "That one's a real spit-fire, isn't she?"

"You have no idea," Jax and I answer in unison.

"You know Rocky's sister, too?" Dom asks while still slurping down his drink.

"What? Mhm. Sure do," I reply anxiously. Because amongst all of the chaos and excitement to get here, coupled with the fact that Dom came so last-minute, my brain didn't once seem to comprehend the fact that both Lil and Dom were going to be here.

*We don't talk about the other partners.*

The most important rule rings through my head.

*Yeah well that's pretty fucking hard when you're trapped on a tropical island with them both and one is your roommate for the weekend and the other is the maid-of-honor.*

Suddenly, the sweat beading down my back has nothing to do with the sun and everything to do with the fact that I don't know how the hell I'm supposed to handle this one.

# WAIT, I KNOW HER

**DOMINIC**

"I think I'm going to die of a heat stroke," I pant out in my seat next to Emerson.

He huffs in exasperation. "You are not going to die from a heat stroke. You're wearing a linen suit for Christ's sake. And it's only like eighty degrees out. And do you feel that breeze?" He holds his hands out in front of him and looks around. "It's fucking gorgeous outside."

I look at him deadpan. "Have you seen the size of me?" He raises his brow and looks down briefly. "Shut up. Not what I meant and you know it. This"—I wave my hand over my body—"is a lot of mass to cool down. So sue me for being a little warm."

Emerson patronizingly pats the top of my thigh, and I narrow my eyes at him. "This wedding is going to last all of fifteen minutes, and then we can go get you a drink. Plus, the sun is going to start going down in an hour."

I let out a dramatic sigh. "Fiiiiiine."

"You two are worse than me and your brother," Theo murmurs in his seat next to Emerson.

"Shut up," Emerson snaps.

"Awe, come on, Emmy. Lighten up." I look around Emerson to find Theo laughing at himself.

Emerson points his finger at his brother-in-law. "Don't you start with that shit, too."

Reaching behind Emerson, I fist bump Theo. Despite my jealousy over him *momentarily* being Mrs. B's favorite, he's actually a pretty cool guy.

Quickly, I pull my phone out of my pocket one last time, hoping to see a message from Lil, and when I don't find one, I silence my phone and put it back in my suit jacket pocket.

Lil is the only other person I'm seeing. She is… an enigma—really. I've never met a woman who is more in tune with her emotions and yet, so guarded from sharing anything too personal. I don't know her last name. I don't know where she works. I don't know who else she hangs out with or even where she's from. But what I do know is that she loves sushi, specifically spicy shrimp tempura. Her favorite movie is *The Greatest Showman,* even though she'll deny it until the day she dies. She always smells like honey and vanilla. She's a terrible singer, but that doesn't stop her from belting every song at the top of her lungs. And even though she is significantly smaller than me, I'm almost one hundred percent certain she could kick my ass.

But most of all, I know that whenever I'm with her, I feel something I've only ever felt with one other person.

Emerson.

That thought in and of itself is completely terrifying. Because just the thought of losing one more person I care about is enough to make me want to collapse like a dying star. But two? Two is unimaginable.

Soft music starts playing over the speakers, and it's enough to pull me out of my internalized panic. But Emerson suddenly goes stiff as a board next to me. "You good?" I ask him, but he doesn't answer. So, I bump his knee with mine. "Hey, Em. You okay?"

He blinks a few times, then looks over at me. "Yeah. Fine. Just—just remember I didn't do this on purpose, okay. I should have told you sooner but—"

"Shush," Mrs. B scolds.

Emerson gives me a sympathetic look before turning around and focusing his attention on the aisle.

The processional starts with Jackson, the best man, walking down the aisle by himself, winking at Theo as he passes him.

Oooo's and ahh's follow as Jackson uses the treat in his hand to bribe, who I'm assuming is Clay and Rocky's adorable St. Bernard puppy down the aisle. Usually, the "ring bearers" come after the entirety of the wedding party, but considering she's a puppy, I'm assuming Jax bribing her with treats was probably the safest bet.

Once the puppy makes it down the aisle, Jax hooks a leash to her flower collar and does his best to wrangle the little ball of energy up front. My attention is so focused on the little cutie that I don't notice the maid-of-honor until she's standing up front.

It takes my brain a few seconds to recognize who is standing in front of me, but when I do, I almost can't believe it. "Lil?"

I must say her name loud enough that she hears me, because when she spots me, her eyes grow wide. Then she looks at Emerson and back at me. A sense of panic marring her features.

"You know her?" Emerson asks.

"Yeah, I know her. Wait, do you know her?" I faintly hear the sound of the music change in the background, but I can't look away from the man sitting next to me and the woman standing next to the altar.

"Yeah, that's Lil. Rocky's sister. That's what I was talking about before—wait. How do you know her?"

"She's the other person—"

"You've been seeing," Emerson finishes for me before sighing heavily and closing his eyes. Slowly, he runs his hand through his black strands and opens his eyes to look at me. "I've been seeing her too, Dom."

*Well, if that isn't a kick in the balls.*

# CHAPTER 7
# MY ROSTER WILL WRECK THIS WEDDING

**LILIANA**

What—and I cannot stress this enough—*the fuck* are they both doing here?

Dominic and Emerson. The best friends. The two peas in a pod. The only two men in as long as I can remember that haven't sent me running for the hills.

[1] And they're both here.

*But why?*

I mean, I knew Emerson was going to be here… he and I have been talking about it for weeks. But why is Dominic here? He was supposed to be hundreds of miles away—an ocean between us… literally.

*They weren't supposed to know that I know.*

Emerson is wearing a beige linen suit, and Dom's is the most perfect shade of deep blue. Both of them are

---

1. Back to Back (feat. Future, Southside) - Nardo Wick, Future, Southside

wearing white linen shirts, each with the top few buttons undone. Suits are a normal part of their wardrobe, and I often see them wearing them. Either before or after their hockey games, but something about seeing them now, outside of a Palm University-sanctioned event, makes it look even better. Almost *natural*.

I don't know what it is about hockey players, but my god, can they wear a suit. It's one of the few things they have in common… well, besides me. Which they are clearly now *very* much aware of.

Dominic is the starting goalie for the Palm University Panthers, and a damn good one at that, from what I've heard and the couple of clips I've seen him share to his socials. He's built like a brick shithouse, which is apparently common for the goalies to be absolute monsters of men. At five foot ten, I can wear my highest heels and still have to make him bend down just to kiss me. However, I will say that the man's ability to throw me around like a rag doll is an absolute plus. And don't even get me started on how flexible he is. He has the most beautiful, golden-brown skin, a couple of shades darker than mine, and keeps his pitch-black hair in a short, faded haircut, but keeps the cutest curls on top that my fingers love to get lost in. Specifically when he's between my thighs. And that light stubble that dusts over his perfectly sculpted jaw is the cherry on top.

Then there's Emerson. He's a few inches shorter than Dominic, but his muscles rival Dom's. His black strands are always styled in the most mouth-watering flow, and his steel-blue eyes twinkle every time he looks at me. And when he smiles, there's a dimple that pops out on his right cheek. Just one. Emerson is also the right defenseman for the team, which means he protects the net and Dom at all costs. *Supposedly*. From what I hear. I really don't know jack shit when it comes to hockey. However, what I do know is that the two of them light up whenever they talk about it. They're like kids at Christmas any time even the mention of the game comes up. And what can I say, I like watching them smile, so I let them yap.

Regardless of how panicked I feel and how disappointed both of their expressions read, I can't help but want to climb them like a stripper climbs a pole. I'm weak when it comes to them. And I'm not weak for anyone, *ever*.

*Ooo, that reminds me. I need to check if Gigi wants to take that pole dancing class I've heard about.*

By the time I hear the music change over for Clay to finally walk up the aisle, Rocky is already standing next to me. But instead of looking down the aisle, his concerned expression is focused on me. "Are you okay?"

"I was about to ask you the same thing," he whispers back to me.

I nod reassuringly because my messiness is none of his business. Especially not now. I gesture toward the end of the aisle where his man is waiting for him.

The smile on my brother's face and the equally blinding one covering Clay's are enough to make my nose burn. Looking up at the sky, I try to hold back the tears that are already wanting to make their appearance.

Clay's practically floating up the aisle, walking alongside Mr. Baker. That's not Clay's father, but trust me when I say Clay's actual father is the biggest piece of human garbage I have ever stumbled across. So when Jax and Emerson's dad offered to walk with him, let's just say there wasn't a dry eye in the house.

Clay joins my brother at the altar, and despite my best efforts, I find myself having a hard time listening to the first part of the ceremony.

*I want nothing more than to look at the two men I can feel burrowing holes in the side of my head.*

"Rocky, do you have your prepared vows?" Yep, that pulls my attention right back down to earth.

My brother goes first, reciting his vows from memory. I could never, but he's always been smarter than me.

"Clayton Aldrich. The man you are. More so, the man I've watched you become." I can see Clay's face as I look around Rocky's shoulder, and there are already tears streaming down his cheeks. "The positivity and humor that you bring to every situation, no matter what your brain is doing, is something I wish everyone could experience. You light up every room with the brightness that is you, Clay, and being able to experience this life with you will be a debt I owe to some higher power, forever. I often ask myself how I could have possibly gotten so lucky. And even though I know I'll never know the answer, I do know one thing: I could never do this life without you. You're my sunshine on the rainiest of days, and I love you more than I'll ever be able to tell you. But I promise you, I'll spend the rest of my life trying."

A sob breaks out of Clay as my tears begin to fall. Fuck, I didn't want to cry; I'm not going to be able to stop now. And the quietest, "I love you so much," from Clay, has me biting the inside of my cheek, trying to hold in the sob that is rapidly crawling its way up my throat.

The longer I stare at the two of them, the more it hits me that I'm afraid I'll never find love like this… I'm a hard person to love. Being a woman who's headstrong and independent isn't what most men look for. That was always the reason my exes ended up leaving, or why men never ended up asking me out. Men have said the wildest shit to me…

"You're too mean." *I tell the truth, and sometimes that is hurtful. Grow up.*

"You act like you don't even need me." *I don't.*

And my personal favorite, "I can't control you." *The thing is, the right man* could *have control if he wanted it, but that's earned, not given.*

I can be a lot and cause problems when I feel the tension building or when things start to become too serious. I don't like feeling out of control. And when you're in a relationship with another person, there's not much you can control about them. The only thing you can *control* is you. That's why I've warned off relationships and instead keep things fun and casual. It's worked out great with Dom and Emerson, but I have a sneaking suspicion that it's all about to change.

*Did you catch my sarcasm there?*

Clay takes a second to gather himself and inhales a shaky breath, once again pulling me from said spiral. "Rockwell Campos. Rocky Baby. Rockman. *My everything* is what I should've called you from the beginning."

Rocky murmurs under his breath, "You did…" And everyone bursts out laughing because it's true. Clay fell fast and hard, and he sure as hell never denied it, either.

"I did, and I regret nothing, because look at us now." Clay's beaming smile says it all as he continues. "I may be your sun, but Rocky, you make that light in me brighter than I ever could have hoped. Or should I say flame? You know, since I'm a Leo and all… Fire sign, and you're my air. The very oxygen I need to breathe." Rocky chuckles at his joke because that's what Clay and Rocky do. They joke. They laugh. They have fun. They're some of the lucky ones. Because they've got both.

*A best friend and lover wrapped up in one.*

"There was a time that I thought the only way I was ever going to be fortunate enough to be loved by someone was to make everything I am louder. Bigger. Bolder. But then you came along—" Clay's voice cracks and I'm officially a goner. "You came along and loved me for everything I wasn't, or what I thought I wasn't. You showed me that the parts I tried to snuff out not only make me who I am but are worth just as much as the rest. And because of that, I have finally learned to find peace in the quiet moments. The small moments. The mundane moments. I have found peace with *you*. In this lifetime, and every one that follows."

Rounds of sniffles sound from the chairs, and I finally chance looking back at Emerson and Dominic, and I can't help but think…

Is there a love out there for me like what I see in my parents? Like what I see in Rocky and Clay?

Will someone ever love me enough to give me all of them?

Will I ever love someone enough to give them all of *me?*

Is that what love is?

If that's the case… do I even want it?

As deep and profound as these questions are, I know that right now is not the time to answer them. But I do know that I have both of my men here. My maid-of-honor duties are done after the reception, and I want to have some fun. And despite the fact that we clearly have some important details to go over, there's no better place to enjoy the present. Everything else can be saved until we return to reality.

My only problem is… now that they both know, how could I ever choose?

*Or do I even need to?*

# CHAPTER 8
# TEQUILA-STAT

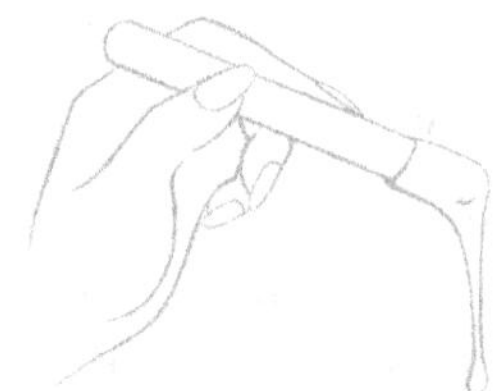

**LILIANA**

I'm practically jogging through the doors where the cocktail hour is being held to find the closest manned bar, and bark out, "Tequila gold, I don't care what kind—stat. You know what, make that a double." The bartender's eyes are about to bug out of his head, so I give him my most unhinged smile. Hopefully that relays that both of my situationships are currently in this very room, and I need some alcohol in me to deal with this new discovery.

We just finished taking pictures for what felt like three hours.

In all reality, it was under thirty minutes.

Come to find out, when the grooms actually love each other, the photographers don't have to try too hard to get good shots.

*Thank fuck.*

But now that pictures are over and cocktail hour has

started, I can feel all eyes are on me. And it's making my skin itch. Because as more people enter, I know the questions that are about to be thrown my way.

*"When's it going to be your turn to tie the knot?"*

*"Are you seeing anyone?"*

*"Gosh, don't you hope your wedding is going to be this beautiful one day? You better get on it if you want to get married before you're fifty."*

How about, *fuck off.*

Thankfully the DJ's voice sounds over the speakers to make a few announcements, and I use the opportunity to dip back out the door I came in, but not before locking eyes with Emerson and Dom standing in the corner, talking animatedly to one another. The conversation seems heated, and I can only assume it's because of me.

*Duh, Lil.*

Knowing I won't have time to give this conversation the focus it deserves before I have to find Jackson for our grand entrance, I decide to take the risk and return to the rest of the wedding crowd.

"And the reason we're all here tonight! Please help me welcome Mr. and Mr. Campos!"

I wolf whistle as my brother and brand-new brother-in-law make their way into the extravagant venue. "That's my brother!" I scream before whispering to myself, "I'm not going to cry. I'm *not* going to cry. You can't mess up your damn makeup, *again*."

The love emitting from Clay and Rocky is enough to have my bottom lip quivering. I'm on the side of the venue closest to the wall of windows that overlooks the ocean. Jax and I did our ridiculously choreographed dance, and now all that's left for me to do tonight is make a speech. Wanting to ward off the vomit that's building in my throat at the thought of making it, I turn to stare out at the ocean and try to gather myself before someone else sees me crying today.

"Fancy seeing you here." Two bodies press in behind me, one on each side.

*Dom and Emerson.*

I spin around to face both of them, finally, and give them a gleeful smile. "Huh, it is fancy seeing both of you here." I try to keep my voice even, like their bodies and presence don't have an effect on me. Even though we all know that's bullshit. My face gives me away every time.

Dom's deep brown eyes are glowing with a rusty hue from all the sunlight beaming in through the windows that are now behind me. Every time Dom stares at me, it's as if he can read every thought racing through my mind before I even have a chance to say it.

Then there's Emerson and his crystal blues that damn-near match the ocean water crashing against the shoreline a couple hundred feet away. His eyes are unlike anything I've ever seen, as if I look at them long enough, they'll have the power to rip me apart and pull me back together.

Dom half-heartedly chuckles, pulling me out of my ogling. "So, Rocky's sister, huh?" I get how sneaky it seems that I never told Dom my last name, but he didn't know me like Emerson's family does. Maybe if either of us wanted more from this—whatever *this* is—I would have brought it up. But we don't. So I kept that little snippet to myself.

And I see the little sting that gives him. He feels like he's been kept out of the loop. But that wasn't my intention, and this was our agreement. I kept my end of the bargain. We agreed to keep whatever all this is very surface-level, just for fun. I can't help that Emerson knew me beforehand, and he didn't. But, despite how sassy I can be, I don't say that. I don't want to hurt his feelings any more than I'm sure they already are. So, instead I say, "Yep… in the flesh. But the better question is, what are you doing here?"

Emerson answers this time. "The twins have the flu and couldn't make it, so I asked Dom if he wanted to come with me, and he agreed… of course."

I give Emerson a look that I'm hoping silently communicates, "You didn't think this one through, did ya?"

And when he smiles slyly back at me, I know the answer is no.

*Men.*

"Of course," Dom reiterates before looking over at Emerson.

The way they're looking at one another, the sexual tension that radiates off the two of them is palpable, and the nosy side of me wants to know more. But that's against the rules, isn't it? Or are the rules out the window now? I'm not sure I know the answer to those questions, either, so instead I say, "You two look *very* dapper this evening."

*Dapper? What the fuck, Liliana?*

Both sets of eyes land on me. Mortified that I just said the word *dapper*, I blurt out, "So are you like… each other's dates then?"

In slow motion, just like in the movies, both of them turn to look at the other, and smiles pull at their lips. Nonchalantly, both of them answer me at the same time, "Yeah…"

"Oh, how the plot has thickened," I murmur while steepling my hands together in front of my chest.

"I don't like when she gets that look…" Dom says to Emerson.

"Yeah, me neither. Nothing good ever comes from that look…"

"That's not what you said the last time we were driving, and you wanted your—" Emerson's hand covers my mouth, actively cutting me off from finishing that sentence.

He leans into my ear and whispers, "And you swallowed my cock up real nice on that drive, didn't you?" I nod my head while his hand is still covering my mouth, and my eyes find Dom's to see if I can gauge where he is with this whole mess we've found ourselves in.

[1]Dom seems to be interested, judging by the heat that's in his eyes, watching Emerson and I together.

---

1.  100 Ways - Austin Hull

"And what happened to not talking about our other hookups?" I ask Emerson when he pulls his hand from my face.

"My other hookup is *him*, Darlin'," Emerson replies.

"You two are it," Dom adds.

"And you two are mine..." I look between them. "Look, I know we have a lot to clear up but... for now... Who's to say we all can't play together?" I let them ponder that question for a second before adding, "We're on vacation; let's just see where the rest of the weekend takes us?"

They quickly nod in agreement as if they had already discussed this with one another. The three of us are silent for a moment before Emerson speaks. "I still can't believe you didn't know Lil was Rocky's sister." Emerson shoves Dom. "Do you not go to her as your esthetician? Literally so many people at school go to her for facials and all their other skin care needs. Dom, you're going to get early wrinkles." Emerson is stressing over Dom's skin, and it may be the cutest thing I've witnessed.

"Have you ever heard me once mention that I go and see an esthetician? Does this skin look like it needs an esthetician?" Dom's waving his hands up and down his face and chest with an "are you stupid" expression.

I raise my hands in innocence. "Dom's skin is glorious. I fear I couldn't make it look any better." I lean over towards him and whisper, but make it loud enough for Emerson to hear, "Unless you need a manzilian... now I can help with that."

The look of pure terror on both of their faces is enough to have me snorting a laugh.

Once I regain my composure, the two of them usher me back to my seat before they sit at their table. The first part of the reception goes off without a hitch, even my maid-of-honor speech, where I got to make fun of my brother for a good ten minutes, and by the end of it, there wasn't a dry eye in the room. Whether that was from laughing or crying, we'll never know.

Now… it's time to shake my ass.

# CHAPTER 9
# ODD MAN OUT

## DOMINIC

This may not be a huge wedding, but I'll be damned if everyone here doesn't know how to have a good time. Since dinner ended, there hasn't been a single second when the dance floor hasn't been the place to be.

[1] And when Mr. Baker and I danced to "Let Me Clear My Throat (Live)" by DJ Kool, I swear I almost died and went to heaven. For a middle-aged man who lives and breathes ranching, the dude's got moves.

I know Lil took a video of it, too, and I'm not lying when I say I want it played at my funeral.

The DJ is a whole vibe, playing the throwback music I wish they would play in the clubs nowadays.

Weddings are always a little bit hard for me. They're a stark reminder of the things, or people, I don't have

---

1.  Let Me Clear My Throat (Live) - DJ Kool

that others do. They remind me that as bright and shiny as the love from another person can be, opening your heart and loving someone that deeply can also lead to somewhere so dark and cold that you're afraid you'll never make it out alive.

However, when I'm surrounded by people like I am tonight, it makes it easy to forget. It makes it all bearable. If only for a few hours.

Now we're to the part of the night where the "older" crowd is all standing around the edge of the dance floor drinking and conversing while the rest of us act like a bunch of degenerates.

I'm fucking loving it.

For the last ten minutes Lil has been sandwiched between Em and I, each of us balancing drinks in our hands, despite the fact that Rocky looks like he wants to murder us every time he looks over. It's a good thing his new husband has him more than occupied. The three of us are well on our way to being tipsy. Not too much where the rest of the night is going to turn into an absolute disaster, but just enough to lower any… *inhibitions*.

Emerson and I had a quick, but frank, discussion after the ceremony. Clearly, there is a lot that the three of us need to discuss, but we knew what we were signing up for when we each said we wanted to see other people. Especially considering the number one rule was that we didn't discuss other partners. As long as we were being safe, that's all that mattered.

It's just, Emerson and I never thought that we'd both be seeing the same person.

That being said, there are two things I'm trying really hard not to let sink under my skin. At least not now. One, it's not a mystery that Lil knew we were best friends. The two of us never shut up about one another, and when we're not with her, Emerson and I are almost always together. She knew, and she didn't say anything. And two, Em and Lil have something I don't have with either of them… their families are now tied to one another. For all intents and purposes, Clay is just as much a Baker as he is now a Campos, which is why he didn't keep his last name. His family, the Aldriches, aren't his family. The Bakers are. And now, the Camposes are part of that family. I'm the odd man out.

*I feel like the odd man out when I'm with these two.*

Buuuuuuut I'm doing what I do best, I'm swallowing it down and putting on a happy face. Because Emerson and I decided that Turks and Caicos was a time for fun. We can figure out all of this shit when we return to reality. As long as Lil is down, which she clearly is based on the way she's eye-fucking me while pressing her ass against Emerson, that's exactly what we're going to have.

Fun.

A lot of fucking fun, actually.

[2] And just when I think it can't get any better, the music changes. The opening notes to the next song play, and Lil's and my eyes go wide. She and I stand still for a moment before pointing at one another. And because Emerson knows me inside and out, he knows exactly

---

2. Animals - Nickelback

what I'm about to do. He's just never seen me do it with Lil. Stepping back, he clears some space around us.

Because let me tell you. We're about to blow the fucking roof off this place.

It takes no more than fifteen seconds into the song for the rest of the party-goers to circle us and cheer us on as Lil and I sing "Animals" by Nickelback at the absolute top of our lungs. At one point, she even grabs my leg and pretends to use it as a guitar.

And when we make it to the bridge of the song, I really hit my stride and practically take on the persona of the one and only Mr. Kroeger himself.

# CHAPTER 10
# TWO FUCKTOYS

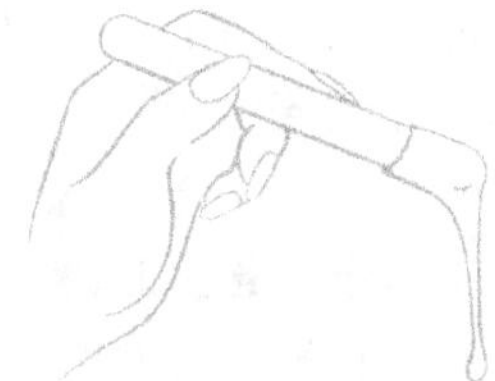

## LILIANA

I take over, screaming the lyrics of "Animals," where the lead singer is going on about the dad being outside the car.

*You might as well call me Chad Kroeger.*

We're still head-banging to the end of the song when I finally return Dom's leg to the floor. I smile up at him, and it's an effortless smile. I never have to try to put on an act for him. I'm just completely *me*. Never once have I thought about my actions before doing them or my words before speaking when he's around. That's the thing when it comes to Dom and I, when we're together, fun will be had, no matter what.

[1] We lost Emerson when we heard the beginning of one of the most iconic songs in the last twenty-ish years. And as I hear the beginning of "If I Ain't Got You" by

---

1.  If I Ain't Got You - Alicia Keys

Alicia Keys, I know the DJ is trying to wind the party down.

I open my arms and Dom does the same, wrapping one around my waist, and grabbing my hand with the other. I hear Clay belting the lyrics somewhere behind us on the dance floor, and I just smile, knowing he's singing directly to my brother.

*And that makes my heart happy.*

As Dom and I rock back and forth slow dancing, my eyes meet his, to find him already looking down at me. "Are you okay with all of this? I know it seems like I lied... well... I guess I kind of did. But, I knew you and Emerson are best friends, and I just have so much fun with the both of you, and I was being selfish because I didn't want to give that up and—"

Dom presses a finger against my lips, effectively silencing me. I stare wide-eyed up at him. "We're here to have fun, right?"

"But what happens when we get back?"

"We will deal with it all later." He winks at me, and I feel butterflies in my stomach. I don't know what it is about him, maybe it's the twinkle in his eye or the way he can always lighten even my heaviest of moods, but when I'm around him I feel such a lightness about me.

"So... we do whatever we want for the rest of the weekend and think about what we want to come of this when reality smacks us once we land back in Florida?"

"I vote that answer." He nods his head.

Grinning ear to ear, I grab his hand and drag him toward the bar where I know Emerson is waiting for us.

I'm sure to sway my hips a little more than normal. "Come on, let's go find my other man."

From behind me Dom replies, "I just got jealous there for a second, and then remembered Emerson's my man too." His playful chuckles might just rival my favorite Nickelback songs.

I spot Emerson leaning against the bar, elbows propped on the countertop behind him, a glass of dark liquor in one hand, and a perplexed look on his face. But as we grow closer, his forehead relaxes and a soft smile spreads. My fuck is he sexy. "You two finished putting on your show?"

I give him a wink and a toothy grin. "You know… we could put on another type of show"—I fist the fabric of his linen shirt, press myself against him, and bring my lips to his ear—"in the room."

Emerson inhales a sharp breath, and Dom chuckles behind me. "Lil said she's down for some *vacation festivities*," he teases before resting his large hand on my waist and pressing up against me. Leaving me sandwiched between the two of them, *again*. And I can't lie and say the weight of their bodies on mine isn't already doing things to me.

They keep this up and I won't even need any foreplay.

*Who am I kidding… this whole damn night has been foreplay.*

Emerson bites his lip as he looks down at me before saying, "My only request is that we have fun for the night in Lil's room because both of you are loud on your own—but together… yeah, we will need to be as far away from our parents as possible."

"Well, good thing I thought ahead. My room is on the opposite side of the resort from the rest of the wedding party," I reassure them.

I did it mainly because I knew I wanted a night with Emerson with the least likelihood of my brother, Clay, or my parents seeing us, but I also knew I would be at max capacity with family members by the end of the wedding night, so I was smart enough to request a room far in advance.

Honestly, that was the first thing I called about when Clay finally told me where he was planning to have their wedding.

And now that Dom is here too, I'm extra glad I thought ahead.

"We have to stop by our room first, I have to grab a couple of things." The glint in Dom's eyes when I look over my shoulder at him says he has something planned, and I'd be lying if I said I wasn't excited to find out what it is.

Emerson downs the rest of his drink, and I have to rub my thighs together at the sight of his throat swallowing down the amber liquid. "Ladies first," he says with a mischievous grin.

I step from between the two of them, and I faintly hear them mumble to one another, but I don't stop to listen closer.

As we all walk out of the space where the reception is currently dying down, I quickly stop and turn around to look at them. "Guess I didn't need to bring my trusty vibrator with me after all. I have both of my fucktoys with me on the island."

They both look at one another, smile, and I wish I were joking, but it happens right in front of me.

They fucking fist bump.

I'd act annoyed if the sight of it, for some ungodly reason, didn't have me giddy with excitement.

*Sometimes I love being me.*

# CHAPTER 11
# BIRDS OF A FEATHER AND ALL THAT...

**EMERSON**

"What is he doing in there?"

"I have not a single fucking clue," I answer Lil as the two of us stand across from one another in the hallway outside mine and Dom's room.

"What could he have possibly brought that he needs to bring back to my room?"

"I wish I could tell you."

"You don't have any idea? How do you not know? He came here with you," she asks from her leaned position against the wall.

"I didn't pack his bag for him," I reply.

She huffs in annoyance. "I mean what does he—"

"Liliana," I snap. Her eyes narrow at me, and I faintly watch as she fights the upturn of her lips. "I don't know what it is, Darlin'. But you know as well as I do that the man can't keep a secret for longer than thirty seconds, so as soon as we get to your room we'll find out. Yeah?"

I fight my grin as she narrows her eyes even further at me. With her arms folded across her heaving chest, she chews her lip before pushing off the wall and sauntering across the hall until she's standing in front of me. Leaning in until her lips brush against mine, she says softly, "Call me Liliana again, I dare you."

[1] I don't budge even a fraction of an inch. "You like it, and you know it."

She huffs a breath, and it takes every ounce of my willpower not to break my stare and look down at the swell of her breasts. The lavender satin dress she's wearing is practically painted on, and they've been tempting me all fucking day. But she and I have done this dance far too often for me to know that she's just waiting for me to break.

So I don't.

Because she knows I'm right.

Lil is a strong woman. The strongest I've ever been around. She doesn't bend for anyone, and very rarely does she break. So someone cutting her off like I just did, especially by way of her full name, would usually be grounds for a swift kick in the balls.

But for some reason, she gives in to me. She likes when I call her out on her bullshit. When I toe the line ever so carefully. When I push just the right buttons. It lights a fire in her, and I'm as addicted to watching it burn as she is to letting it consume her.

______________

1. Lovesucker - Haiden Henderson

"I—"

The door next to me opens and Dom's large frame appears. "Well, what's going on out here?"

Lil gives me a look that screams "keep it the fuck up and see what happens" but instead she looks over at Dom and asks, "Care to share with the rest of the class what you were doing in there?"

A mischievous grin takes over his face. "You'll seeeee."

I huff a laugh and roll my eyes, knowing good and well that whatever he's up to, it's no good.

Lil points a finger at him. "You're lucky you're so fucking cute."

Dom shrugs. "I know." Grabbing Lil's hand, he leads her back down the hall, toward the other end of the resort.

I follow the two of them as they walk hand in hand through the weaving halls, watching as they effortlessly connect with one another. Filling any moment of silence with jokes and laughter. As people pass us they smile at the two of them, unknowingly pulled into their orbit just as I always am.

And for a moment, I find myself entirely too envious of their relationship. Of the way they seemingly fit together so perfectly. Of how, just like they did during their two-man Nickelback performance, people flock to them. How, whenever they're around, I'm just the grumpy guy in the background that they feel like they have to overcompensate for. Even though neither of them would ever intentionally make me feel that way. I know that it's just my own insecurities playing tricks on me.

But as I watch them, they just feel so natural. So... effortless.

And yet, when Dom looks over and smiles at me, and Lil follows suit, shooting me her usual devious wink, the tension I'm suddenly feeling in my chest eases a little.

Because even though I was behind them, in the background, they didn't forget about me.

And not being forgotten... well, it feels like a gift.

"Here we are!" Lil says excitedly.

Dom stops in his tracks, and he and I look at each other in confusion. Because we're no longer *inside* the resort, and instead we're standing outside in front of what appears to be a sliding patio door.

Lil pulls a keycard out of her clutch and waves it over the sensor next to the door. It makes a beeping sound followed by an audible click. She wraps her hand around the handle and pulls it open.

In unison, Dom and I lean to the right to look inside what appears to be a giant oceanfront suite.

"What *the fuck?*" I ask.

Lil pinches her brows. "What? Like it was hard? All I had to do was bat my eyelashes at my new brother-in-law, and he folded faster than a lawn chair. Don't tell Rocky, though."

The two of us stand there gawking at the immaculate suite as if she's opened a portal to another planet.

*Here I thought our room was nice.*

Lil rolls her eyes and starts walking backward into

her "room." Despite the darkness, the full moon reflects the perfect amount of light off the water just a few yards away, casting the perfect glow. So I'm faintly able to see as she reaches under her arm and pulls down the zipper of her dress. Slipping her arms out of the delicate straps, she lets it pool at her feet. Leaving her standing before us in nothing but a pair of heels, white lace panties, and a matching bra. "If the two of you don't get in here in the next five seconds I'm going to take care of myself. I brought my vibrating besties after all."

Dom and I exchange a brief glance before racing inside and sliding the door closed behind us.

# CHAPTER 12
# GO AHEAD... KISS

## DOMINIC

The moment the door latches behind Emerson and I, I'm reaching for her. "Uh uh," she says before pointing her finger between the two of us. "Shirts. Off."

I eagerly follow her directions, but Emerson tilts his head in her direction, narrowing his eyes. A shit-eating grin spreads across Lil's face, and she raises her brows. Emerson exhales a heavy breath, takes off his jacket, and slowly undoes the buttons of his shirt. A hell of a lot slower than necessary, and I know it's just to get Lil more and more riled up.

My fingers twitch at my sides, eager to touch her, but I wait as she drinks us in.

"Jesus fucking christ," she huffs in what almost sounds like disbelief. "I'll never get over how beautiful the two of you are."

Emerson goes to move toward her, but she stops

him again. "Liliana," he warns, and her eyes light with mischief.

"Before anyone moves another inch, I need something from you first."

"Name it," I answer eagerly.

"Kiss."

"What?" Emerson asks.

"I want the two of you to kiss. Right now. In front of me."

Em tilts his head. "Why?"

[1] "Because, I know the two of you are more than just friends. It's abundantly clear now that I see the two of you together. And I need to know if seeing the two of you together is something I can handle." She says it as if it were a question, but judging by the way she is pressing her thighs together at the mention of it, I'm pretty sure she already knows the answer.

I don't know why Emerson is suddenly feeling gunshy, but it won't do. Shooting Lil a wink, I turn to him and reach out to grab at the waistband of his beige slacks. With one swift pull his chest crashes into mine. His eyes bounce between mine as I reach up and thread my hand through his wavy hair. "Quit pretending like you don't want to show her what I do to you," I murmur against his lips.

His lips twitch as he fights a smile. "Just shut up and kiss me you—"

I crash my mouth to his. Despite our newest revelations, and both of us being wrapped up in Lil's orbit,

---

1. Friends- Chase Atlantic

I've wanted to have my mouth on his all day. I've wanted the taste of him on my tongue. And when he moans into my mouth, I forget for a moment that Lil is even here.

I'm lost in him.

Just like I always am.

That is until I hear Lil let out a shaky breath followed by a breathy, "Fuck."

Emerson pecks my lips once, twice more, before stepping away from me and slowly making his way over to her. With her heels on she only has to tilt her head ever-so-slightly to meet his eyeline.

Reaching up, he firmly grips her jaw in his hand, and an expression crosses her face that I've never seen. Almost... *nervous.*

"I hope you enjoyed that, because that's the last time you're going to be bossing me around." The deep timber of his voice sends a chill down my spine and all the blood to my cock. Fuck, I love when he gets like this.

*And why my voice is the one that makes the money, I'll never know.*

"Maybe for today, at least," she bites back.

I swear to fuck, Emerson practically growls, and I can't help the moan that slips past my lips at the sight before me. Emerson in nothing but his slacks, and Lil in the sexiest set of lingerie I think I've ever seen and a pair of heels. The light of the moon casts the perfect glow along the ridges of their bodies.

It's fucking mesmerizing, and they haven't even done anything yet.

Despite his hand still firmly gripping her jaw, Lil looks over his shoulder at me. "You just gonna stand there and watch?"

"Honestly," I reply. "I'm fucking thinking about it. There's no shame in my cuck game."

She lets out a laugh so pure I swear it could bring me to my knees. "How about you save the watching for next time? Get over here," she demands.

*Next time.*

She wants there to be a next time.

More than happy to oblige, I step toward her before I remember what's in my pants pocket. "Hold on," I rush out.

Quickly, I grab the small microphone and my phone out of my pocket. Opening the app on my phone, I quickly sync the two of them together and press record before setting them on the nightstand next to Lil's bed.

When I turn to face them, Emerson's arching a brow at me. "Seriously?"

"What? I have a schedule to keep and you interrupted my recording session the other day. Plus, I have a feeling I'm going to want to remember this until the day I die."

I'll keep to myself that it was Emerson's brother Jax that helped me figure out what equipment I needed, and this little mic picks up even the quietest of sounds. He is a computer genius after all.

Emerson rolls his eyes but smiles, and Lil looks from the small microphone back up at me. "Any objections?" I ask, never wanting to do anything anyone isn't comfortable with. This is already treading into uncharted waters for me, but I wasn't kidding when I said I want to remember this forever. But if they say they don't want to, I won't.

End of story.

Lil hesitates for a moment before asking, "No one will know it's me?"

"Not a soul. I swear."

Emerson leans forward and brushes his lips against her ear. "The thought of every person that listens knowing how hard I can make you come... fuck, Darlin'. Just the thought of it is making me hard."

"But they won't know it's me," she answers breathlessly.

"I will." He gently nips at her lobe, and a shiver wracks her body. I watch as his fingers flex around her jaw.

Lil's eyes go to my crotch, easily spotting my dick tenting my pants. They stay there for a moment before her stare makes its way back up to mine. She bites at her bottom lip before saying, "This better be the best sex of my life."

My eyes meet Emerson's for only a moment before he nods in my direction. "You can fucking count on it, Darlin'."

# CHAPTER 13
# HOW THE TABLES HAVE... FLIPPED?

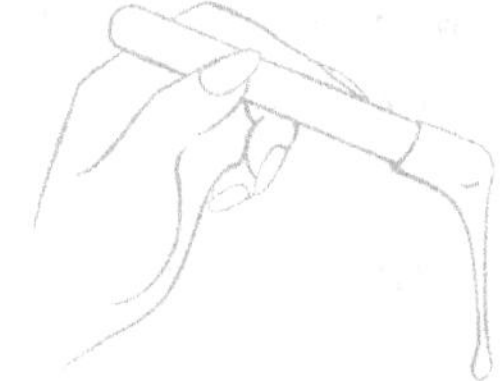

## LILIANA

The consent.

The care.

The comfort Emerson and Dom have given me separately before the thought of the three of us together was even a blip on the radar. All reasons why I find myself drawn to them. Addicted.

But the anticipation of what's to come now that we're all together… My imagination is running wild and has me clenching my thighs together to dull the growing ache between my legs.

Any ounce of softness left in Emerson evaporates as he grabs the back of my neck, pulling me into his body. I tilt my head back in anticipation, thinking he's going to crash his lips to mine, but instead, he hovers right above them, just out of my reach. His voice low as he instructs, "Since you clearly want to be a brat tonight, let's put this fucking mouth to good use." Emerson's brows raise as he waits to see if I'll protest, but instead, I drop to my knees. The smug smile he's sporting says plenty. "There's my *good* girl."

I whimper.

I fucking whimper.

*I mean, what's a girl with a praise kink to do when she hears words like that?*

Dom steps up next to Emerson, and my eyes meet his. Even beneath the glow of the moonlight his eyes shine down at me. They're like the color of the richest cognac, and every time they look at me, I feel them warm my center as if I took a shot of the liquor itself. His stare lingers for a moment before biting his fist and moaning. "Fuucckkk, Honey, look at you on your knees for both of us while you still have those heels on."

His open appreciation of me goes straight to my cunt.

Then I remember Dom's recording every second of this, and a groan crawls its way up my throat. I reach up to unbutton his slacks, and he follows suit with Emerson. In unison they both pull their pants down along with their briefs, freeing their throbbing cocks. I start at the inside of their legs, just above the knee, and run one hand along each of their muscular thighs. I stare at their faces, as their eyes watch my hands make their way toward their eager cocks. But before I reach where they want me most, I reach around and firmly squeeze a cheek on each of them. "Your asses are to die for."

Emerson scoffs. "Coming from you, Darlin'... Did you see yours in the dress you just peeled off?"

I smile up at him with my arms still wrapped around both of them, pulling them closer together. Leaning forward, I run the flat of my tongue up the full length of Emerson's cock. His head falls back against his shoulders, and the sound he makes washes over my body like the finest silk. Dom's eyes bounce between me and Emerson. Once I'm done, Emerson's face comes back into view, and he commands, "Again."

Now it's my turn to raise my brows. I'll happily give him the control, but he's not getting all of my attention. That shit isn't going to fly. So instead, I dismiss his order and look over at Dom. "But Dom's being a good boy waiting so patiently."

Not missing another beat, I wrap my hand around Dom's cock and slide him between my lips. With my eyes on his, I nod my head towards Emerson. Dom grabs the back of Em's neck and brings his face to his. Their lips meet in a passionate kiss, and their tongues dance a dance it's clear they do often.

They know one another's bodies just as well as I know each of theirs. Now… we all need to learn how to dance together.

Humming, I suck as much as I can of Dom into my mouth. I lose myself in the delicious rhythm of bringing him pleasure when I'm suddenly ripped off his perfect dick.

"What the fu—" I'm cut off by being picked up from under my arms and tossed on the bed. The squeal that comes from me doesn't even sound human.

Dom's eyes heat, and his chest heaves as he looks down at me. "I was about to come down your throat…

and we are just getting started," he growls while crawling his way up my body. He slides my panties down my legs, but leaves my heels and my white see-through lace bra on.

Dragging his tongue up my thigh, he stops to suck and mark my skin. "I'd rather breed this tight little cunt." He pauses to drag his tongue up my slit. "And as it drips out, watch him fuck it back into you." The moan that leaves Emerson from his place behind Dom has me squeezing my thighs together around Dom's head.

The mouths on these two are going to kill me...

I also have no clue where the breeding talk came from. We've always been cautious using condoms, and I'm on the insertable ring for birth control, but I won't lie and say I'm not panting at the thought of being filled with *them*.

[1] The forbidden.

The one thing I've never experienced.

But we can talk about that in a second. Right now, I want to come. No, I *need* to come.

I tease a broody Emerson that's staring at Dom, and I spread out on the bed. "Don't be shy, bring me that cock up here, big boy." And he obeys. My threesome dreams are coming true. If I could fist pump, I would, but they would probably think I'm losing it.

*Actually, just Emerson. Dom would probably fist pump right along with me.*

I flip over to my hands and knees so I can suck Emerson a little better, and instruct Dom, "Eat this cunt

______

1.  Forbidden Fruit (feat. Kendrick Lamar) - J. Cole, Kendrick Lamar

from the back like the good boy I know you are." I give him a small shake of my ass, and he laughs.

But instead, he slides under me on his back and wraps his large hands around my hips. "Sit. I want to watch you swallow his cock while I eat."

"Oh how the tables have… flipped, or whatever that saying is." I laugh at myself, but that laugh turns into a gasp when he pulls me down onto his face and sucks my clit between his lips. The stubble lining his jaw and upper lip is giving the best stimulation between my thighs.

The man may be Palm University's star goalie, but eating pussy is where he truly shines.

As I get lost in Dom's glorious mouth and what it's doing between my legs, Emerson climbs up to kneel on the bed. His leaking cock is right in front of my mouth, practically begging for me to suck it.

"Open that pretty mouth, Darlin'." I look up at him, waiting, and he knows what I want. "Please?" Emerson asks in an exasperated tone.

I moan my response, "Mhm, that's better."

Dom grabs my hips and starts rocking me back and forth, which only spurs me on. Shamelessly I rub my cunt harder along Dom's face, just like I know he loves.

Before I realize what's happening, Dom has me on the brink of an orgasm.

Emerson can tell I'm right on the edge, and he growls, "Come on his face, brat."

His words are what push me over the edge, and Dom is sure to lap up every ounce of my release.

Once I'm out of the orgasm haze, I look down at Dom as he licks his lips. He lifts me with his strong arms and slides himself up so his upper body is now under Emerson's spread-out legs. He runs his hands over Emerson's thighs, groaning. "This view will be ingrained in my head until the day I die."

Now sitting on Dom's stomach, I ask, "Since it's only us..." My eyes bounce between both of them as their lust-filled stares snap in my direction. They're silent for a moment, so I continue. "Right? I've only been with you two."

"Yes, it's only you two for me," Dom reassures me.

"I haven't been with anyone else in over a year. Before that, no one for much longer than I would like to admit..." Emerson says a lot shyer than I've ever heard him be. And fuck if seeing him momentarily nervous around me doesn't give me butterflies.

I clear my throat. "Then, if you two are fine with it, I would like to be... bred and filled... or whatever it is you said earlier." I look at Dom, hoping he knows I'm talking to him, but not wanting to say his name because of the recording.

I swear to god, growls come creeping up both of their throats before Emerson answers, "I've never fucked anyone without a condom."

"Neither have I," Dom adds.

I fidget nervously on top of Dom, and he gives my thigh a reassuring squeeze. "Same. So this would be a first for all of us..."

I look up at Emerson to gauge where his head is,

and he has a wicked gleam in his eyes. My eyes find Dom's, and he has a matching expression. "I'm on the ring. So we are good in the pregnancy prevention department. Well, one out of every hundred, but that's with any birth control, sadly," I ramble, but it's true. It's the reason I have always used condoms. Plus you never know what kind of new STI is bouncing around, especially in a college town. And the last thing I want to sound like is someone who wants to "trap" anybody with a baby. Even though I know, if it came down to it, Emerson and Dom would step up if they had to. They're those kinds of men.

In reality, it would be a bigger trap for me. Motherhood is nowhere near on my radar, especially as I watch Gigi handle her newborn son Charlie, all on her own. You'll never catch me saying I don't want kids because, well, you never know. But as a new business owner at twenty-two, that's the last thing I need in my life right now.

Dom reads my facial expression, and asks, "Are you sure about this?"

"Yes. Sorry, I was in la la land, imagining how bad being a single mother at this age would be."

Emerson's big hand grabs my jaw and forces me to look at him. "Listen to me this one time, Darlin'. You would never be a single mother if it were either of our babies."

*See, told you.*

I let his sentence sink in, and it shouldn't, but it has my stomach in knots and my traitorous pussy fluttering. "We would never leave you to raise another human we helped create. I hope you know how genuine I am when I say that."

Dom grabs my hips in a silent reassurance and nods. "I watched my mother struggle to raise me for half of my childhood by herself... I would never even think about leaving you to raise my child. Hell, I would stay and raise it even if it was his."

In the year I've known him, Dom has always spoken so highly of his mother but hardly ever mentions his father. If he does, it's either in passing or by accident. And whenever he does, a sudden somberness takes over him. I have a sinking feeling I know what happened to his dad, but I've never asked, and he's never openly told me. So, for now, I'll leave it be.

Part of me expects them to be lying, but as I look into their eyes I *know* their words to be true. Because in them is a care and passion that lights my soul on fire. That's exactly what Dominic and Emerson do; they light me on fire more than anyone ever could in my past.

*Fuck* this wasn't supposed to get this deep, but this is a huge step to take with a person, let alone two. Be that as it may, I don't want to lose the momentum of the moment, so I give them both a reassuring smile. "Okay, okay, enough with spilling our guts. Let's do it." I look back at Dom's cock. "How you two kept your boners that whole time, I'll never know."

"I'm about to fuck this pretty cunt bare for the first time. How could I not be rock solid?" Dom jokes, before lifting me one more time so I can slide my knees under me to hover above his length. Reaching down to notch him at my entrance, the feeling of the throbbing head of his cock sliding against my aching cunt, begging to be filled, is nothing shy of forbidden. He gives me another nod and reassures me, "You don't have—" He cuts off mid-sentence as his head breaches my entrance after what feels like ages of waiting.

The pure ecstasy of there being nothing between us is something I can't even describe.

"Fucckkk," Dom grits out, his jaw clenched.

I'm sliding up and down his length, and when I go to throw my head back in pleasure, Emerson grabs the sides of my face. "Open up. I bet we can have him filling that tight cunt up in under a minute with the view of you swallowing my cock."

And open I do.

He slides his cock between my lips, and I start bobbing up and down on his length, again. With my right hand I begin to work my clit in tight circles, trying to milk an orgasm out of Dom and myself.

"I don't know where to look. Fuck this is too hot. Come on my cock, Honey." Dom almost sounds like he's in pain, and I know he's trying to hold off his orgasm.

But it's no use for me. It hits me hard and fast. Washing over me in a quickness I've never experienced as both of them keep using my body for what they need.

A few more grunts leave Dom as he fucks into me, and he's yells, "I'm coming—Fuck, I'm coming." Well shit… Dom didn't even need the view of me swallowing Emerson up.

I don't know if it's another orgasm or still the same one, but my toes are curling and my vision blurs before I close my eyes and let it take me under. I don't want air if this is what drowning in them feels like.

Emerson pulls out of my mouth and lays down beside Dom, and in one swift move he's pulling my half-limp body off of Dom's cock and hovers me over his own. Despite my sudden exhaustion, I start to rub my cunt up and down Emerson's length, coating him in another man's cum.

Another man, but not a random man.

His best friend.

Dominic.

The groan that leaves him just from the erotic sight of what I'm doing has my lower half fluttering. "Please fuck me. Fuck your best friend's cum back into me."

Dom hisses from beside Emerson's head, "Fuck, you two are so hot."

I make the same move, gripping Em's length, and notching him to my dripping entrance. "You're sure?" He lets me get my question out, but that's it. He slams into me, and that's all the reassurance I need. He wastes no time as he grabs my hips and starts fucking me.

"Look what you're doing to him, Honey." I don't know if Dom is letting the filth fall from his lips because of the recording or if this is his new normal, but the sideline commentary is going to send me into orbit for the third time today… or would this be four?

*Who the fuck even cares?*

Reaching over, Dom starts circling my clit, and whispers, "Let him feel that tight cunt of yours strangling his cock too."

*I swear to all things holy my eyes cross and enter the back of my head.*

I'm so overly sensitive, that it takes the two of them no time to bring me to the edge of an orgasm for what *has* to be the last time tonight. I don't think I have anymore in me. But I'll sure as fuck beg for this last one at this point. "Em, please let me come on your cock."

"I like it a lot better when this pretty mouth of yours is being used for begging." Emerson smirks while reaching up and running his thumb over my pouty lips, and I open willingly to suck his thumb into my mouth.

And that's what does him in.

I feel him stutter with his thrusts, and a look of pure ecstasy lines his face. "*Fuck.* I'm filling this beautiful cunt up, Darlin'." His cock twitching inside me has my walls tightening around him, and my hand wrapping around Dom's, willing him to stop rubbing my clit that feels like it's on the verge of falling off. But not before I'm falling over the edge of yet another orgasm.

Eventually, Emerson pulls me off of him and lays me between the two of them, and in this moment all I can think about is how lucky I am to be here.

They each drape an arm and leg over me in some kind of protective, comforting effort, and I couldn't feel more at home. But the panic is quick to show its head when I think about how attached I could get to this feeling.

To them.

Together.

This is all for fun.

We're just on vacation, having a good time.

Feelings aren't supposed to be getting involved… at least my feelings aren't.

# CHAPTER 14
# SLUTTY CARWASH

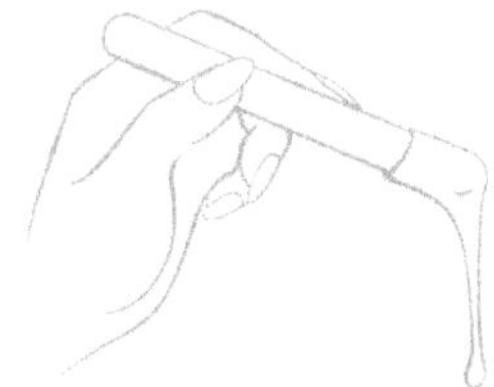

## LILIANA

I'm finishing up in my salon suite after a week of entirely too many clients. In fact, the amount of work I've had to do this week should be illegal after a tropical vacation. *Especially* after a tropical vacation where I got fucked into oblivion by two insanely hot hockey players.

*But… a girl's gotta work.*

Despite how busy I was, my head kept floating back to the resort, and it was always at the worst times. Like during clients' appointments. One flash of the memory of being between Emerson and Dominic and I'd be blushing like a virgin in a whore house. And it didn't stop at just that one time between the three of us.

No.

The two of them stayed in my suite while we fucked like rabbits for the rest of vacation. Not a surface in that place was left untouched. Hell, we even fucked in the private pool, and the chairs were put to very good use as well. Even recorded a few more audios for Dom—which I can't wait to listen to when he finally uploads them.

The joy I feel knowing random people are going to hear me get fucked three ways to Sunday, all while keeping my anonymity, has me practically jumping for joy.

I don't want to remain anonymous because I'm embarrassed by what happened between the three of us, quite the opposite actually. I just don't want it affecting Dom's career as an erotic audio creator. A lot of his fans are wildly obsessed with him, and I don't want to get between him and all of *that*.

We haven't had the chance to talk about what happened yet, but we're definitely going to need a group debriefing at some point in the near future. The guys had to jump back into their crazy hockey sched-ules, and my week at the salon has had me crawling to my bed by the end of every night. I was lucky if I even made food for myself. I don't even want to admit to the amount of food I had delivered to me.

But now it's Friday and I have the weekend off, and Brittany, my last client, mentioned there is a fundraising car wash just around the corner at the university. My poor Betty girl is disgusting, and she is in desperate need of a bath.

*Yes, my old Honda Civic is named Betty.*

So I decide I'll be an adult for three-point-five seconds and get my ole girl washed off. Plus, it's for a good cause.

That is my thought process until I pull up in the small line and see one of the shirtless guys in the shortest swim trunks I've ever seen holding up a sign that reads: Palm University's Hockey Team. He flips it to the other side. It reads: "Get your slutty car wash here!"

*Goddammit.*

And of course, just as I'm about to bail because the first encounter I have with the two of them post-sexcation *cannot* be at a shirtless car wash, a car pulls in behind me, boxing me in. My only hope is I get the other group of guys that doesn't include Dom and Emerson.

But as the line moves forward I realize that luck isn't on my side.

And what's worse… the moment I see the two of them, standing in front of me, shirtless, water glistening across their muscular chests under the Florida sun, I forget why I didn't want to be in their lane in the first place.

What's a girl to do?

*Sue me.*

## CHAPTER 15
# SUDS & BUDS

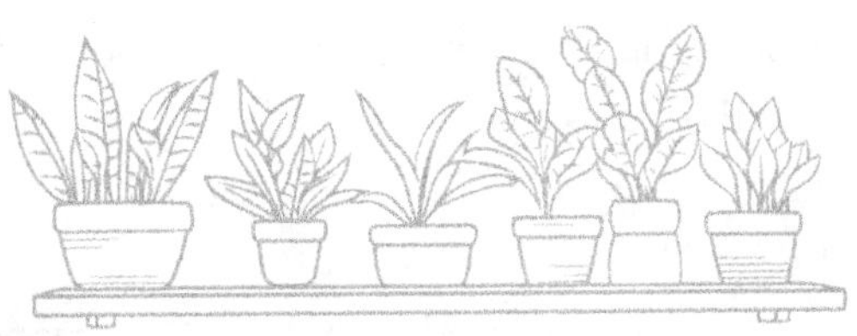

**DOMINIC**

"Banner," Cole groans from the other side of the parking lot. "Not this song *again*."

[1] It's me. I'm Banner. The series of events it took for them to come up with this nickname never fails to amuse me. But then again, what's a hockey player without a ridiculous nickname?

My last name is Foster, which then turned into Banana Foster, which quickly proved to be too long. Banana lasted all of two days before I had to put an end to it. I just couldn't. So then they collectively decided on Banner—which they swear sounds like banana, even though it doesn't. But I'm not one to look a gift horse in the mouth. So, I accepted it and moved on.

Em says it's fitting considering sometimes I have the

---

1.  Pink Pony Club - Chappel Roan

*77*

persona of Bruce Banner. You know, the Hulk. Especially on the ice.

Anyway, I just turned on "Pink Pony Club" for probably the fourth time this afternoon over the wireless speaker. Because let's face it, this song fucking slaps, and I will never not shake my ass to it. Plus, the ladies love it. "It's the price you pay for letting me be DJ for the day, Cap."

Cole's last name is Evans, and weirdly enough he looks kind of like Chris Evans.

Evans. Chris Evans. Captain America.

You get it.

"Baker, please get him under control," he groans.

Because Emerson is well, Emerson; he's just Baker.

Huffing a laugh, he drops his sponge in the bucket at his feet. "If I had any control over him whatsoever the song would have never played in the first place."

We've never told any of the guys that the two of us hook up. Not that we're embarrassed but because, quite frankly, it's none of their business. However, they do know that the two of us—more often than not—are attached at the hip. And none of them are blind. They see the way we act toward one another. Even though we never show blatant public displays of affection, we never shy away from one another. If the guys suspect anything, they never bring it up. And if they did, I know that despite the occasional razzing, they'd be nothing but supportive. My team is filled with some of the best men I know.

I grin widely at him before looking back over at

Chris. "You're looking a little dry over there, Cap. Remember, the girls like the abs looking *moist.*"

"For the love of god, please stop saying moist," Emerson groans, and I can't help but laugh.

The car we just finished with drives off, and the next one pulls up. I'm so busy shaking what my momma gave me—have to lure the ladies in somehow—that I don't even notice the car that pulls up until I hear Em curse, "Well, fuck."

Through the windshield of an all-too-familiar Honda Civic, I see the adorable face of Liliana Campos.

She looks equal parts horrified, embarrassed, and turned on.

Honestly, that's her usual expression anytime I'm around.

I love it.

This is the first time we've seen her since we got back from, what I'm now referring to as, our "sexcation." As amused as I am, I'm also vividly aware that this is less than ideal. The moment we landed, the three of us got sucked right back into our regularly scheduled programming. Emerson and I with school and hockey, and Lil with her business. Hell, outside of practice and our game yesterday, I've barely even seen Emerson. We haven't even stayed at each other's places since we returned, and we rarely run into one another on campus anymore. With it being our senior year, he and I are both busy with our respective senior year classes. Him in journalism and mass communication, and me in audio engineering. Safe to say our classes don't cross over whatsoever.

Outside of both of us sending Lil the occasional lunch or sweet treat, because the woman constantly forgets to feed herself while she's working, we've barely even had time to communicate. Let alone go into detail about what all of *this* means now that we're home.

And as much as I want to hear her every thought about the subject, a hockey team carwash on campus is not the time or place.

"She seriously needs to get a new car. That thing is an accident waiting to happen," Em says under his breath.

I roll my eyes. He's such a grouch sometimes. "You and I both know she's attached to that car," I tell him as one of our teammates starts hosing down the relic.

"I'll buy her a new one then."

I side-eye him. "You think that woman would ever let you *buy her* a car?"

Emerson huffs a dramatic breath. "Yeah, you're right."

"Plus, I already have it scheduled for a maintenance appointment for next week. Cap is going to drive it there one afternoon when I take her out to lunch."

The corners of Emerson's lips curl, and he pats me on the shoulder. "You're smarter than people give you credit for."

"Ummm, *thanks?*"

"You're welcome," he answers smuggly before patting me on the ass and grabbing his sponge out of the bucket.

Wanting to ease what I know is Lil's monumental

level of discomfort, I saunter over to her driver's side window and tap the glass. She exhales heavily before lowering it. Bending at the waist I rest my forearms against the door and peek my head inside. Still looking out the front of the car, she holds out a five-dollar bill between two fingers. I snatch it from her and say, "I'm assuming you didn't know this was the hockey team's carwash?"

I curl my lips in to fight the laugh that's wanting to fall out as she dramatically turns her head in my direction.

*Fuck, she's pretty.*

"What do you think, Dominic?"

I can't help it, I lean forward and plant a chaste kiss on her pouty lips. The only person paying attention right now anyway is Emerson, and I can't see her and not kiss her. "I think you're about to get the best car wash of your life, Honey."

I tap the inside of her door twice before righting myself and looking over at Emerson. "Sponge me, Emmy. We got a show to put on."

Emerson rolls his eyes but tosses me the sponge, and I don't miss the way he shoots Lil a wink through the windshield.

I also don't miss the way her cheeks turn pink at the gesture.

Just as the queen, Miss Roan, begins the last chorus, I fold myself over the front of her car, pressing my sudsy pecs right against the glass. And when I hear her laugh come from inside the car, I feel like I've won the lottery.

# CHAPTER 16

# I'M HERE...

**EMERSON**

I'm not going to lie, spending my Friday afternoon fundraising via shirtless car wash wasn't exactly how I wanted to spend my day, but it had its perks.

Seeing Lil after a week with little-to-no communication was like a breath of fresh air. Hell, I've barely even had the time to text except the message I send her every morning reminding her to lock up her apartment because she literally always forgets.

One time I walked right into her place at ten o'clock at night while she was in the shower.

Safe to say I was beyond unimpressed.

Anyway… that was perk number one. I'd be lying if I said I didn't miss her this week. My every unoccupied moment was spent thinking of her and everything that happened back at the resort. And when I wasn't thinking about her, I was thinking about *him*.

Perk number two is currently sitting shirtless on my

counter eating a spoonful of peanut butter. I might shake my head at his antics, but seeing him be, well, him this morning was just what I needed.

And when I wasn't thinking about the noises Lil made as she was between us, or the look that Dominic would give me as she moaned in pleasure, I'm stuck thinking about what all of this means. When I'm playing hockey, all I can think about is what if she picks him over me. When I should be studying, the thought of Dom realizing that Lil is a better fit for him than me, or that we're simply better off as best friends—that's where all of my focus is. And when I lay down in bed at night, the one thing that is at the forefront of my mind is that eventually, I'm going to get pushed to the side.

Cast away.

Made less important.

An afterthought.

Because that's been the story of my life for as long as I can remember.

*Emerson will be fine. He always is.*

*We don't have to worry about Emerson.*

*If anyone can handle it, Emerson can.*

I don't want to be an afterthought to them. I don't think I could handle it. So the best thing I can think of is to avoid the temptation. To be sure we're all on the same page. To make sure the rules are crystal clear.

"Out with it already."

My head snaps up to find Dom raising a brow at me, empty spoon in his hand as he swings his feet back and forth on the counter. Of course he knows I'm spiraling. He always does.

This is the first time I've seen him outside of hockey this week, and I guess now is as good of a time as any. "We gotta talk about it."

"It?"

I look at him deadpan. "Don't play dumb."

Dom just stares back at me. Ugh. He's going to make me say it. He does this to me all the time. He knows how in my head I can get, and just because I don't word-vomit all over the place like he does, he tries to force my hand.

And it almost always works.

Like right now.

I take a deep breath, then explain, "We have to talk about what we want out of this." I gesture between the two of us. "And what we want out of the relationship with Lil." He still says nothing. *So annoying.* "Because even though I really like her, I love you. You're my best friend. Whether we're fucking or not, I don't want to lose *that.* I—" I look away from him, not wanting to meet his eyeline as I confess something so vulnerable. "I *can't* lose us."

He's quiet still, and I'm about two seconds away from saying, "Just kidding, nevermind," when I hear the clang of the spoon against my granite counter. Then, his hand reaches out and fists the front of my Panthers T-shirt and pulls me to him. I stand between his legs, still not meeting his eyes as mine focus on the ridges of his muscular stomach. He refused to put his shirt back on after the car wash, something about, "The show must go on, Emmy."

"Emerson," Dom finally says, his deep voice soft

and full of concern. "Look at me." Shoving my embarrassment aside, I force my eyes to finally meet his, the color of the richest whiskey, shining with compassion and understanding. He gives me a soft smile before saying, "I'm not going anywhere. Lil or no Lil. Sex or no sex. You got me."

"That's easy to say now," I mumble. But I regret it almost the moment the words leave my mouth. Because one thing Dom isn't, is a liar. When he says something, he means it.

But he doesn't react to me questioning his morals, instead he gently tightens his hold on my waist and adds, "Yeah it is. Because you were my best friend first. Before anything else, that's what you were. It's what you are now, and it's what you'll always be."

I've never explained to Dom the reason I constantly feel this way, but the man's not dumb. Regardless of how often we tease him about being all looks and no brain, he's actually insanely smart. And what's more, he can read me like a book. Anyone really. For a twenty-one-year-old hockey player in college, he is weirdly in touch with his emotions, and everyone else's apparently. "So what do you think we should do?" I ask him.

He thinks for a moment. "I think… I think we should have this conversation with Lil. She's part of this now. No more secrets. No more sneaking around. Which means we all have to be on the same page." He's right, so I nod my head in agreement. "So we'll text her and see if the three of us can talk tomorrow, okay?"

I exhale a long breath. "Okay."

Then, a mischievous smile takes over Dominic's face

as he plays with the hem of my athletic shorts. "But for now…"

*There he is.*

"Seriously?" I ask, mocking exasperation.

He rears back in shock. "I've been staring at you shirtless and sudsy all afternoon. Sue me for being a little horny."

I place my hands on his thighs, reveling in the way his quads feel beneath my grip. "A little?"

Dom shrugs. "Okay, a lot. But it's been a week, and seeing you all shy just now really sent me over the edge."

I can't help it. I tip my head back and bark out a laugh. "You're impossible, you know that?"

"Impossibly irresistible." He wiggles his brows at me.

"Shut up," I laugh as I shake my head.

"Okay," he replies before grabbing the side of my head and crashing his lips into mine. I groan into his mouth, all the tension from just seconds ago almost instantly leaving my body.

*Fuck I've missed him.*

And because I live alone, and I'm not opposed to fucking where I eat, I use my hold on his thighs to slide him backward on the peninsula counter. He lets out a low chuckle, clearly amused that he got his way, before he turns himself, lying parallel to the length of the counter. I climb up and kneel between his legs and stare down at him. Wanting my lips on his, I fold myself over him and slant my mouth over his.

I get lost in him. Lost in the way he tastes. The way

his warm body feels against mine. Lost in the way his hands roam over me. And forever lost in the way he has the power to quiet my mind when I can't seem to do it myself.

I pepper kisses across his jaw, loving the way the stubble pokes at my lips. And when I nip at the skin along his neck, he lets out a soft moan as he runs his fingers through my hair. With the exception of my yearly close-crop cut at the start of summer, I mostly wear it in a flow. Typical, I know. But they call it "hockey hair" for a reason. The stereotype holds up. Dom grabs a fistful of it, pulling my lips away from his neck. With a heavy breath, he pants out, "Clothes. Off. Now."

[1] Placing one quick kiss on his full lips, I kneel between his legs and throw off my shirt. The two of us continue to work delicately, careful to not heave our giant asses over the side of the counter, and remove the rest of our clothes.

With me resting back on my knees, Dom sits upright, his legs spread around me. His chest pressed against mine. Our heavy breaths coming in unison. His eyes staring into mine. Despite being on my kitchen counter, the whole moment feels extremely intimate. Like if he stares at me like this for too long it could have the power to rip me apart until he can see every thought. Every feeling. Every desire. The weight of his stare is almost too much for the type of *relationship* that we're in.

---

1.  THE WITHDRAWALS - Kae

And yet...

I find myself wanting to get lost in it.

I don't have time to think about it long though, because a strange look crosses his face, and a moment later he blinks it away. Reaching over the edge of the counter, he pulls open my junk drawer and blindly moves his hand around until he finds one of the packets of lube I threw in there a couple months ago after the *first* time we fucked in here.

Because honestly, guy or girl, you never know when you're going to need it.

I watch as he takes a corner of the packet between his teeth and rips it open. He squirts some into his hand before reaching between us and wrapping his fingers around my hard cock. My head falls back, and I let out a wanton moan the moment his skin makes contact with mine.

"You wanna fuck me, Emerson?" his deep voice rasps in my ear.

His hand works up and down my shaft as I groan out, "*Yes.*"

Dominic nips at my ear, causing my head to snap forward. My eyes burrow into his. "Then fuck me."

*He'll never have to ask me twice.*

Raising up on my knees, I place my hand in the center of his chest and push him backwards. Dom rests his hands on my waist as I rest one arm on the countertop beside him and use the other to notch the head of my cock at his entrance.

Sometimes, the two of us spend a good amount of

time doing prep work and foreplay, and sometimes… well, sometimes neither of us can be fucking bothered. He'll likely feel it in the morning, but I'll be sure to treat him with the best aftercare once we're done.

The two of us have done this enough and are comfortable enough with one another to do this carefully. We know each other's limits and know how to tell when the other is uncomfortable. Which makes these rushed moments, the ones filled with so much lust and desire, that much more possible.

Slowly, I press the head of my cock into him. "Oh *fuck*."

Every time. It feels so fucking good.

*Every.*

*Single.*

*Time.*

"Emerson," he moans my name as his fingers flex against the skin of my waist. I sit there for a moment, letting his body adjust to me. But a moment later, Dominic uses his hold on me to slide me deeper inside of him. And when I'm as deep as I can go, a shaky breath leaves his lips, dusting against mine. "Remember when I said to fuck me?"

"Yeah," I answer softly.

"Fuck. Me."

A slow smile spreads across my face and I do just that. I fuck him on my kitchen counter. I fuck him so good he doesn't even need to touch his cock before he's coming all over his abs. Painting his golden-brown skin like a perfect work of art. And when I come deep inside of him, the two of us hop off the counter, clothes strewn about my kitchen floor, and fuck again in my bed.

And in my shower.

And in my bed again.

Only hours later, do we fall asleep for the first time together in over a week.

# CHAPTER 17

# AUNTIE LIL

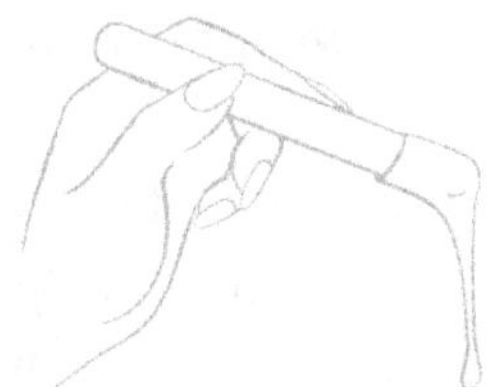

## LILIANA

I'm busy cleaning my apartment on a glorious fall afternoon—as glorious as fall can be in Florida. I'm counting my blessings because at least it hasn't been in the nineties for the past week.

[1] All of my windows are open, fresh sheets on my bed, and I have my cleaning playlist going, which is all old 2000's hip-hop and R&B. Music that you can shake your ass to but also clean the whole damn house simultaneously. And when I hear "Salt Shaker" come on, I'm sure the neighbors are begging me to shut my windows.

Not thirty seconds into the song, there's a knock on my front door. I let out a huff, hoping it's not the fancy-ass apartments' security. Not that I couldn't get out of it. My brother-in-law owns the whole building after all. I roll my eyes as I open the door but immediately put

---

1. Salt Shaker - Ying Yang Twins

them back into normal position when I see who's on the other side.

"Oh, there's Auntie's sweet little Prince!" I say excitedly. Sticking my arms out I make grabby hands at my favorite little neighbor, Charlie.

He comes to me willingly because babies are obsessed with Liliana Campos.

*What's not to love, honestly?*

Having a neighbor with a baby has been a win-win for me. I get to be fun Auntie Lil but don't have the full responsibility of having a child of my own.

Gigi, my favorite grown-up neighbor, says, "We heard the Ying Yang Twins and couldn't resist. Charlie will have good taste in music one way or another."

With him propped on my hip, I wave my arm, gesturing her into my apartment, and then head over to the balcony door to shut it. The last thing I need is my number one man crawling off through the railing.

I plop Charlie on the freshly cleaned floor so he can explore and grab a couple of toys I keep stashed here for him, while Gigi and I take up our usual spot on the couch. I lower the music a tad so that we can catch up. I'm not really Charlie's aunt, obviously, but since Gigi and I became fast friends a little over six months ago, she bestowed the title of honorary Auntie on me. It's a name I wear with great pride.

I didn't know she was my neighbor for the longest time, though. That is, until one Saturday I was listening to a newborn baby screaming bloody murder for what felt like hours. Wanting to make sure everything was okay, and that a small infant wasn't left in the apartment alone, I knocked on the door directly beside mine, and what I was met with was nothing I had ever experienced. An exhausted mother bent over in what looked like pain, bags under her eyes that could've been registered as their own zip code, and a screaming Charlie in her arms.

We stared at one another for a good thirty seconds before I introduced myself and explained that I could hear her baby and wanted to check on them. She immediately started to cry. The kind of cry that hurts your soul to watch. A cry so bone deep, it seemed that every tear that rolled down her cheeks held the weight of the world within it. There was no way I could have left her there to deal with whatever she was going through alone. So I did what I would hope any other woman would have done—or what I hoped they would do for me if I was in her shoes—and I wrapped my arms around both of their crying forms. Scooping Charlie up in my arms, I told her to go shower while reassuring her I wasn't going to go anywhere with her brand new baby. It was my new mission to get him settled. To give his poor mom some reprieve.

And that's exactly what I did.

"How have my two besties been? It feels like I haven't seen you two in forever." It's only been two weeks, but just in those two weeks, Charlie's clearly gotten the crawling thing down pat.

*I've noticed they gain new skills so fucking fast when they're little like this.*

I still remember her explaining the day I met them that she had to have a C-section to deliver Charlie only three days earlier, and that her parents had just gone back to their home, which is about twenty minutes away, that morning. She was in pain and couldn't get the baby settled, and she just sobbed to me because she felt like a failure. I, of course, explained that she wasn't a failure, and that even though they say it takes a village to raise a child, some people don't always have that luxury, and that it's *okay* to struggle a little without one.

From that day on, though, I became her village. And I did it gladly.

Since then we've pretty much had an open-door policy. If she needs me, she lets me know. No one, and I mean *no one*, should have to go through raising a baby on their own. *Especially* when the father is the biggest piece of shit known to man and isn't helping in any way, shape, or form.

*But I digress. Another story for a different day.*

"We've been good. I was tired of being cooped up in my apartment. And honestly, I don't know what it is about your apartment, but he'll be fussy all day, and we simply set foot in here and he's a completely different kid. It's like magic, I swear." Gigi chuckles, while watching him try to pull himself up on the coffee table before falling back on his butt when he loses his grip.

"I think they like seeing new environments. Even though he stays here pretty often, it's just different, ya know?"

"Yeah..." she says, staring off into the distance but not really focusing on anything.

"Are you okay, babe? Not to sound like a"—I

whisper my next word even though Charlie doesn't know what any of it means yet—"*bitch*, but you look exhausted."

"He's going through a sleep regression and teething, and I haven't had a full night's sleep in probably six months."

I huff a faint laugh because six months *is* the entirety of this kid's life but… semantics. "I know you're iffy about it, and never want to put me out, but I'm going to offer again and again. Let me keep him tonight, Gigi." She looks over at me, and for the first time I think she might actually be convinced. So I keep going. "You'll be right next door if anything happens. And it's only a couple of hours until his bedtime anyway. I know what to do. I've watched him at bedtime before, and he's more than comfortable with me doing it."

"What about him waking up—"

I cut her off. "I'm off all weekend, so even if he's up partying all night, we'll just party together. But I promise he'll sleep. And I don't mind if he does wake up. I need you to rest. I worry about you, Gigi."

She's staring off again, mulling over my words. She's a volleyball player at Palm University but redshirted this year to have Charlie and care for him until he's a little older. So while being a full-time student in her third year of college, she's also a full-time mother. A single mom. Her only reprieve is that her parents are a short drive away and that the two of them are so loaded, they're more than willing to help Gigi pay for college, her apartment, and anything else she and Charlie would need.

Financial help or not, sometimes I still don't know how she does it, but I help out whenever I can, or nights like this when I force her to let me help.

Finally, she looks at me and says, "You know what… yeah. I'm going to say yes this time. I need help, and I'm not afraid to say that."

"That's my girl! You hear that, Charlie? We're partying tonight."

He lets out a squeal and looks like he's trying to clap his hands like he knows exactly what we're talking about. Gigi and I both start clapping right along with him regardless.

"Okay." She huffs out a breath. "I'm gonna go grab his stuff. I'll be right back."

"I still have his Pack 'n Play," I yell after her as she makes her way out my front door. Taking a quick look at Charlie to ensure he's still occupied, I grab my phone to look and see if I've missed anything important or if there are bookings from clients that need to be approved. The first thing my eyes see is:


***Dom has added you to the group chat**


***Dom changed the group chat name to "Fearsome Threesome"**


***You changed the group chat name to "Lil's Bitches"**

DOM THE DON

Hey my group chat name was good!

EM AKA BIG BOY

Lil's group name is better. I'd happily get on my knees anytime for her.

DOM THE DON

???

EM AKA BIG BOY

*sigh* you too, Dominic

I simultaneously laugh and roll my eyes. I vividly remember telling each of them, *several times*, that group chats are the bane of my existence. Clay has tried multiple times to add me to a group chat with him and my brother. I have left said group chat, every time.

The constant pinging of notifications on my phone is enough to send me over the edge most days.

Does that make me sound like a bitch? *Maybe.*

Do I care? *Not really.*

And right on cue, another message comes through, and my eyes are rolling.

EM AKA BIG BOY

What are you doing Lil?

DOM THE DON

Yeah we miss you

I snap a picture of the back of Charlie's head as he plays with a soft book and send it with my next message.

ME

I'm on baby duty right now.

DOM THE DON 🎙️

Em she has a kid and we didn't even know 👤

EM AKA BIG BOY 💪

How did we not know this?!

Why did Rocky never tell us he was an Uncle?!

Oh dear god. These two are ridiculous.

ME

You both know good and well this is not my child.

EM AKA BIG BOY 💪

...riiiiiight.

Anyway, coffee date tomorrow so we can go over everything that happened on the fuck-cation?

ME

Is this convo going to be coffee shop safe?

DOM THE DON 🎙

Yeah it'll be fine.

We can whisper 😌

I know you love when I whisper in
your ear.

ME

I will come under one condition.

EM AKA BIG BOY 💪

Yes ma'am?

ME

If I am going to be part of this group
chat, please, for the love of all that is
good and holy, say everything you need
to say in one message. I cannot
mentally nor emotionally handle
message after message after message.

Dominic... I'm talking to you.

DOM THE DON 🎙

...Yes, ma'am.

EM AKA BIG BOY 💪

Thank you for that, Darlin'

ME

I aim to please. See you guys
tomorrow.

The second I lock my phone, I hear the sound that I
would compare to a grown man shitting himself, but

instead of a grown man it's the giggling six-month-old sitting on my floor.

*You brought this one on yourself, Liliana.*

From there on out, besides the occasional text to his mom, I don't so much as have a second to check my phone for the rest of the evening until after Charlie lays down for the night, and I set it on the nightstand next to my bed. And even then, I can't seem to muster up the energy to do my nightly doom scroll. Instead, I absolutely pass the hell out.

Auntie Lil is officially *exhausted*.

# CHAPTER 18
# ARE RULES MEANT TO BE BROKEN?

**EMERSON**

"Do you think she's bailing?" Dom asks nervously as the two of us stand near the floor-to-ceiling window at the front of the coffee shop. We were supposed to meet Lil ten minutes ago, but she's still not here yet.

I don't know why he's surprised. If he and Lil have spent as much time together as she and I have, it's very apparent she's not an overly *punctual* person. Actually, now that I think about it, outside of her work, I don't think I've ever seen her on time to anything.

I'm not entirely sure what keeps that woman from being on time, but what I do know is that she wouldn't just bail on us.

Checking my phone one last time to see if she texted before sliding it into my shorts pocket, I tell Dom, "Come on. Let's just order for her and find a table."

He looks up and down the block out the window

before sighing heavily. "Fine. But if she's not here in ten more minutes I'm going to her apartment. Something could be wrong."

"How many times have you stormed into her apartment when she was late for something?" I ask as the two of us get in line.

Dom side-eyes me. "More times than I'd like to admit." I can't help it. I snort an obnoxious laugh. "Shut up," he deadpans.

I don't. I chuckle all the way up to the register because I know he's a hundred percent serious. Lil usually flies by the seat of her pants, and despite Dominic's usual carefree demeanor, he's insanely over-protective, which means I know that him not knowing where she is or if she's okay probably tests every ounce of his patience.

It's not that I don't worry about her, or her safety, but I know how late is *too* late when it comes to Lil. She was once twenty minutes late to a movie, and didn't so much as bat an eye. I'd say it bothers me, but I'd be lying. Honestly, I always like the way she looks when she comes flying in. Cheeks all rosey from being in a rush, and eyes blown wide as she looks for me, only for a full-fledged smile to cross her face once she finally spots me.

But Dom's not me, and I love how protective he is. So, I pat his back sympathetically as one of the employees starts taking our orders. "What can I get you, gentlemen?" the small blonde on the other side of the counter asks with a smile.

"I'll take a vanilla sweet cream cold brew," Dom replies, giving the employee a soft smile.

"And I'll just take a coffee. Hot. Black."

"I'm a man and I drink my coffee black," Dominic mocks under his breath before I jab him with my elbow.

"Can we also get a large hot dirty chai? How many shots of espresso does that come with?" I ask her.

"Two," she replies brightly.

"Better make it three."

"Oh," Dom pipes up, rubbing the spot where I elbowed him. "Could we also get a double chocolate muffin?" He looks over at me. "That woman loves her chocolate."

The woman rings us up, Dom pays, and I add some cash to the tip jar. "You guys go ahead and find a seat. We'll bring it out when it's ready."

Dom and I find a table big enough for three tucked into the corner of the cafe so we're far enough away from any prying ears but still close enough to the front windows so Lil can see us when she finally comes breezing in.

As if the thought itself summoned her, the front door swings open, followed by a head of dark strands blowing in the summer breeze. And just like I was hoping, her eyes scan the room before landing on Dom and me. Eyes wide, cheeks pink, and a smile so pure I can feel it in my toes.

She sits down in a huff in the chair beside Dom, the morning sun casting the perfect glow against her sage-green eyes. "I'm so sorry. I severely underestimated how much work watching Charlie all night was going to be. I didn't set my alarm because I was sure he was going to have me up at the ass crack of dawn. Thankfully he decided to sleep in a little bit this morning, but that means I did too. *Ohmygod* I need copious amounts of coffee, or I fear I might actually die." Dom and I both chuckle at the woman in front of us. "I'm going to go order and then we can talk about—"

"Here you go!" the same woman from behind the counter announces as she arrives at our table. She sets mine and Dom's coffees in front of us before looking down at Lil. "I'm assuming this one is for you."

"It is. Muffin too," I tell her.

She sets both items down in front of Lil. "Holler if you need anything else."

Lil brings the hot mug to her nose and takes a whiff. "Hmmmm." I swear the sound goes straight to my cock, and I have to shift in my seat to keep myself from getting hard. "Is this a dirty chai?"

"Extra shot. Had a feeling you were gonna need it," I answer.

She takes a long slow drink, closing her eyes as she savors its taste. When her eyes open, she looks right at me. "If I wasn't already sleeping with you, I definitely would be now."

For the second time this morning, I laugh a truly genuine laugh. I seem to be doing that a lot around both of them.

Lil looks over at Dom and runs her hand down his arm. "Thank you for the muffin, Baby."

Dom beams with pride. "I know how much you like your chocolate," he says with a wink.

"Hell yeah I do." She rips off a small piece off the top of her muffin and pops it in her mouth. My eyes home in on the way her full lips move. "Alright, boys. Hit me," she mumbles around her muffin.

"We wanted to hear what you had to say first," Dom answers.

Lil's shoulders stiffen ever so slightly before taking a deep breath. She busies herself by brushing her hands together, clearing off any muffin crumbs that stick to her delicate fingers. Dom and I wait, leaving her to garner the courage to say whatever it is she has to say. "I-I really enjoyed what happened in Turks and Caicos."

Dom gently sets his large hand on her wrist, gently stroking it with the pad of his thumb. "So did we, Honey."

She offers him a soft smile. "And… and I think—no, I know—I know I want more of it. Of *that*. With both of you."

Lil looks between the two of us nervously as Dom drops his chin in my direction. I set my hand on top of her free one. "So do we, Sweetheart." I'm not sure where that nickname came from but it just felt right. And judging by the way her blush deepens across her cheeks, I'd wager a bet she likes it too. "But I think if we're going to do this we need to establish some ground rules."

"Agreed," Dom replies.

"Me too," Lil adds.

"Okay." I look around the room then back to where mine and Dom's hands rest on hers. "How do we feel about other people seeing the three of us in public?"

Lil looks to Dom. "Emerson and I already have a pretty established relationship. We're not outwardly affectionate in front of other people, not because we don't want to be, but because it's nobody's business honestly. But then again, I don't think anyone would necessarily be surprised if they found out."

*He's right.*

"I'm not much for PDA," Lil adds. Dom and I start to lift both our hands in unison, but Lil flips hers over and grabs onto them. "But… if I want to touch the two of you in public, I'd like to be able to. If that's okay with you?"

Dominic beams. "Hell yeah, it's fine with me."

She looks to me and I nod my head. Continuing, I ask, "Is everyone still in the same place we were before? We just want to have fun?" The two of them nod in agreement. "Then we all have to be on the same page. No more secrets."

"I don't think any one of us should see anyone else," Dom blurts out. "I mean—I just—this is complicated enough. I don't want to add other people into the mix."

"I agree," Lil answers.

"None of us were seeing anyone else anyway," I answer nonchalantly.

"Two of us are allowed to spend time with each other without the third one present?" Lil phrases it as a question, but I have a feeling it's not.

But judging by the way Dom slightly stiffens, I'd gather that makes him just as nervous as it does me.

However, it wouldn't be fair to Lil. Dominic and I spend a lot of our time together. It's part of being on the same team. So, to make her spend time with both of us all of the time wouldn't be fair since we can't be held to the same standards.

As if he were reading my mind, Dom and I nod in unison.

"If at any point, one of us wants to be done, we need to be up front about it. If this"—I point between the three of us—"is meant for us to have fun then that's what it should be. *Fun.* If that's no longer what's happening it needs to be clear." What I'm about to say next is something I thought about all night while I was lying in bed next to Dom. My best friend. My person. And as I stare across the table at him, sitting next to Lil, the woman who has the power to be our undoing, I realize there's no way I can't not say it. Before anything, my friendship with Dom has to come first. He's the only person I've ever felt truly *sees* me. Always. And that's something I can't lose. No version of any relationship is worth that risk. So taking a deep breath, I rush out, "And if one of us wants to be done, I think we *all* need to be done."

Dom's eyes widen for a moment, but just as quickly as shock takes over his face, it just as quickly morphs into understanding. His eyes soften and he tilts his head at me. He doesn't even have to say anything, and I know he understands. Then I look over at Lil, who is busy looking at Dom as he looks at me. And I see it. I watch as she finally grasps what he and I feel for one another. It's something few people are privileged enough to find. Because with or without sex, he is my person.

And finding someone who will love you like that is a rarity.

She smiles softly at him before turning her head to find me already staring at her. Letting go of my hand, she reaches up to cup my face, grazing her thumb along the corner of my mouth. "I think you boys got yourself a deal," she says softly.

"Hell yeah we do," Dom sounds from across the table.

Finally, the three of us go about drinking our coffee, getting lost in normal conversation, but one thought continues to plague my mind as the three of us sit at this little table tucked in the corner of the cafe.

If finding someone who will love you the way I know Dom loves me is such a rarity, when Lil held my face in her hand, when she looked at me as if she could see into the depths of my soul, like she could see me for everything I am and am not, why did it feel like I just might be lucky enough to experience such a rarity twice?

Is anyone ever really *that* lucky?

# CHAPTER 19

# WHAT'S THE PRICE?

## DOMINIC

"Atta boy, Banner!" Daisy, aka Casey Flowers, the team's first-line left defenseman, yells as he and Emerson skate over to me. They both clap me on my padded shoulders after I stopped a goal attempt from our second line.

We have a home game tomorrow night, so we're having a light scrimmage and practicing some plays before we face South Tampa, one of the season's bigger rivals.

The save was nothing overly impressive, but regardless, my teammates never fail to hype me up. That's what we all do for one another—day in and day out.

I couldn't have asked for a better group of guys to play with over the last four years.

Besides my mom and the Bakers, they're the closest thing I have to a family.

"Alright!" Coach Bailey yells. "One more and we'll wrap it up for the day."

Cap, our first line center, and Patty, aka Patrick, our second line center, face off on the dot to my right. I can hear the two of them chirping at one another from here. It's nothing serious, just lighthearted banter between teammates, but hockey isn't hockey without a little chirping.

Coach blows the whistle and drops the puck between the two of them as we run the last play of practice. As the puck makes its way toward the other side of the ice, I watch as Emerson momentarily turns his head and winks at me through the visor of his helmet.

The surly bastard has been unusually flirty since our talk with Lil at the cafe the other day. It's been a complete one-eighty from how he was the day of the car wash. So much so, it's kind of giving me whiplash. It's been nothing but stolen glances, flirtatious smiles, brushes of the hands, and he hasn't even been trying to hide the fact that his eyes are on me the entirety of the time we're in the locker room.

If I didn't know any better, I'd say the man's more than ready for round two of our fearsome threesome.

*No, Dom. Lil said if you called it that again, the only thing you'd be fearing is, and I quote, her fingers as she gives me the worst purple nurple of my life.*

*I didn't even know anyone past the age of fifteen gave purple nurples, but whatever.*

Anyway, as Emerson skates away from me, I have to force myself to get back into the zone. Because the faster this practice is over with, the faster we can finally meet up with our girl.

ME

Lil, how do we feel about subjecting Emmy to our favorite spot?

HONEY

Please tell me you're not joking?

ME

I would never joke about something so serious.

HONEY

This is going to be the best night of my life.

Wait, is it okay if I bring Gigi?

ME

Of course, the more the merrier. As long as we get you to ourselves later.

The dots appear and reappear on my screen a couple of times before she finally answers.

HONEY

Thank god... I've been dying over here.

EMMY

As excited as I am about the "later" part… Either of you care to fill me in on where we're going?

Turning my head, I stare at him as the two of us walk out of the rink and into the parking lot toward our cars, not wanting to miss the expression on his face when Lil tells him.

Finally my phone dings in my hand, but my eyes remain glued on Emerson.

HONEY

Thursday night is Karaoke night at Jack's. Prepare to be fucking swooned, Baby.

Emerson sighs so loud I'd be surprised if you couldn't hear it all the way across campus, meanwhile I tip my head back and bark out a laugh before texting her back.

ME

Pick you two up at the usual time, Honey.

HONEY

Can't wait.

Emerson turns his head dramatically, giving me his best "what the fuck" look, but I don't even let him get a word out before I point my finger at him. "Don't you even start. You're the one who's been giving me 'fuck-me' eyes all week. This is the price you gotta pay if you wanna get with all of this." I point my finger up and down my body, and an uncharacteristically huge smile takes over Emerson's face.

God, I fucking love it when he smiles at me like that.

[1] It's so rare. So genuine. Sometimes I feel like I've struck gold when I witness it.

"Oh, so now I have to pay a price?" he asks as he takes a step toward me. Scrunching my face up, I pretend to think about his question, even though we both know I'm full of shit. Laughing, he wraps his hand around the strap of my duffle and pulls me to him, leaving my chest pressed against his. "You and I both know I could have you on your knees right here in this parking lot if I wanted to," he says, his voice low and sultry.

I can almost feel all the blood in my body shoot straight to my cock. "What is with you this week?" I ask, feeling breathless.

He shrugs before tipping his face further, leaving his lips brushing against mine as he says, "Just feeling... *lucky* lately, I guess."

As I search his eyes, I can tell there's more weight to that statement than he leads on, but the ringing of my phone prevents me from digging further. I groan, and he presses a chaste kiss against my lips, despite being in the middle of the hockey rink's parking lot. Then, his body is gone, leaving my chest feeling cold despite the warm Gulf air. "Text me what time you're picking me up," he says as he climbs into his Jeep Wrangler.

---

1. fake love don't last (feat. iann dior) - mgk, iann dior

"Who said I was picking you up?"

He looks at me deadpan. "Dominic. If you're dragging me to karaoke, I'm going to need alcohol. You're driving." Then he shoots me a wink before pulling his Aviators down from where they rested on his head and driving away.

*Cheeky, motherfu—*

My phone continues to ring, reminding me of why I'm standing here, Emersonless.

I look at the screen to find my mom's face and slide the green button across the screen. "Hey, hold on, Mom."

I open the door to my F-150 and climb in, connecting my phone to the Bluetooth. Emerson constantly makes fun of me for driving a truck as a college student, and I admit, I don't necessarily *need* to drive a truck. Still, when you're as large as I am, options are limited on vehicles that provide ample enough room. It's the first thing I bought when I started making decent money with my audios.

Plus, I won't lie and say I don't like it.

"Can you hear me?" I ask as I pull out of the stall and head toward my apartment.

"Hi, Sweetie. I was just calling to check on you. Haven't heard from you in a while." My mom's soft voice fills the truck, and I can't describe it, but it instantly puts me at ease.

She's been my safe space for as long as I can remember. My soft place to land. My constant. Even when everything fell apart around us she was there. Ever present. The way she cared for me never wavered.

I'll spend the rest of my life trying to repay her for everything she's done for me.

It's the least I can do.

Especially after everything she's already been through.

"Sorry, Mom. It's been a crazy week since we got back from Turks and Caicos."

"Don't apologize for having a life, Sweetie. I know you're busy. I just wanted to do a quick check-in. How's school? Oh! How's work been? Numbers been good?"

My mom knows what I do. I don't hide this from her, and I'm not embarrassed of my job. When I told her, though, my one condition was that under no circumstances can she ever, and I mean ever, listen to any of it. Nor can she share it with any of her friends. I think I would literally combust from mortification. Hell, I went as far as making Googling my voice acting name off limits.

*I'm taking no chances.*

"School is good. My senior year classes are hard, but not impossible. I actually am enjoying a bit of a challenge this year. And work has been really good. I've seen a steady increase in subscriptions, and I've been making well beyond my means, so that's all a guy can really ask for."

I can't see her, but I know she's smiling on the other end of the phone. "That's so good to hear. I watched your game last week, by the way. Sometimes I still can't get over how you and Emerson play so well together. I'm so proud of you both. For everything you've been doing. Not just hockey. This is a hard season of life, and you are navigating it beautifully. I'm glad you have each other."

*If she only knew.*

"Thank you, Mom. Have you been okay? I know this is always a hard time of year for you."

Guilt nags at me. I should have been better about calling her. But I've just been so swept up in everything. In Emerson. In Lil. I need to do better. Mom deserves better.

She sighs softly. "I know it is for you too, Sweetie."

I fidget nervously with the seam of my shorts. "It's not me I'm worried about, Mom."

Her silence speaks volumes. She wants to push me more but knows it's no use. Finally, she says, "I'm doing okay. Every year, it gets a little easier. I will never be able to fill the hole that your father left. But slowly, other things I love are making the vastness of his absence hurt a little less, like stacking bricks around the side of a well. Soon, I'll be able to lean over and see the hole he left and admire it with love and longing, rather than falling into its darkness. That's all I can hope for. And for you too, Dominic."

As I round the corner of my block, memories of my dad flash through my brain. I was twelve when he died. One night, he peeked through my door to tell me goodnight, and the next morning, he just didn't wake up. But I did. And Mom did. And the sounds of her screams as she woke next to his lifeless body are what woke me.

Those screams have followed me. They're impossible to forget.

Like a constant reminder that no amount of love can keep a person in your life.

Because if that were the case, my dad would have lived forever.

Tears sting at my eyes, and I bite the inside of my cheek to keep them from falling. This isn't about me. This is about Mom. Every year, as we near the anniversary of Dad's death, I get a pit in my stomach. I worry about her constantly. I lost my dad, but she lost her person. The love of her life.

But she's right. Every year, it gets easier and easier for her. I know it will never go away, that kind of pain never does. But for her, it seems as if it's morphed from an all-consuming pain to a dull ache. One that sneaks up on you from time to time, rather than constantly being at the forefront of your brain.

I wish that were the case for me. I wish I could think about him without hearing those screams.

I wish.

Clearing my throat, I simply respond, "Hey, Mom, I'm about to pull into the parking garage, but I promise I'll be better at checking in. Okay?"

And just like I know when she is smiling, I don't need to see her to understand the look of concern that covers her face. But once again, she doesn't push. "Okay. I love you, sweet boy."

"I love you too, Mom. I'll call you soon." I end the call using the button on my steering wheel before she says something else that will make the tears finally fall.

I can't do this today.

I don't want to fall apart today.

It's supposed to be a good day.

So, as I pull into my parking spot, I close my eyes, take a deep breath, and recenter myself.

Because tonight isn't about the darkness of my past.

It's about the light in my present.

And I'll be damned if I'm going to let those memories tarnish it.

# CHAPTER 20
# DOWN BAD X
# TWO... OR THREE?

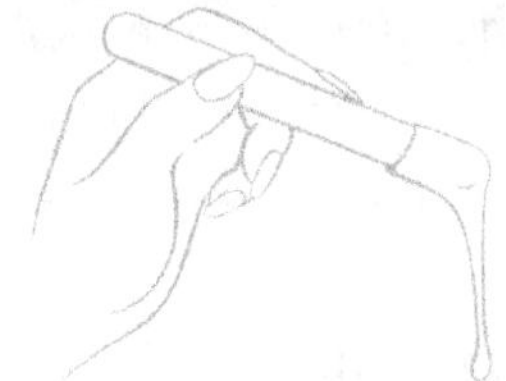

## LILIANA

I'm on my way home from work after the guys texted me about going to Jack's. It's a little hole-in-the-wall bar here in Pensacola, and it may just be my favorite place.

You wouldn't catch me dead in one of the fancy bars that charge twenty bucks for a watered-down tequila soda.

Gigi had mentioned while we were FaceTiming earlier that her parents were keeping Charlie for her tonight and that she wanted to hang out. She was almost done with her homework, and I convinced her that she needed to treat herself with a little night out. And what better way to do that than belting out your favorite songs in a bar on the beach?

She knows who Emerson and Dom are and that I have been seeing them both. But she certainly doesn't know of our new *arrangement*. Honestly, I think she might actually be pretty proud of me. She hasn't talked much about her sex life, being a mom to a newborn and all, but I have a feeling my pocket-sized redhead has a side to her that no one knows. I'd lay any amount of money down that the woman is an absolute firecracker in bed.

Thank god she's not wasting it on that fucking jerkoff.

I just hope she finds someone someday that's worthy of her. Who knows? Mr. Right might be waiting in the wings, ready and willing to serenade her with "You're Beautiful."

*Only one way to find out.*

I'm pressing my code into my front door before shoving it open. It's the newest addition to my apartment. Emerson ended up installing it because I always forget to lock my door, and with the fancy keypad, it does it on its own. Kicking the door closed behind me, I throw my purse and oversized cup—my weapon of choice if ever needed—onto the kitchen island. This apartment used to be Clay's, and I had to come in and redecorate the whole goddamn thing. It was too dull. Too clean-cut for my liking.

Of course, I asked Clay before I started, but once I got the okay, it was so on.

I ended up painting the whole place—really, only

one or two walls per room. I might be a little on the adventurous side, but I couldn't do the wild colors on every wall. I love the eclectic look; I'm convinced it's the closest to my haywire personality.

My favorite space is the living room. The wall on which the TV is mounted is a mauvy pink, and every decoration in the living room is either pink or gold.

Rocky calls it *throw-up pink*, but I just call it my happy place.

Heading to my room, I strip out of my—surprise, surprise—pink scrubs, to get ready for our night out.

My fingers are crossed that I have the time to shower by the time Gigi arrives. She had to run and drop Charlie off at her parents' house. I told her to come in once she got back, and we could jam out to music and pregame before the guys came to pick us up.

Once I'm done with the fastest shower I've taken in a minute, I'm opening the glass door, drying off, and shrugging into my getting-ready robe just in time to hear my front door open. I yell, "I hope that's you, Gigi, and not a serial killer." In all reality, I know it's her. She's one of the few people who know my new door code.

"It's me, babe! I raided my mom's liquor cabinet just like the old days. You want a margarita?!"

Knowing her parents, it's safe to assume that's some high-quality tequila she has, so of course I scream, "Hell yes! Can I have salt on my rim? It's up in the cabinet, and the marg mix is in the fridge!"

Thankfully I didn't need to wash my thick-ass hair, or we would've been here another two hours, minimum, waiting on me. A few minutes later, Gigi strolls into my oversized Jack and Jill bathroom, setting our margaritas on the counter. "Can you do my eye makeup? I did everything else, but whatever magic you use to put your eye makeup on, I don't possess."

"Of course! You want to curl my hair while I do my makeup, so we can save a little time?"

"Duh." She's already scavenging through my cabinet below the sink, where she knows I keep my wand.

We sip our margaritas and gossip, like the goddesses intended.

*This, this is girlhood.*

Once our hair and makeup are done we head to my closet to pick out a cute outfit.

She brought a couple different options with her from her closet. I would love if we could wear one another's clothes, but the girl is maybe five foot two on a good day, and I tower over her, so most of my stuff would swallow her whole.

Not to mention, Gigi may have just had a kid, but you wouldn't know unless Charlie's with her. She is a MILF to say the least. I know moms go through all kinds of healing mentally and even some physical things you can't see.

I keep a handful of business cards for one of the other suite owners in my building. She's a pelvic floor therapist, and I hand them out to my clients who joke about peeing themselves. It's always the, "It's very common to pee yourself, but it's not normal" spiel. Each one of them who has visited Gina down the hall was so thankful. Hell, even I go to see her. Sports can fuck with your pelvic floor if you're not careful, and I was not careful whatsoever.

Not to mention, a strong pelvic floor can help make good sex great, and like, who wouldn't want that?

She pulls out some black barrel jeans that I know would look so cute on her, but then I spot the leather mini skirt she has tucked away, probably thinking I wouldn't see it. "Nuh-uh. Put those down." I point to the leather skirt. "That. Put it on. Ooo, pair it with that band tee," I add pointing to the black Metallica shirt.

She huffs and puffs but eventually starts to put everything on. Heading into my closet, I find my obnoxiously hot-pink leather mini skirt and a black faded Oasis crop top.

There's nothing more fun than matching with your bestie and going out to the bar. A bar that we're going to be severely overdressed for, but who cares?

I walk out of my closet, and Gigi is already dressed in hers, turned away from me, and looking in my full length mirror. I can tell by the look on her face, she's analyzing every bit of her appearance as if she's not the one of hottest ladies in town. And that just won't do. "Oh my god, that's it. Yes! Yes! Yes!" I let out a whistle of appreciation. She turns around to face me, pink crawling up her cheeks.

"You don't think it's too much? This is the first time I'm going out after having Charlie. I think the sexiest thing I've put on since he was born was a pair of jean shorts." I see her lip starting to quiver. I can only imagine how overwhelming this moment must feel.

"Ahh ahh, no crying. You're a hot bitch. It's not too much. You look amazing. We're going out to have a good time, but if you hate it or get sad, you say the word and we'll get the hell out of there. The boys will be just fine without me." I smile at her, and she gives me one back, though it doesn't reach her eyes. I want her to feel good and remember that she can still have fun even though she has a baby now.

That's what best friends are for.

Two disgusting tequila shots later, we're jumping in the back of Dominic's truck to head to Jack's.

"Give me bluetooth. I'm not listening to country music right now." I'll never admit it to Emerson, but I have *really* been loving the older 2000's country music, which tracks because it's my favorite time period for everything.

Instead of wasting time setting my phone up, he hands me his unlocked phone and lets me scroll through his music app. I feel eyes staring into my skull, and I turn to look at a gaping Gigi. My brows immediately pull together. "What?"

She leans in and whispers loud enough for me to hear her over the T-Pain I currently have blaring through the car's speakers. "He just gives you his unlocked phone?"

My brows pinch and I respond gently, "When

there's nothing to hide, this is how it is, sweets." I just want to hold her; she has been put through so much with guys, but instead, I smile and let it go.

I'll eventually talk praise and worthiness into her.

She deserves the world, and I want to be here to witness her finding it.

Gigi slowly turns her head to face me. "Oh shit… you've got these two down bad for you." We're at a high-top table tucked along the wall while Dom and I are waiting our turn to get up there and sing our hearts out.

I give her a sheepish look that quickly turns into a devilish smirk when I see the look on her face. "I fear they've got me down bad, too, babe. We're keeping it fun for now, but more often than not I'm fucking swooning over the two of them and everything they do for me." Then I lean in closer to her barstool and whisper, "And do *to* me." I nudge her shoulder, making her giggle.

"God, I'm so jealous." She laughs. "Actually, I'm not. I've barred men from my life for the foreseeable future."

I hate that she's lost all hope in men, but honestly they don't have much going for them usually anyways, and then throw in the shitty situation and the worst baby daddy in the world, and I'd be right there with her on the banning-men train too. "You'll find your person, if you want to, of course. No one *needs* a partner if it's something you don't want, but in that same breath, you deserve to have someone who will worship the ground you walk on, Gigi."

And right as those words come out of my mouth, the guys are back with the drinks, and the DJ is announcing our names to come up to the stage.

[1] "Our next duo is singing a song from the pop legend herself! *It's Britney, bitch.*"

---

1.  Gimme More-Britney Spears

# CHAPTER 21

# I'M ON YOUR TEAM NOW

## EMERSON

"Here you go, Gigi. Got you another one. Malibu and Diet Coke right?"

Her smile pushes up her freckled cheeks as she takes the glass from my hand, yet her eyes look almost shocked. As if she can't believe I would take time out of my day to get her a simple drink. "Oh. Thanks, Emerson."

[1] I sit down in my seat next to her as the crowd continues to cheer on Lil and Dom. I think they're on their third song, and they aren't showing any signs of stopping. I'm both equally jealous and in awe of how in sync the two of them are. I always am.

Even Gigi, who is apparently best friends with the woman currently giving me "the eyes" as she belts Dua Lipa's "New Rules" at the top of her lungs, has her eyes

---

1. New Rules - Dua Lipa

glued to the stage. Albeit she looks more amused than in awe of Lil.

But, despite how desperate I am to get the two of them to look at me the way this entire bar is looking at them, I'm even more desperate to get my hands on them. I watch as Dom pulls her close, pressing Lil's back against his chest, as the two of them sway back and forth singing—to be frank, I'm half-tempted to storm up there, pull them off the stage, and take them home right this minute. But I know if I interrupt what Dom is referring to as "their moment," they will be beyond pissed.

Forcing myself not to get a hard-on, again, I refocus my attention on the redhead across the table, who I didn't even know existed until we picked them up from their apartment building. "Why do I feel like I know you from somewhere?" I ask her.

"Hm? Oh, probably because I played for the volley-ball team. Or play? I played freshman and sophomore year. Took a… a break this year. I'll play again next year, though." She takes a long drink of her rum and Coke through her straw as I recall a small redhead playing in the back row for the school's volleyball team when I went to a couple of games last year.

"You played libero, right?"

Her eyes widen in surprise, as if she's shocked I even knew what that was. "Yeah, I did."

"So does your year off have anything to do with who I'm assuming is your baby?" And we're back to shock. Should I have asked it so bluntly? *Probably not.* Dom's always telling me to "soften the blow" of my delivery, but sometimes it just comes out without thinking. "Lil never told us about him, if that's what you're worried about," I clarify. "But she did mention she was watching her neighbor's baby the other day. Kind of putting two and two together here."

What looks like a mix of guilt and embarrassment passes over Gigi's face, though I'm not sure why. Being a mom is nothing to be ashamed of. "I never—" She inhales a deep breath. "I never asked her to keep me and Charlie—that's my son's name by the way. I never asked her to keep us a secret. Honestly, I'm a little surprised she did. Because I've heard plenty about the two of you." I can't help it, I puff up my chest a little at the thought of Lil telling her friends about me. "I guess she just saw the situation I was in, a single mother, living alone with a new baby, and decided to protect me. To keep me safe. I love her for that, honestly. The world's a scary place."

"You got that right." Which is exactly why I finally installed the automatic lock on Lil's door.

"Nice job on the lock, by the way," Gigi says with a wink.

*What is she? A mind reader? It's a mom thing. I just fucking know it.*

"I could get you one too, you know?" I say nonchalantly, but once again, Gigi looks as if I just offered her the fucking moon. The woman plays every thought out across her face.

"Why would you do that for me?"

I'm confused. "What do you mean? You just said so yourself. You're a single woman, living alone with a new baby. The last thing you need to worry about is whether or not you're safe in your own home. Plus, if you're important to Lil, you're important to me. To us," I say as I nod in the direction of Dom, who is now sweating from all the gyrating his hips are doing.

"That actually would be amazing. I—I'll pay you back for it, though!"

I wave her off and take a drink of my whiskey. "Don't even worry about it. I have a half-off code from when I bought Lil's, anyway."

*I don't, but she doesn't need to know that.*

"Just make sure you give the code to Charlie's dad before he comes to get him next time," I add, and Gigi's face pales.

*Hello, mouth. Meet foot.*

I pinch my face up in regret as Gigi looks down at her lap. I want to reach for her. To apologize. But I get a sense she's a lot like me. She doesn't need or want to be emotionally coddled. She wants the space to process her thoughts and feelings in her own time. I think that's why everything plays across her face so vividly. She's actively thinking. Always processing.

So, I wait.

I wait until she finally takes a deep breath and looks up at me. "That's probably another reason Lil never said anything about me and Charlie. Charlie's dad— actually scratch that—Charlie's sperm donor is pretty popular on campus. Plays football actually. He's in one of the school's fraternities. She probably didn't know if you were close to him or not. The last thing I need is that piece of shit knowing anything else about me."

I think that's the first time I've heard this woman swear all evening. I wrack my brain, trying to think of someone on the football team who has mentioned that he has a kid, because it's true, Dom and I are pretty close with a decent amount of them, but I cannot for the life of me think of a single one of them ever mentioning Charlie. Let alone Gigi. With that being said, one name comes to mind from that team. One, and I use this term very loosely, *man* who would be a big enough piece of shit to have a child and pretend like he doesn't exist. To be quite fucking frank, I'm honestly surprised the asshole is as popular as he is. I have never, and I mean not once, had a good interaction with this waste of space. My protective instincts flare because, like I said before, if Gigi is important to Lil, then she's important to me. So is Charlie. Gritting my teeth, I ask the question I already feel like I know the answer to. "Who is he?"

"Weston Parker," she answers softly.

"I fucking knew it," I grit out.

"For the most part, he leaves us alone. Hell, when I told him I was pregnant, he practically ran the other direction. Wasn't there when I gave birth to Charlie, has never spent any time with him, didn't even sign his birth certificate. But every once in a while, he likes to just show up. Like he's trying to blow up any bit of progress I've made. Seeing him be god's gift to football and the campus shining star is bad enough, but to see him and know he wants nothing to do with—" Gigi's voice cracks ever so slightly, but she covers it up quickly. "But to see him and know he wants nothing to do with that sweet boy makes me see fucking red. Every time I see him I want to burn the world down around him." Suddenly she stops, and her eyes go wide, clearly worried she's said too much. "Anyway." She fakes a smile. "That's me in a nutshell. Aren't you so glad Lil's my best friend?"

I reach across the table and grab her hand. "Actually, yeah. I really am."

And that's the truth. I can see it already. I can see the way Gigi and Charlie make Lil a better person. In only the few hours I've seen the two of them around one another, I've witnessed a side of Lil I don't think I'll ever be privy to. And I love that for her. And I love that for Gigi and Charlie. They deserve to have people in their corner who want to be there. That much I know for certain.

Another thing I know for certain, next time I see Weston fucking Parker I'm going to have a hell of a time not punching him in his pretty-boy face.

Gigi gives me a soft smile as the music around us fades, and Lil and Dom finally exit the stage. The two of them make their way over to us, breathless, and when Lil spots my hand gently resting on Gigi's she simply smiles and asks, not an ounce of jealousy in her voice, "What's going on here?"

Gigi's cheeks pink in embarrassment, so I look up at the two of them and say, "Just getting to know one another."

Lil's eyes search mine, and I know that she knows I know. But instead of commenting on it, she bends over, kisses my cheek softly, and whispers in my ear, "Thank you."

Out of the corner of my eye, I see someone bend over next to Gigi and grab something off the floor as Dom sits down next to me, and Lil makes herself comfortable in my lap. The man stands, black clutch in his hand, and taps Gigi on the shoulder. "'Scuse me, ma'am. Is this yours? It was on the floor."

"Ford?" Dom asks, standing back up. He grabs Ford's hand and pulls him in for a hug, patting him a couple times on the back.

Ford Acosta is first baseman for the school's baseball team. He's a little bit of a surly fuck sometimes, which I can appreciate about a guy, but he's as good as they come.

"Hey, guys. Didn't mean to interrupt, I just saw this on the floor as I was walking by and wanted to get it back to the lady here."

"Her name's Gigi. Well, Georgia actually," Lil rushes out from her spot in my lap, and I pinch her side. "Ow!" She slaps at my chest. "What was that for?"

"Don't even think about it, Darlin'," I mumble in her ear because I know exactly what's going on in that pretty head of hers.

"Me?" She places her hand on her chest, feigning ignorance. "I'm not doing anything."

"Keep it up and I'll make you pay for it later," I snarl playfully.

"Hmmm." She wiggles, rubbing her ass against my crotch. "I like the sound of that. But"—she subtly points her finger across the table—"*look.*"

Ford and Gigi aren't even paying attention. He's just staring down at her in awe and she back up at him. Like a couple of deer in headlights. Finally, Ford clears his throat and hands her her bag. "Georgia is a beautiful name." Gigi grabs the bag from him, and I don't miss the way their fingers brush up against one another a little longer than necessary. But Gigi doesn't speak. She just smiles at him, stunned into silence. Ford tends to have that effect on women. I'm not gonna lie. He's a good looking dude.

A few seconds later, Ford finally lets go of the black clutch, and takes one last look at Gigi before looking at the three of us. "You all have a great night. I'll see you around."

Lil giggles in my lap as we watch Gigi's eyes follow Ford to the other side of Jack's.

*Well, that's interesting.*

# CHAPTER 22
# PLANT DADDY

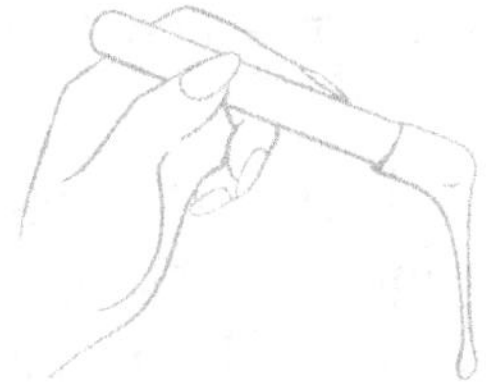

**LILIANA**

"**D**om, baby, why don't we come here more often?" I huff and pretend to pout as we walk up to his second-floor apartment. "I love coming to your place." I drag my nail down his black, faded, and cropped Disturbed T-shirt.

*God he looks so fucking hot.*

*How many drinks have I had tonight?*

*Not that many, but enough to be tipsy.*

But being with these men, these insanely sexy, charming, wonderful men, I feel high. Euphoric even. Just being in their presence makes me feel like I'm fucking floating.

"Because your place has you, Honey," Dom purrs in his audio erotica voice, and it has my pussy reacting like it always does. The devilish smirk he's wearing says he knows exactly the effect it has on me. Emerson's huffing like a bull on the other side of me, trying to wrangle our drunk dumbasses into Dom's apartment, before we wake up the neighbors from fucking on the steps.

Emerson finally opens the door to Dom's apartment, and we're immediately transported into what feels like the Amazon rainforest. A serene, spacious two-bedroom apartment that is covered from floor to ceiling in plants. I honestly don't even know what color the walls are in here between all the vines and branches lining the walls.

He's at max capacity for anything else decoration-wise with all the plants he keeps in this damn apartment. This man has everything you can imagine. I won't pretend to act like I know the first thing about these things, but I do know that he's in groups on social media to buy, sell, and trade them.

Yes.

Buy, sell, trade fucking plants.

We've had to drop plans multiple times and drive halfway across town to pick up a piece of a plant. It's not even a full plant; it's a damn piece of root or something that he'll plant and baby until he has the thing snaking and wrapping up the wall. I'm pretty sure he's doing some witchcraft over them or something, but I don't have the evidence to prove that theory...

Yet.

It's bizarre, but it's what the man loves, so Emerson and I sit and watch him enjoy his plant babies as he heads straight to the kitchen sink to fill up his watering can that says, "My plants are my happy pills," and I watch as he moves over to the hanging baskets by his balcony door.

He reaches up, and a sliver more of his stomach comes out of his cropped shirt, and I let out a low whistle. "You better put that slutty stomach away, or I won't be controlling myself much longer." Something about watching him care for a living thing while simultaneously showing me pieces of bare skin has me clenching my thighs together.

Even if that something is just a plant.

Emerson is leaning up against the island, one leg crossed over the other, openly appreciating the view of drunk Dom alongside me. I watch as his eyes rake up and down Dom's gorgeous body. His ass in those jeans should be illegal, and don't get me started on the dimples on his back that are out to play because the man can't be bothered to pull his jeans up while he's watering his plants. Emerson groans. "Dom, you keep taunting me with that ass, and I'm going to have to redden it."

Dom looks over his shoulder and teases Emerson some more. "What you gonna do about it, *Emmy*?"

Oh he hates it when we call him that.

In what feels like half of a second, Emerson is crossing the room to Dom, pressing his front into Dom's back, and I move over to the couch to get a better view of what's about to go down. "What did I say about calling me that?"

"Hmmm…. I'm having a really hard time remembering," Dom jokes, then moans as Emerson's hand slides down the front of his jeans.

We had the best night tonight. Dom and I sang our hearts out until we shut down the bar. I even got Gigi up there with me once. It was genuinely the perfect night.

Once we dropped Gigi off at her apartment, we came straight here. We could've easily gone to my apartment right next door, but I didn't want to traumatize Gigi with what I know is about to be a wild night of sex.

*Or at least, that's what I'm hoping.*

Before I know it, Emerson's knees hit the ground, and he's unbuttoning Dom's jeans like it's his only mission on this planet. He doesn't even pull them down his legs all the way, just enough to free his throbbing cock. They're halfway down his ass, and the way the top of his cheeks are hanging over the waistband of his jeans, makes me want to crawl over there and bite it.

But I don't.

Actually, I change my mind on what I want out of this night entirely.

I prop a pillow up behind me on the end of the couch, facing them. I spread my legs wide with my knees up, and I let my skirt ride up my thighs, baring my pussy to them.

"Lil, Honey, why so far away?" Dom asks with a pleading look in his eye. I watch those eyes roll to the back of his head as Emerson sucks him to the back of his throat. He starts pumping his hand up and down Dom's soaked shaft in sync with his mouth, dare I say better than I ever could.

"I think I just want to watch you two tonight..." I hesitate a little. "If that's okay with both of you."

Emerson pops off of Dom's cock to reassure me. "Of course you can watch, as long as you rub that pretty cunt while you do." The smirk on that man's lips before taking Dom back between them is just plain devious.

"Emerson, you look awfully pretty with my fat cock stretching that mouth open. Eyes watering for me, while you're trying to hold back your gags." Dom grabs the sides of his head while still looking down at him and starts controlling his movements more, going deeper and deeper. "Fuccckkk, I love when you're on your knees for me." Dom's dirty talk in the heat of the moment may be my new favorite thing. Yeah, his audios are great, but nothing compares when you experience Dominic Foster in real life. Nothing I could hear through a set of headphones could top the real thing.

I hear Emerson's whimper from Dom's words and that has me picking up speed as I circle my clit, my release already near. Emerson has the same idea. Unbuttoning his jeans, he pulls out his cock. I can tell from here it's painfully hard and leaking at the tip. I lick my lips, fighting the urge to walk across the room and take it into my mouth.

"Tap my leg if it's too much," Dom whispers. "But I know my man can take it." He looks over to me and adds, "I want to hear you coming with me. Both of you."

A chorus of whimpers is our only response, and Dom only uses that as fuel to his fire.

I love that both of them can be just as submissive as

they are dominant in the bedroom. There's nothing more attractive to me than someone who knows exactly what they want and is not afraid to ask for it.

*My kryptonite.*

Emerson hums around Dom's cock, the wet slurping sounds fill the otherwise quiet apartment. I don't think I can handle it much longer, so I plead, "Em, make him come. *Now.*"

And fuck does he listen.

I see his cheeks hollow, and Dom opens his mouth like he's going to say something, but can't quite get the words out. Em has rendered him speechless. That has me tipping over the edge. "*Fuck.* I'm-I'm coming."

Dom pumps in and out of Emerson's mouth two more times, growling, "Swallow it. Swallow me like the good boy you are."

My eyes are glued to them as I begin to catch my breath, and Emerson comes right along with us, all over his hands and jeans that are still barely down his thighs.

A small giggle falls from my lips. Who knew watching a man water his plants would start this?

[1] Flopping back on the couch, I can't quite get my giggles to subside as I say, "Well I think we all thought tonight was going to be a wild fuck fest, but I think that was even better."

---

1.  So What - P!nk

# CHAPTER 23

# THE MORNING LIGHT

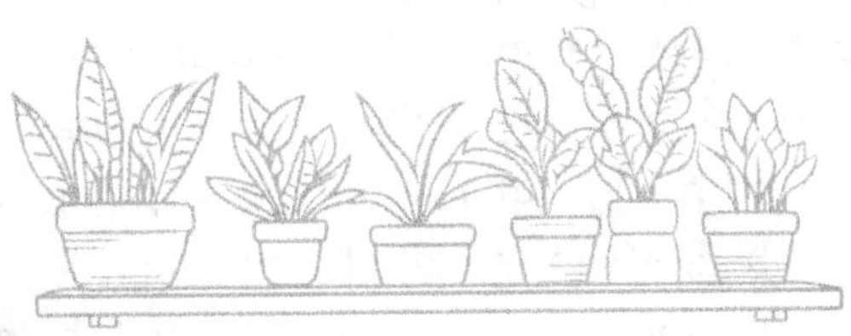

## DOMINIC

Raising the spatula to my mouth like a microphone, I sing at the top of my lungs,[1] "Build Me Up Buttercup," as if I were a member of The Foundations myself. I've been singing along with the songs on my perfectly curated "Cooking breakfast for my boo thang" playlist for the last fifteen minutes and shaking my ass in nothing but briefs and a pair of socks —because despite it being Florida, my floors are always fucking freezing in the morning—in between perfectly executed pancake flips.

The coffee finished brewing about five minutes ago, and I heard a round of groaning—not the sexual kind, but the "oh my god I hate the morning" kind—about two minutes ago, which means Lil and Emerson should come grumbling into the kitchen any minute—

---

1. Build Me Up Buttercup - The Foundations

"What is even happening right now?" Lil groans from behind me.

*Now.*

Turning on the balls of my feet, I point my microphone at the two Grumpy Guses in front of me, both of them wearing matching looks of both annoyance and confusion. Emerson is in nothing but a pair of cotton shorts, long hair looking disheveled, and Lil is in nothing but one of my shirts, strands of hair falling out of the braid she slept in. Neither Lil nor Em are big fans of the morning, but if anything is going to get them out of bed, it's the smell of a fresh pot of coffee. Despite their pinched expressions, I can't help but admire how fucking cute the two of them look standing next to one another, sleepy and annoyed, in my kitchen.

I urge the two of them to sing along, waving my spatula in their direction, even though I know good and well I have a better chance of sprouting wings than that happening. But I do it anyway.

Emerson looks me up and down before asking, "Who are you? Joel fucking Goodsen?"

I playfully raise my brows at him, not even the least bit phased by his scowl. "Get me a button-up and some tighty whities, and I'll bust out the moves right here and now, baby."

He rolls his eyes, but I see the corners of his lips twitch. "I'm too tired to understand what either of you are talking about," Lil adds. "But for the record, I only came out here because I smelled coffee."

"Same," Emerson adds.

"But this"—Lil points at me, moving her finger up and down my body—"is an added bonus."

I shoot her a wink before stepping forward and pressing a soft kiss to her forehead. "Morning, Sweetheart."

"Mmm." She smiles up at me. "Good morning."

"Grab yourself a cup of coffee. Your creamer is in the fridge."

Her sleepy eyes suddenly widen in delight. "Cinnamon coffee cake?"

"Sure is."

Her brows pinch together. "But I—you—I don't spend the night here that often. How did you know to get it?"

Well that's easy. "I usually keep a container of it in the fridge so I have it in case you need it. I usually drink it with my morning coffee or this crabass over here will drink it with his when he stays here so it doesn't go bad."

A slow smile spreads back across her face as if I just reached up into the sky, grabbed the moon, and presented it to her. But it's just creamer. Simple, really. Regardless, I'll take that smile whenever I can get it. I press one more soft kiss to her lips followed by another on the beauty mark above her top lip.

She squeezes my arm gently before stepping around me and heading for the coffee pot, and I hear her mumble to herself, "Fuck yes. Chocolate chip pancakes."

I puff my chest out in pride as my eyes move to Emerson before he speaks, his voice low and rough. "I will never understand how you're like this in the morning. It's like you shit fucking rainbows."

I bark a laugh, but he's not wrong. Mornings have always been my thing. For most of my childhood it was when I got to spend time with my dad. He worked long hours in the evening, so those were usually spent with Mom dragging me to and from games and practice. But those few hours before school, when the only sounds outside were the birds chirping and the neighbor's sprinklers going off, that's when I got to spend time with Dad. Sometimes, if it was nice enough, we'd go outside and he would slap shots into the small goal we kept in the driveway. I did my best to block them, and sometimes I even managed it. However, looking back on it, I'm pretty sure those are the ones he let up on just so he could see the smile on my face when I stopped it.

I'd help him make breakfast, and the two of us would have it on the table ready to go by the time Mom woke up. Didn't matter if we cooked scrambled eggs or a continental breakfast. The smile on her face every morning was like she won the lottery.

After Dad died, I knew that was one thing I wanted to keep doing for her. A small way I could make her life easier somehow. Even though some mornings I could practically see the memory of Dad flash in her eyes before she'd softly kiss my head and quietly eat her breakfast. The only sound then was her sniffling as she tried to hold back tears.

Regardless, the habit has kind of always stuck. Most days I don't even need an alarm.

The same does not go for my best friend. Even when

we're traveling for games and the two of us have to share a room, I feel like I'm trying to get a fifteen-year-old boy out of bed for school.

Liliana is no better. Some mornings she buries herself so deep into her pillow, I genuinely worry she's going to get stuck there.

But I'll take their grumpiness any morning I can get it.

"Am I going to get a good morning kiss from you too or are you just going to keep snarling at me?" Emerson's sleepy eyes stare at me deadpan, so I add, "The sooner you give me what I'm looking for, the sooner you get pancakes and coffee."

"And they're really fucking good," Lil mumbles from behind me. I look over my shoulder to find her sitting on the counter, cup of coffee in one hand and a stolen pancake in the other, half of it already in her mouth.

Chuckling, I turn around and face Emerson. "Tick, tock."

He rolls his eyes, *again*, before grabbing the spatula in my hand and yanking me to him. With my front pressed up against his, I can feel the effects of the *morning* pressing against my stomach, letting me know he's not as annoyed as he lets on. Then he mumbles against my lips, "You're lucky there's chocolate chips in those pancakes."

My smile grows wider, if that was even possible. "Just trying to do myself a favor."

He huffs a laugh before pressing a chaste kiss to my lips. "Good morning, *Dominic*."

"Good morning, *Emerson*."

I feel his cock twitch against me before he kisses me once more and heads over to where Lil is sitting on the counter.

Turning back around, I watch as he pours himself a cup of coffee and adds a splash of the creamer to it. Usually he drinks it black, but because he knows I keep it stocked here for Lil on the off chance she needs it, he's sure to help me drink it instead of letting it go to waste. Then, he steps in between her spread legs, one hand resting on her bare thigh, the other holding his coffee, bends down, and takes a bite out of the pancake in her hand. Her face lights up as she giggles at him, and the muscles along his back flex as he moves his hand up and down her thigh.

The mornings are where I find peace. They're when I feel centered. They're when I feel *whole*. Like, for just a couple hours, my life isn't missing anything. Or at least that's what I thought.

Because as I stand here in my kitchen, staring at the two of them, I realize that all this time, I think I was wrong. I try to wrack my brain for the last time this sense of peace has settled in my chest. Suddenly, the thought crashes into me like a freight train. I haven't felt this way since the day before my dad died. All these years, all this time, I've used the sunrise as a way to find solace, but it's only now, looking at the two of them, that I understand, I was nowhere close.

And as much as I want to get lost in the joy that is that moment, another thought hits me. This feeling, this *joy*, was already taken from me once. It was snatched from my grasp without a second thought. The person who made me feel whole was taken from me, leaving me grasping for pieces of him in the morning light.

If the someone with that power over me was taken from me once, it can be taken from me again.

And I just know… I *know* that'd I'd never survive it the second time around—or third.

# CHAPTER 24
# BABY DADDY TORTURE

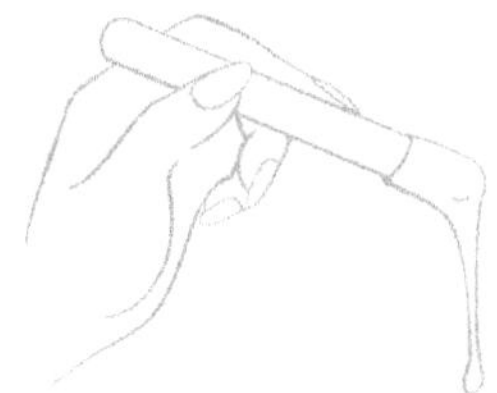

### LILIANA

I'm back at my apartment later that day, relaxing on my couch, full from orgasms, coffee, and chocolate chip pancakes. I have one of my headphones in as I listen to the female main character in this book getting railed by her three boyfriends, when my phone starts to buzz.

GIGI

We ran into Wes at the grocery store...

He didn't even acknowledge Charlie

I'm not going to put in writing what I want to do to that piece of shit...

I'll be over there in a second

The way a book boyfriend would never. I roll my eyes because I've had just about enough of Charlie's sperm donor.

Does it shock me that he acted like Charlie doesn't exist?

*Nope. Not even in the slightest.*

Does it make me want to murder him any less?

*Also no.*

A quick murder would be too easy on him, though. I would want him to suffer—no, I would *need* him to suffer, and not your normal suffering. Psychological warfare level of suffering. Suffering on the same level that Gigi has had to endure as a single mother because he is literally scum of the fucking earth.

I would put one of those labor simulators on him, strap him to a bed, poke and prod at him for a good thirty hours, and then mock a C-section. And I wouldn't stop there either. I would have him take care of one of those baby simulators we had to have in health class, ensuring it's on the worst level. If he can't keep it alive, then he's locked up for murder.

Is that psychotic of me?

*Maybe.*

Do I still want to do it?

*Abso-fucking-lutely.*

The knock on the door pulls me out of my murderous spiral. Probably for the better because it was only going to get worse as time went on. I'm sure whatever she's about to tell me will only add to the wishful torment.

She stands inside my door with Charlie on her hip, looking like she's on the verge of a breakdown. Then, completely unprompted, Charlie's hands reach out to me as he babbles away. But then he says, "Li, Li," and we both stop in our tracks.

My eyes find Gigi's, and it's like that was the straw that broke the camel's back—the floodgates have been released. Quickly, I pull her inside and kick the door closed with my foot. The three of us stand in the entryway as my best friend breaks down in front of me.

Between sobs, Gigi gets out, "He said your name before dada…" Her voice cracks, and she lets out a soul-deep sob, causing tears to prick at the back of my eyes.

"Da da da da," Charlie mocks. Gigi's head snaps up, and she hits a new level of hysterics I didn't even know was possible. She's hysterically laughing with tears running down her cheeks. To the point that I'm starting to get worried…

Thinking quick on my feet, I pull out my phone with my other hand and text for some backup.

**Lil's Bitches**

ME

Operation: get Gigi to forget the sperm donor. I need help.

DOM THE DON

On it. We'll be there in 10

EM AKA BIG BOY

Why am I kind of scared to know what's about to happen?

Should we have bail money ready?

DOM THE DON 🎙️

I'll always bail you out sugar tits 😌

I wrap Gigi and Charlie in a big hug, and it hits me again how similar this is to when we first met. But this time is going to be different. I'm sick of watching her break down in front of me because some dickwad refuses to see how amazing these two beautiful humans are. So, I'm taking her out for a lunch date. I need her mind off of him and what just happened, and out of the house, even if we were just out last night.

[1] She was doing so good last night—honestly, the past couple of months—but all it takes is seeing him once to bring up all of the past hurt. Most of the time, I don't think it's so much hurt as it is mourning Charlie's chance of having a father. That's the only person she truly cares about—her son.

"I'm sorry, babe. You both deserve so much better than him," I whisper against the side of her head. We stand in the doorway like that for a few minutes until Charlie starts to squirm, wanting to get to his toys.

Doing her best to wipe away her tears, Gigi and I get Charlie settled in with his favorite noise-making toys, which are reserved for my apartment and mine only, when my front door opens. Gigi and I spin around to find Dominic and Emerson standing in the doorway, looking down at the three of us on the floor. They go wide-eyed when they spot Charlie, but Dom is quick to

---

1. Kerosene - Miranda Lambert

walk over and squat down to our level. "Hi there, little man."

Almost immediately, Charlie's arms reach toward him as he makes grabby hands up at Dom. "Can I pick him up?" Dom asks Gigi before even touching Charlie.

She smiles softly before nodding her head. I look at Gigi, because normally Charlie hates men, to the point of not even looking at them most of the time. But as I watch Dom pick him up, Charlie only has a look of pure awe on his face for my big man. My heart fucking melts.

Dom spins to face Emerson, and with all the excitement in the world he shouts, "Look, he likes me!"

Dom stands beside Em, and Charlie reaches over to touch Emerson's face quizzically. Emerson blows his lips together on Charlie's hand before giving Charlie the biggest smile. Charlie giggles uncontrollably as Dom hands him over to Emerson, the three of them lost in their own silly, little-boy bubble.

"He-he never does this," Gigi whispers to me. "These two really are good guys, aren't they?"

Looking at the two of them with Charlie makes me want to scoop my ovaries out and hand them over to them on a silver platter. "They happen to be two of the best men I know." The happiness they fill me with is truly nauseating, and I'm definitely keeping that to myself. Because admitting it out loud would make this entire thing feel all too serious for something that is supposed to be "just for fun."

So instead of sabotaging myself or forcing ovulation,

I slap my hands on my lap before standing. Holding my hand out to Gigi, she grabs it and stands from the floor. I look her dead in her red-rimmed eyes and say, "We're having ourselves a girls' day, baby."

## CHAPTER 25
# MR. MOM

**EMERSON**

"Did you test it on your wrist?" Dom asks as I hand him Charlie's bottle.

I look down at where he sits on Lil's couch with Charlie in his arms. "Yes, Mr. Mom."

He beams with pride as he puts the bottle in Charlie's waiting mouth. Little man's chubby hands do their best to wrap around the bottle as he guzzles it down. "Oooo, I like that. Say it again."

I look at him deadpan. "Don't make it weird."

While Charlie drinks his bottle, I turn on ESPN just in time for the NHL Panthers game against the Bruins. Draping my arm along the back of the couch behind Dom, the three of us settle in for what should be a pretty good game.

I'm not going to lie, when Dom and I walked in and I realized exactly what it was Lil needed help with, I was slightly nervous. But within approximately two seconds, I could tell that me, Dom, and Charlie were going to be fast friends. Despite how comfortable the three of us were with one another, Gigi was reluctant to leave us with her son. Not that I blame her. She doesn't know Dom nor I all that well, and it's clear she and Charlie's history, or lack thereof, with men isn't all that great. But when Lil, so lovingly I might add, mentioned that if so much as a single hair on Charlie's head was harmed while they were out she would, and I quote, "Chop our balls off and shove them down our throats," we knew that messing this up in the slightest wasn't an option.

And you know what, I don't doubt it for a fucking second.

Threats or no threats, Dominic and I are fucking killing it. The girls told us to hang out in Lil's apartment, since we were familiar with it anyway, and Charlie has more than enough here for us to keep an eye on him for a few hours. Honestly, I don't know how neither of us have noticed all of this baby shit before. Probably because every time we've been over here the only thing we're thinking about is being inside of our girl.

Lil and Gigi have been gone for about four hours. Charlie is on his second bottle and about ready for bed. We've done tummy time, read *several* riveting books about a blue truck, and played with anything we can find that lights up and makes noise. Everything is picked up, the sushi we had delivered is waiting for us in the kitchen, and now all we are waiting on is for Charlie to fall asleep.

He may only be six months old, but he's a fucking trip. For his little body, he has such a big personality. I honestly couldn't even imagine not wanting anything to do with this kid. There isn't a mountain I wouldn't move for him, and he's not even mine. Christ, this is the first time I've met him.

I look over at Dom, expecting him to be watching the game, only to find him staring down at Charlie, likely thinking the same thing I am. "He's really fucking cute, isn't he?" I ask, rubbing my thumb along the back of his neck.

"Yeah," he sighs, eyes still on the almost sleeping baby in his arms. "He's really fucking cute." Finally he looks over at me and points his finger in my direction. "Don't get any funny ideas."

I snort a laugh. "I don't know if you noticed, but we don't have all of the necessary equipment required to make one of those."

His lips turn up. "I don't know if *you* noticed, but we're sleeping with someone who does."

My hand gently wraps around the back of his neck. "Does Lil seem like the type of woman who would have a child before she was ready?"

He doesn't even need to think about it. "True."

"Would—would that be something you wanted? Kids?"

He tears his eyes from mine and stares at the TV. We both know he's not watching the game. "I don't think I've ever let myself think about it. Having a child is—

it's like having a part of you, the best part, the most vulnerable part... the most essential part, the one thing that keeps your soul from shattering into a million pieces—it's like having that outside of you. Where anything can get to it. That's..." He lets out a heavy sigh. His next words are so quiet I almost don't hear them. But I do, and it breaks my heart a little for him. "I can't think of anything more terrifying."

I know why he feels that way. He's my person. Some days I know him better than I feel like I know myself. Which is exactly why he's never let himself love someone as deep and soul-consuming as I know he's capable of. I also know him well enough to not push the subject any further. Which is why I simply say, "I think you'd make a great dad someday."

His eyes meet mine again, and he gives me a soft smile. "So would you, Em."

The sound of Charlie sucking on air refocuses our attention. Kid can slam a bottle better than some of my friends can slam a beer. "Come on, let's go lay him down. I'm fucking starving."

Dom huffs a laugh as we take Charlie to Lil's room where she and Gigi set up the Pack 'n Play. Between the living room and the twenty steps it took for us to get in here, he's somehow wide awake again. Dom elbows me with his free arm. "Quick, sing him a lullaby."

"Do I look like I know any damn lullabies?" I hiss.

"Think of something," he whines.

I sing the first thing that comes to mind, a song that I could sing from start to finish, any time, any where.

It takes all of five seconds for Dom to figure it out. "'Neon Moon'? Really?"

"Shut up. It's the first thing I thought of," I rush out before continuing.

*I grew up on a ranch in Montana. Sue me.*

"You're so singing this next time we go to karaoke."

"Shut. Up. And sing the fucking song."

Smiling ear to ear, Dom sings the rest of the song with me. The two of us swaying and bouncing to the beat. However, I have no idea why the fuck I'm bouncing when I'm not even holding the baby.

*Wait, is this why moms are always rocking side to side when they're standing in line at the grocery store?*

By the time we reach the last chorus, Charlie's eyes flutter shut, and his tiny lips pop open.

*Success.*

"I really think my ovaries are actually going to explode," Lil's hushed voice sounds from behind us.

Dom and I turn around to find her and Gigi standing in the bedroom doorway, both their phones pointed in our direction. Dom and I were so busy serenading Charlie to a country classic that we didn't even hear them come in. But judging by the heart eyes the two of them are sporting, they're more than happy they snuck up on us.

"I think that was the cutest thing I've ever seen in my life," Gigi says, pocketing her phone and clutching her hands to her chest.

I point my finger between the two of them. "Hush. We just got him to sleep."

Lil curls her lips in, trying not to laugh as Dom lays

Charlie down in the Pack 'n Play. The two of us give him one last longing look before sneaking across the room to shove the two giggling women out the door and closing it behind us. Gigi opens her mouth to speak but I stop her. "If that video ever sees the light of day, the two of you are in so much trouble."

Dom scoffs. "God forbid the world sees that you're anything but a crabass."

Gigi shoots me a wink before the four of us head back out to the living room. Dom asks, "You girls good if we stay and eat our sushi? We weren't sure when you were going to be back, and Mr. Man in there helped us work up an appetite."

"Of course," the girls say in unison before Gigi looks between us. "Thank you for watching him. I needed this afternoon. I feel... well, I feel much better."

Reaching out, I put my hand on her arm. "Any time, Gigi. Really. Charlie is the best."

"Yeah," Dom agrees, California roll already stuffed in his mouth. "I think he might be my new best friend."

"Say that again and I won't give you any of my dumplings," I tell him over my shoulder.

"I can always get one of those dumplings," he says pointing his chopsticks at my ass.

"Boys," Liliana scolds, but her smile lets me know there's no real heat behind it. "Please don't traumatize poor Georgia. She's been through enough today."

"Actually, this whole thing is interesting. I find it quite entertaining," Gigi admits, with a humorous smile on her face.

"And you," Lil spins to face her. "Don't encourage them."

Laughing, I make my way to the kitchen to grab some food, and the four of us settle into comfortable conversation about Charlie and their afternoon of tacos and margaritas.

# CHAPTER 26
# HUMP DAY FESTIVITIES

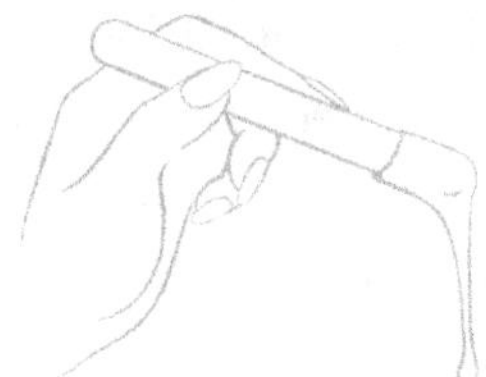

## LILIANA

It's my day off, and I'm waking up in between two warm bodies with every limb imaginable wrapped around me. The smile on my face is so huge it's stupid.

Last night, we passed out right as our heads hit the pillows, the three of us all utterly spent. Shit, we barely even had the energy to kiss one another goodnight. We haven't had sex since Turks and Caicos. None of us have felt the need… or the rush.

*It's all just felt* right.

I never thought this kind of happiness or peace was possible, but with Dom and Emerson by my side, that's all I feel.

Usually, Dom is up well before me—up before the sun somedays, too—but this morning he's snug as the proverbial very large bug in a rug. So, as their quiet little snores fall from their lips, I climb my way out from between the two of them and head into the kitchen. I start my favorite salted caramel coffee from the local shop down the road and grab all the stuff I need to make some blueberry muffins, before throwing some bacon on a baking sheet, knowing those two need some protein, too.

Pulling the bacon and muffins from the oven, I hear the patter of footsteps. Last night, just like the other night at Dom's apartment, was some of the best sleep I've had in a long time. I don't know if it was the fact that I was snuggled between two warm bodies, or that I felt as if I was as safe as I could possibly be, or maybe a bit of both, but whatever the reason, I know I want more of it. And as I'm leaning against the kitchen counter with my coffee in my hands, it hits me that not only do I *want* more of that feeling, I almost feel like I might *need it*.

But that admission suggests more than I'm equipped to deal with before I've finished my first cup of coffee, so I swallow it down. For now.

Emerson and Dominic come into view, and I can't help but chuckle. "Momming wore you two out, didn't it?"

Dom whines, "Yessss, but it was so much fun." He dramatically flops down on the stool on the other side of the counter. "I don't know how Gigi does that every day."

"And all on her own..." Emerson adds with a somber look on his face.

That right there is how he gets me. Emerson *notices*. He notices everything. Most men wouldn't even think about Gigi struggling as a single mother, but he does.

"That's exactly why I try to do what I can to help her out. She's planning on starting volleyball her senior year, too…" It makes my eyes sting just thinking about her not being able to do what she wants to do, but I have a plan to help out with Charlie as much as possible. They're my family now too.

Emerson's expression slowly shifts to pride, and I know whatever he's about to say is most likely to have me sobbing. "You're a good woman, Liliana. And an even better friend."

[1] We sit here in a comfortable silence, sipping our coffee, grazing on the muffins and bacon, when I hear a knock at my door. And before I can even move toward it, the chime that tells me the code was entered correctly goes off, and the last voice I want to hear echoes through my apartment. "Lil Lil! Your favorite brother is here!"

*Correction: my favorite brother-in-law.*

*My only brother-in-law, actually.*

My eyes go wide as I look at Emerson and Dom, who are currently shirtless in my apartment. Whipping my head back to the door, I see Rocky stroll in behind Clay.

Clay spots the guys and immediately greets them with more excitement than necessary for this early in the morning. "Emmy! Dom! What are you two doi—"

Rocky smacks his chest, cutting him off. "Yeah, what *are* you two doing here?"

My brother raises his brows at Dom and Emerson,

---

1. Holy Smokes - Bailey Zimmerman

but I quickly cut in. "We had a slumber party, clearly." I roll my eyes at my brother's wannabe, macho big-brother shit. "We're not doing this, *'She's my sister, you can't do this or that.'* Got it?"

I don't know why or when he started behaving like this, and my parents have never acted all protective over me with men. They know damn well I can hold my own and are proud of me for it. But, apparently, Rocky hasn't received that memo as of late.

My brother doesn't answer me. Instead, he crosses his arms over his chest as his eyes remain locked on the two men sitting at my counter. Emerson looks less than phased, albeit almost perturbed by the interruption, while Dominic is wearing a shit-eating grin on his face, knowing good and well Rocky is more than capable of drawing his own conclusion as to what is going on here.

Clay comes over and wraps his arm around my shoulder. "Well, what do we have on our off-day to-do list?" He leans in closer and whispers, "Rocky's been keeping me locked away since the honeymoon, and I'm going stir crazy."

They stayed in Turks and Caicos for a week-and-a-half after their wedding, and I couldn't have been more jealous. Clay is a little social butterfly, though, so I'm sure he's been eager to spend time with someone besides my surly brother. It doesn't help that his best friend Jackson, Emerson's older brother, moved across the country with his new husband. But, Rocky and Clay are prepping for their pro league to start soon, and that's a full-time job in and of itself. So they'll be more than busy before they know it.

I knew the two of them were coming over today. But with everything that happened yesterday, it totally slipped my mind. So here we are, standing around while Rocky, Emerson, and Dominic have some sort of imaginary dick-measuring contest in my kitchen.

"Well, what do you want to do today, Clay?" I smile up at him, thankful that he's not probing about what's going on when he very easily could.

"Umm, should we go?" Emerson asks.

"Nonsense. You both are more than welcome to stay. I wanna hang out with the guys too. It's been too long. And if I can't have my best friend here, his brother is the next best thing." Some days I genuinely think Clay misses Jax more than Emerson does.

"Gee thanks, Clay." Emerson scoffs while I do my best to fight the laugh threatening to burst. "We can stay for a bit but have a late afternoon practice. So we'll be out of your hair then."

"Yay," Rocky mocks, his face void of all excitement or amusement. Total shocker.

*This is either going to be great or an absolute shit show.*

# NOSY FUCKING NELLIES

**EMERSON**

"Well, I think it went great!" Dom claps me on the shoulder as the two of us walk through the locker room doors.

I sit down on the bench in front of our lockers and glare up at him. "And how exactly do you think that went great? All Rocky did was glare at us the whole time while Clay and Lil tried to fill an hour of uncomfortable silence."

"Okay, and?" He sits down next to me. "You glared at him just as much as he glared at us. He could have very easily punched us in our dicks, which he did not. And considering it was very apparent as to why we were there, I'm very thankful my balls are still intact. And three." He holds up three fingers in front of my face, and it's taking every ounce of my willpower not to bite them off. "We're two guys that he went to school with, his friends for all intents and purposes, that are fucking his sister. At the same time. I don't blame him for being a little overprotective. I would be too."

*Fucking his sister.*

I don't like the sound of that. Not even in the slightest. I mean sure, we haven't all had sex since Turks and Caicos, and we didn't even have sex last night. Dom and I were just shirtless from sleeping. But it's not because we didn't want to have sex. It just hasn't happened organically again. And that other night at Dom's was... I don't even have words for what that was. Knowing she was so turned on from the sight of Dom and me that she reached between those pretty legs of hers and...

No. Nope. I can't get hard. I'm about to get undressed in a locker room full of men. Men that I have zero interest in showing my boner.

[1] Refocusing my attention on Dom, and not the blood rushing to my cock, I ask, "Is that what we're doing? Are we *just* fucking Lil?" Because I know what we said, and I know what the "rules" are... but is that actually what's happening here?

Dom's eyes go wide, and I watch as his Adam's apple moves as he swallows harshly. His mouth opens as if he's about to speak, then closes again. I wait a moment, before it opens again. "I—"

"Who's Lil?" Patty's voice sounds from the other side of me. *Goddammit, I know better.* "Wait." *Fuck, fuck, fuck.* "Are you talking about Lil Campos?" *Well, secret's*

---

1. Kiss Land - The Weeknd

*fucking out, I guess.* I shoot Dom an apologetic look. "Are you guys fucking Liliana Campos?"

"My dudes." Daisy comes from the other side of the locker room, holding his hand out for a high-five. *Great. So this is a team fucking meeting now.* "Niiiiice."

I stare him down, until he lowers his hand. Turning to Patty, I seethe, "Can you please keep your fucking voice down?"

Patty looks between me and Dom. "Why? Is this a secret thing? Oh! Are you two fighting over her? Come on now guys, bros before hoes. You know this."

"Jesus christ," Dominic mutters.

"No, we are not fighting over her."

"So you *are* both fucking her? May I repeat… Niiii-ice." Daisy holds out his hand again, but when I reach out to punch him, he uses it to cover his dick.

"If someone utters the words 'fucking her' one more time I'm going to lose my shit. And it's nobody's busi-ness what Dom and I are or *are not*"—I look at him as I enunciate those words—"doing with Lil." It's not lost on me that the two of them haven't asked about what Dom and I are doing with each other.

"Wait, isn't Lil like your sister-in-law or something now?" Patty asks.

*Fucking hell. I cannot with these two today.*

Dominic snaps his head in my direction. "Holy shit. Is she your—"

"No, Dominic. She's not."

*I think I'm getting a migraine.*

Daisy eyes the two of us suspiciously. Not that I'm surprised. The nosy little fucker sees and hears everything. He also can't keep anything to himself to save his life. Which means the whole school is going to hear about this by the end of the day.

"If the two of you don't go away and get dressed for practice I'm going to—"

"Ooooo, we made Banner angry. 'You won't like him when he's angry,'" Daisy mocks. Dominic fakes like he's going to get up, and Daisy holds his hands out in front of him in surrender. "Okay, okay, okay. I'm going now."

He retreats to the other side of the locker room while Patty chuckles next to me before going about whatever the hell he was doing before he decided to be Nosy fucking Nellie.

"Well, good thing we weren't trying to keep this a secret or anything." Dom sighs next to me.

"Yeah. Good thing," I agree, not missing the fact that Dom never had a chance to answer my question. Nor did it seem like he wanted to. But before I get the chance to pressure him about it, my phone dings in the side of my duffle bag.

Pulling it out, I find a message from my brother.

JAX

You and Dominic are fucking Liliana Campos?!

*There's that* fucking *word again.*

# CHAPTER 28
# PREPARE TO BE WOOED

**DOMINIC**

My phone only rings twice through the speakers of my truck before she picks up. "Miss me already?"

I scoff. "It's been two days. What do you think?" Of course I miss her. I miss her the second I'm not around her. Which is starting to become a serious problem, and yet… I can't get myself to stop. Being with her, being with *them*… It's starting to feel like I'm addicted. Like I'm addicted to the most dangerous drug. Because, I know, that in the end it'll hurt me. Every hit just buries me deeper and deeper. But I can't stop. I want more.

I don't know how to stop.

Her laughter floats through the speaker. "I think you can't get enough of me." *If only she knew how much.* "But before we get to whatever reason you called me about, you or Emerson care to explain why everyone that's come in here the last two days is asking me how the two of *you* are?"

Ah shit. Knowing there's no use in denying, I come clean about our little locker room incident. "Emerson and I were talking about you in the locker room before practice on Wednesday. Daisy heard. He's a fucking loud mouth and has no idea how to keep a secret."

"I see…" Her tone is hard to read. I can't tell if she's pissed or indifferent.

"I'm sorry, Honey. I promise we weren't going around telling everyone about our business. It was an accident. If you want we can—"

"Dominic."

"Yeah?"

"It's totally fine. I promise." I can hear the smile in her voice, and I immediately loosen my grip on the steering wheel. I'd ask her if she was sure, but Lil isn't one to sugarcoat whether or not she's okay with something.

"How about I make it up to you tonight? Dinner?"

"Em coming too?"

"Nah, he has a paper to write for his media ethics class. Told us to go have ourselves a Friday night." I was momentarily bummed he didn't want to come, but then I remembered I haven't had a minute alone with Lil since before Turks and Caicos. And as much fun as I'm having with this little threesome, I miss that. Just as I crave time alone with Emerson, I want that with her, too.

*I don't know how to stop.*

[1] She doesn't even hesitate, which puts a smile to my lips. "I'm in. I have one more client, but it should just be a quick eyebrow wax. I can come clean up in the morning, so just give me..." She goes silent for a moment. "Give me two hours? I need to wash my hair tonight, so that'll be a whole thing."

I huff a laugh. "Sounds good, Baby Doll."

"What should I wear?"

It's actually the perfect Florida day. It's not too hot outside, the humidity is low, and there's just the right amount of breeze. Perfect evening for what I have planned. "Something casual. Wear comfy shoes."

"Okaaaaay," she replies, but I know she wants me to elaborate. Not gonna happen. My girl deserves to be wooed. And woo her I will. Once she realizes I'm not going to explain further, she sighs dramatically before saying, "Fine. Casual it is. See you soon, Baby."

"See you soon, Honey," I answer before hanging up the phone, just in time to pull into the parking garage of my building.

Grabbing my phone out of the cupholder, I see a text from Emerson.

EMMY

Have a fun night. Send pics.

ME

I just saw you twenty minutes ago.
Need a dick pic already?

---

1.  305 - Jordan Adetunji, Bryson Tiller

He answers immediately.

EMMY

Not what I meant and you know it. I
need a new lock screen.

AND NOT ONE OF YOUR PENIS.

Laughing, I pocket my phone and head upstairs to get ready for a night out with my girl.

I knock on the door to Lil's apartment as I—for some weird reason—anxiously wait for her to answer. She knows I'm here, plus I know the code to her door, so I could easily just walk right in. But, I'm determined to make this a proper date. Which means, here I stand, bouquet of dahlias in hand, waiting for Lil to answer the door.

We've been hooking up on-and-off for a year now, and yet, this is the first time I think I've taken her on an actual date. Don't get me wrong, we've gone to parties here and there, met up for coffee or lunch, and we've spent countless nights wrapped up in one another, but I've never taken her on an honest-to-god date. Which, I am now kicking myself in the ass for because, dick move, Dom. But seeing as how the entirety of Pensacola now knows most of our personal business, or at least they think they do, I figured now is as good of a time as any.

I hear a loud thud followed by a couple of muffled curses, which causes a smile to pull at my lips, before Lil unlocks and pulls her door open. The smile on my face falls in a split second, and my mouth pops open in awe. Because even in what should be a "casual" outfit, Liliana Campos steals my fucking breath away. She's rubbing at her elbow, which must have been the loud thud I heard, as she looks me up and down, a small smile of approval on her lips. It lights me on fire. "Why didn't you just come in?" she asks, slightly out of breath.

I hold out the flowers. "Because this is a date. You don't just barge into your date's apartment. You knock like a gentleman."

She raises a brow. "Oh so you're a *gentleman* now?"

I nudge the flowers further in her direction, and she takes them from me. I watch as she sinks her face into the top of the bouquet, closes her eyes, and draws in a deep breath. When she opens them and looks back up at me, I reply, "When I want to be." Before she can get another word out, I reach out, wrap my hand around her arm, and bring her to me. Lifting the arm she was holding, I bring her elbow to my lips. "Kitchen counter?"

She scoffs. "I've lived here long enough. You'd think sooner or later, I'd stop acting like it jumps out at me."

I chuckle before kissing the small red mark. Then I drop her arm and place another small kiss on her lips. As featherlight as it may be, my entire body lights up at the touch. She smiles against my lips before spinning on her feet and walking back into her apartment. "Let me just put these in a vase, then we can go."

Following her inside, I close the door behind me. I lean against the wall, cross one foot over the other, and put my hand inside my shorts pockets as I watch her mill about the kitchen. She's wearing a simple outfit, light-washed skinny jeans that are cuffed at the bottom and have holes on each knee, a tight-fitting black tank top that's tucked into the jeans, and a pair of black-and-white-checkered vans. Her long dark hair is down and straight, with her aviators perched on top of her head, and her makeup looks light and effortless.

But with the way I'm looking at her right now, she might as well be dressed in a black-tie gown. She's beautiful. Perfect.

Swallowing the lump in my throat, I push off the wall and go to her. I have the inexplicable urge to have my hands on her. So I do. As she stands at the counter, carefully cutting each stem on each flower before putting it in the vase, I wrap my arms around her waist, pressing my chest against her back, and drop my chin to her shoulder. We stand there just like that for the next few minutes until she's done. Once the flowers are arranged just how she wants them, she pushes them back so they rest in the center of the countertop and turns in my arms. Wrapping her arms around my neck, she says softly, "Thank you for the flowers, they're beautiful."

I press a gentle kiss to the tip of her nose, staring into her sage-green eyes the entire time. "You're welcome, Honey."

Her eyes dance between mine for a moment before she finally unwinds her hands and pats the center of my chest. "Alright, let's go. You gonna tell me where we're going?"

"There's some live music down at the farmer's market on the boardwalk tonight. I figured we could grab dinner and drinks down there before a round of night-glow mini golf. How does that sound?"

She melts against my body at the suggestion. I knew it was the perfect idea. Lil isn't impressed with fancy clothes and expensive restaurants. Sure, I'd still love to treat her to those now and then, but what really impresses this woman is the simplicity and quality of your time with her. She just wants to know that you're listening, that you care enough to do something you know she'll truly enjoy. And Liliana Campos loves good food, good drinks, great music, and anything competitive. She bats her eyelashes up at me. "It sounds absolutely perfect."

"Then let's get this show on the road, Baby Doll."

# CHAPTER 29
# PUTT-PUTT TO TIED UP

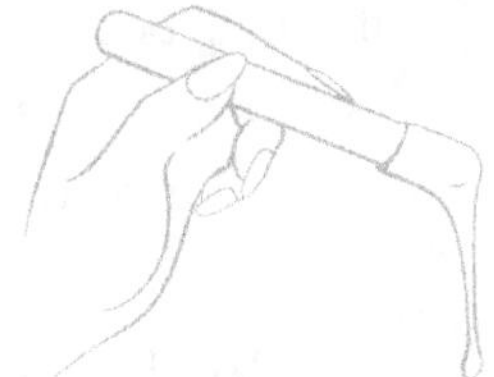



"Hole in one! Fuck yes!" I yell, throwing my putter up above my head.

[1] Dom ducks down like I'm going to whack him with said putter, and I playfully shove at his shoulder when he stands back to his full height. "I wouldn't hit you with this! I'm not that uncoordinated!"

"I never know with you." He smirks at me then, smacking my ass as I walk toward the hole to get my ball. If he gets a hole-in-one with this one, too, I'm going to scream.

There's not a chill game of anything with me. Everything is a competition, *especially* mini golf. Like Ricky Bobby says, "If you ain't first, you're last." Judging by the way he's been laughing under his breath all night, he's well aware of my competitive streak. Be that as it

---

1. Cannibal - Ke$ha

may, he doesn't take it easy on me, and I appreciate that about him. And by some miracle we're still tied on hole seventeen. That last hole-in-one got me the point I needed to get ahead.

*Or lower?*

I have no clue how golf scoring works; I know you want the fewest points… or strokes. And I sure as hell know a hole-in-one is precisely what you want.

My luck runs out though, because after the eighteenth hole, we end up tied, and honestly, beggars can't be choosers. No one wants to deal with me when I've lost a game.

Once the two of us return our clubs, he walks me back to the truck and opens the door for me. He's being the utmost gentleman tonight. Normally, being chivalrous, or *gentlemanly*, isn't something that I get my panties in a bunch over. But, when he opens my door, or pulls out my chair, his face lights up. Who am I to take that away from him?

Once he's behind the wheel, I turn to him. "Where to now, Dom the Don?" Pink crawls up his cheeks at the use of the name. I find it so ironic that's what causes him to blush because when he's "Dom the Don," I listen to him say the filthiest things.

"Back to your place, Honey."

"Oh? Am I getting lucky tonight?" I joke, knowing damn well I'll be jumping his bones the second we step foot into my apartment.

I watch as his eyes darken. An evident hunger takes over him. A hunger for me. With his eyes still locked on me, he puts the truck in drive, and my pussy throbs at the masculinity of it all. "You get whatever you want from me tonight. I'm at your mercy."

Dom and I haven't had any *just us* time since before the three of us started this arrangement, and I won't lie, I've missed one-on-one time with each of them. What's more, I've been saving a little treat for an occasion just like this one.

The sexual tension in the elevator ride up to my apartment is palpable, and Dom is making no effort to hide the way he's staring at me. Like he wants to eat me alive. But tonight, he's the prey. And he's about to find out.

I love a man who can submit to me just as well as he can dominate me. I don't care what anyone says, that's the most masculine thing a man can do. And what's even better is the fact that he and Emerson are so confident in their sexuality. They're confident in the idea of their partner wanting another and respectful enough to allow all of us to be open about it. Their willingness to share me, well, it makes me want to climb them like a fucking tree.

Unable to take the distance any longer, I press my chest into his, pushing until he's against the mirrored wall of the elevator. His eyes leave my face for the first time since the elevator doors closed. I can feel the heat of his stare as it trails down to the swell of my breasts. A soft groan slips from between his lips, and it's enough for me to wrap my arms around his neck, pulling his lips to mine. He's quick to wrap his big hands around my waist, spin us around so I'm the one against the wall, and pick me up. My legs snake around him as he holds under my ass.

Our kiss is pure heat.

Passion.

*Desire.*

We can't get enough of one another. When the elevator dings, signaling we're on the fourth floor, Dom doesn't even break the kiss. He starts toward my apartment, pressing the code to my door while holding me with one hand.

A competent man shouldn't be this much of a turn-on.

*But he is. My god, is he ever.*

Kicking the door closed behind us, he sits me on the kitchen island. But I have different plans.

Just as he's about to lower his lips to my neck, I place my hand on the center of his chest. "I want you naked, flat on the bed, waiting for me. I'll be in there in a second."

It's like he snaps out of the haze he was just in, and immediately answers, "Yes ma'am."

I take a couple of deep breaths, clearing my head, and head toward my spare bedroom. Before he came to pick me up, I laid out my favorite lingerie and a couple of silk ties on the bed.

Quickly slipping off my clothes, I put on my crotchless, black leather thong and the matching bra. I walk to the full-length mirror that's in the corner of the room and take a second to admire myself. This isn't even a bra… it has the the straps and hooks of a regular bra, but other than the underwire, nothing is covering my tits.

*I look hot as fuck, if I do say so myself*

Hopefully Dom likes it.

With one last look, I spin around, grab the silk, and head to my room, where I *know* Dom is waiting for me patiently.

"Ready or not, here I come, Mr. Foster," I purr, stepping through my bedroom door.

*And fuck, is he ready.*

He's spread out on my bed, completely bare. His corded arms are up behind his head, causing his muscles to flex. I may not know much about hockey but I do know that it's an incredibly physically demanding sport. And every time I see him or Em naked, I find myself incredibly thankful for it.

Eventually, I feel the weight of his stare on me. I watch as he takes me in, eating me alive with his eyes. And I've never felt more powerful in my life.

I'm still soaking in his huge frame lying on my bed and entirely at my mercy. He's waiting for me to give him instructions, and that fact alone has my feet floating over to the side of the bed. I'm careful to take my time walking over to him, swaying my hips, and holding eye contact.

"Lil… you look—" He pauses. I've made him speechless, apparently, but then he continues after taking a deep breath. "You look so fucking… *hot*. Is hot bad to say? Drool worthy. Sultry? Sexy? Spank me, madam?"

I was trying to stay serious, but I'm snorting a laugh before I know it. His face morphs from scared to howling in laughter right alongside me. This is what I love about Dom. We can be serious when we need to be, but we're all too quick to laugh until our stomachs are cramping.

*Love.*

I've found myself using that word when I think about them more and more lately.

He stops laughing as I climb onto the bed to straddle him. The way he's looking up at me has me grinding my aching core against him. I look down at where our skin is touching and moan. "You're very distracting right now—lying here naked and helpless." His cock is pressed to his stomach, and I watch his face as he realizes my panties are crotchless, and my wet heat is rubbing all over him. "This pussy is already soaked for you… But I have some very fun plans for tonight."

I bring up one long piece of silk right over his face, running it between my hands. "What are you going to do with that, Honey?" he asks, but the half-smirk on his lips tells me he knows exactly what I'm about to do.

Running my hands up his stomach to his broad chest, I lean down to press my lips to his. I can tell he wants to take charge and crank the heat up with this kiss, but he lets me keep the pace. As my tongue dances along with his, I scoot my ass up his stomach, allowing me to get closer to his arms above his head, then whisper, "I'm going to tie you up and use you like my own personal fucktoy."

"Hell yessss," he moans like I'm already fucking him. I'm not—my tits are just right above his head, and he pulls his chin up, running his nose and mouth up the length of my breast. Without warning, he's sucking my nipple into his mouth, and the moan that escapes me is not the "in charge woman" vibe I'm wanting to give off.

So I tighten his wrists together a little bit tighter to get his attention. "Did I tell you to use that mouth on anything yet?"

He looks up at me with my nipple between his teeth now, and I swear to god if he's about to start being a brat I—"No, you didn't. I know something I can suck on though. Scoot that pretty cunt up—" I cut him off by doing just that.

I grab onto the top of my metal bed frame and use it for balance now that his hands are securely in place, and he can't help me. Before lowering down fully, I instruct, "If you can't breathe, knee me in the back." Most men probably wouldn't have the flexibility, but Dom is a goalie. He can do the splits in his sleep. Safe to say I'm not worried.

He nods, and I don't waste another second before lowering myself onto his face.

Then I say the only thing bouncing around in my head, "Imagine this, but Em is sucking your cock at the same time. Or I could be rubbing this cunt on his face, and you could have his cock down your throat." I know it's just us right now, but even when I'm only with one of them, the other's always on my mind. The moan he lets go tells me he's enjoying the fantasy, and it also feels amazing vibrating my clit.

At a sickening speed, Dom has me coming and sliding off his face back onto his chest. His deep brown eyes are gleaming under my pink fairy lights that hang around my bed, accentuating how breathless and needy he is.

I straddle him. "Would you like this pussy wrapped around your pretty cock?"

"Yes, please," he begs. *Beautifully, I might add.* "Whatever you need. I'm yours to use tonight, remember?"

I run my finger from just below his pit, down his wide rib cage, and trace from the top of his V-cut to where I'm sitting. "I love to hear a good boy beg."

I notch his head at my entrance, and in one swift motion, I slide down, taking him to the hilt. I throw my head back in pleasure and start bouncing as I find my rhythm.

"I don't know how long I'm gonna last..." Those words are music to my ears. It's got me rocking and bouncing with abandon.

*Is anything better than making a man come quicker than they like to?*

His eyes are squeezed shut, like even looking at me will have him coming sooner. He's beyond beautiful, tied up, and letting me take whatever I need from him.

So I do just that.

I start circling my already sensitive clit, trying to make us both cross the finish line together. I'm not going to tell him, but I'm right there already too, and the feeling of his cock pressing against the spot inside of me with every grind of my hips has my eyes crossing.

With a pained expression, Dom grits out, "Lil, Honey… I'm going to—"

"Come. Fill me, Dom. *Please, Baby*," I beg. And like the good boy he is, he listens.

Deep inside of me, buried to the hilt, Dom fills me. His cock pulses with his release, and I make sure to get *every* drop.

I slump back, placing my hands on his knees, but his cock is still inside of me. As I slowly lift myself off his half-hard cock, a satisfied groan leaves his lips as he stares between my legs.

Reaching down, I insert two of my fingers, while watching him watch me. "Let me put that back where it belongs."

# CHAPTER 30

# YOU CAN ALWAYS CALL YOUR MOM

## EMERSON

I'm flipping through my cookbooks as I search for the perfect recipe, but I'm unable to find exactly what I'm looking for.

I know what I want to make, I can picture it in my head. I've just never made it by myself before—but I know the one person who has hundreds of times. Grabbing my phone, I try to call my mom. Shocker to literally no one, she doesn't answer. For a woman who constantly harps on her children about calling her more often, she's really good at not answering the damn phone. I know there's no use in calling my dad because he's just as bad.

[1] Pulling up the app where I can see my friends' locations, I find Jackson at our parents' house. Which tracks, because it's Friday afternoon, so he and Dad are

---

1. New To Country - Bailey Zimmerman

likely sitting down for lunch inside. I'm certainly not jealous of the fact that Jackson is back working on the ranch again—even though I know he's absolutely loving his life right now—but I am *definitely* jealous that he gets to enjoy Mom's cooking again.

Relenting to the fact that this is the only way I'm going to get what I need, I call my older brother.

After just a couple rings, he answers. "Hey, man. What's up?" His voice is muffled, and I just know he's talking with a mouth full of food.

"Eating lunch in the house?" I ask.

"Mhmm," he replies before taking another bite.

"Is Mom there?"

"Don't wanna talk to me?"

"Unless you suddenly know how to bake, then no."

"God you're always so grumpy. Yeah she's here. Hold on, let me put you on speaker." The line is silent for a moment before he says, "Here she is, Momma's Boy."

I roll my eyes. "I'm not a Momma's Boy, you fuc—"

"Hey, Sweetheart." Mom's light voice floats through the phone, and I cut off any expletives I was about to throw out. "Why didn't you just try calling my phone?"

A small smile tugs at my lips. "I did, Momma. You didn't answer. Do you even know where your phone is?"

I just know she's patting at all of her pockets and looking around the counters. "Well I—"

"I think I saw it out on one of the fence posts. Musta left it out there when you were feeding this morning," Dad grumbles.

"Dawson," Mom sighs. "If you saw my phone sitting on a fence post, why would you not bring it in?"

"I don't know. Figured you left it there for a reason," he answers.

"Why on earth would I leave it—"

"Mom," I interrupt.

"Oh. Sorry, Sweetheart. What is it you needed?"

I try not to be surprised that the conversation was steering away from me, even though I'm the one that called. "Could I have your créme brûlée recipe? I'm trying to find one but none of them seem like the one you make."

"Of course! Hold on, let me grab it."

I can hear her ruffling through the cabinets before Jax pipes up. "So who's this for? The boyfriend or the girlfriend?"

"What?!" Mom almost shouts as I hear Dad choke on his lunch.

He can't see me, but I *know* he can feel me flipping him the bird right now. "Seriously, Jax?"

"Sorry," he replies. And I can't see him, but I *know* he's smiling, and he's not the least bit fucking sorry.

Not acknowledging his fake apology, I say, "I don't have a boyfriend or a girlfriend."

"Then why did your brother just say—"

"He's been *seeing* Dominic and Liliana Campos."

"Jackson," I hiss.

"Like, Rockwell Campos' sister?" Mom asks.

"The one and only," Jax answers.

Mom's voice suddenly sounds much closer to the phone. "Emerson. Does Dominic know? I mean, I knew something was going on with the two of you. It's obvious you aren't just friends but—Does Liliana know?!" She gasps. "Emerson Baker, I raised you better than that, you do not—"

I can hear Jackson trying not to bust out in laughter.

*Kill me. Just kill me now.*

The last thing I want to do is explain the dynamics of my throuple with my mother when I'm not entirely sure of it myself.

"Mom! Would you—I'm not—you guys—*ugh!* I'm not cheating on anyone. Yes, they both know. No, Dominic isn't my boyfriend. No, Lil isn't my girlfriend. We're all just having *fun*. It's nothing serious"—*Is it, though?*—"now can we please spare me the indignity of explaining my sexual relationship to my parents and just give me the recipe?"

Everyone is silent for a moment, and it suddenly dawns on me that my mother's main concern wasn't the fact that my brother said I had a boyfriend *and* a girlfriend. No, her concern that I was being a piece of shit. Nobody even batted an eye at the fact that I could have more than one consenting partner. But then again, nobody cared in the slightest when my brother married a man. I find myself being momentarily thankful I have such an accepting family... until my mom says, "Well isn't this exciting? Oh my gosh, we'll have to get a bigger bed for your room for when the three of you come and visit."

I drop my head forward, letting it smack the cabinet in front of me. Jackson just howls in laughter.

"Cat, just get the boy his recipe so he doesn't die of embarrassment," Dad pleads.

"Alright, alright," Mom relents. "I'll just send you a picture of the recipe card, Sweetheart."

"Thank you, Momma. Love you," I groan. Forehead still pressed against the cabinet.

"Love you too. Let me know how it goes. Have a fun night!"

"Byeeee, Emmy," my brother sing-songs, and I hang up without another word, sparing myself anymore humiliation.

*I also make a mental note to punch Jackson square in the dick next time I see him.*

A second later, a text comes through from Jackson with a picture of the recipe card.

I do a quick scan of it and add the ingredients I don't have to my grocery list.

I stopped by Lil's suite yesterday morning in between a couple of her clients and my morning classes to bring her a coffee. *And* to ask her on a date.

When she asked how she got lucky enough to have two one-on-one dates in the same week, I simply shrugged and said, "I can't let Dominic Foster have the upper hand."

Even though the three of us know there's no competition, I don't feel the slightest bit threatened at the thought of them spending time together without me. Honestly, it makes me kind of… *happy.* I want the two of them to have a strong relationship with one another, and I want Dominic to see that getting close to someone on a deep level is okay.

Lil is coming over for a late dinner, as she has a couple of clients this evening. But that actually works out in my favor because our practice ran a little long this afternoon, thanks to our 0–1 loss last night, and I still have to go to the grocery store.

I could have easily taken Lil out tonight, but I wanted this to be different. I want her to see that I'm capable of being more. I want her to see what I feel for her when I can't always put it into words.

*Probably because you don't want to admit what's happening, dumb fuck.*

Pushing that thought to the side, I grab my wallet, keys, and grocery list, and head to Delectable Desserts for top-of-the-line créme brûlée ingredients before going to the grocery store. Because I'll be damned if this night is anything less than perfect.

# CHAPTER 31

# THE L WORD

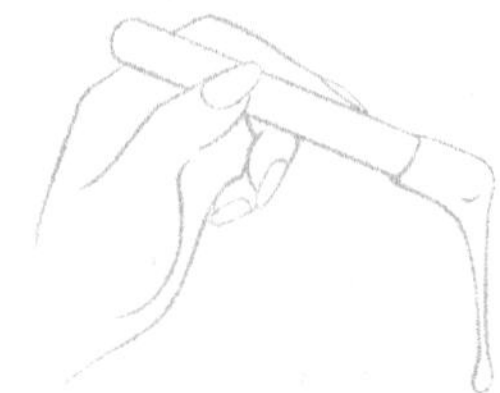

## LILIANA

"I brought wine, sweet cheeks!" I yell through the front door of Emerson's house.

When I don't get a response, I slowly creep into the living room. The Bakers—as in Emerson's parents—bought this house when Jackson, their oldest, was accepted to Palm University. There's a total of four Baker boys, and they were banking on all of them coming to the same school. So they decided to save themselves some money in the long run and invest in a house they could all live in, rather than pay for four rounds of campus room and board. It was a smart move, in my opinion, but now it's only Emerson here, and I worry about him being lonely in this place all on his own now that Jax has moved back to Montana.

As I walk through the spotless house and into the kitchen, where I hear music and the sound of dishes clanking, I stop and lean against the wall. Emerson has an apron wrapped around his neck and waist, and I get lost in the view of his muscular back flexing under his dark grey Henley. I don't know what it is about a man in a kitchen cooking, but nothing makes me want to hit my knees faster.

He moves on from plating whatever he has made for us and places the pot back on the stove. When he finally spots me leaning up against the wall, he clutches his chest. "Oh my god, you scared me!" He pants before taking a deep breath. "But it is perfect timing." Rushing over, he pulls a chair out for me to sit in. "Sit. I'll take this and put it in the fridge for later." He leans down, kisses my head, and murmurs, "I have a special wine pairing for dinner." Pulling back, he shoots me a wink, and I swear to all things holy, I don't think I can possibly survive Emerson Baker in an apron.

The table is already set with wine glasses, glasses of ice water, and all the silverware we'll need for what looks like a multi-course meal. I haven't eaten at a set table in way too long, and the thought of it has my stomach groaning. Between running my own business and me being the only one living in my apartment, I often find myself eating a quick dinner on the couch while catching up on the latest episode of *Yellowstone*.

*Because I'm not ashamed to admit I eat up the way Kevin Costner looks riding that horse.*

Emerson sets my plate in front of me before grabbing his own and sitting down across from me. He looks at me anxiously as he waits for me to dig in first. "Em, this looks so good." I take the first bite of a perfectly cooked steak, which melts in my mouth. Then the veggies, which are also perfectly cooked, and what have to be homemade mashed potatoes. I'm groaning and moaning after each bite. "This is the best thing I've ever had in my mouth."

He watches me as I eat, only occasionally taking bites of his own food. But as the food disappears on my plate, I watch the smile on his face grow. I'm not even overexaggerating either. I've genuinely never tasted better food. "How did I not know you could cook?"

He shrugs. "We've never talked about it… and if it makes you feel any better, I just started getting good, now that Jax has moved out. Take out, and the couple of things I was good at cooking, got old fast."

I nod because I feel all of that way too hard. I look up at him in between bites, and he's still staring at me. "What? Do I have food all over me or something?"

"No, I just love seeing you like this." There's the *L word* again. It's there—not even in the back of my head. It's a spoken word, out there in the open. Sure, he didn't say those three words one right after the other, but he still said it. In regard to me. But I don't say anything about it. I don't trust my brain to get words out properly right now.

Instead, I ask the question that's been eating at me for the past couple of weeks. "Is it just me or does it make you sad too that we could've been doing things like this the whole time?"

"Do what?" he asks, his brows pinched in confusion.

"This." I gesture between the two of us. "The real dates. You and me. Me and Dom. I just feel like we spent a year together but not really *together*. You know?"

He nods in understanding. "We were doing what felt right at the time. But this, this feels right *now*. I wouldn't change a thing about how we've gotten to this point," he answers, his stare not wavering for a second. "I'll always be thankful for any second you let me in your orbit, Liliana Campos."

And there it is, Emerson being the sweetest soul when that's the last thing my confused head needs. I give him a warm smile before we finish with dinner in comfortable silence. I just sipped the last bit of wine in my glass when Emerson says, "Okay, one last surprise —well, a couple of surprises once we get out there."

I huff. "This has been enough surprises for a lifetime already, Emerson." Everyone knows I hate surprises, but they seem to keep coming. I tease, "No more surprises from either of you two for at least a few months."

He's up out of his seat and pulling mine out. "Trust me, you'll love this one. Come on." Grabbing my hand, he pulls me to my feet, and we head out the back door. That's when I see it. A little blanket set up out in the yard under the quickly darkening night sky. "We're far enough out from the city lights to see some stars on a good night... and tonight is a good night." He's being shy, which is so different from how he typically acts. I like this side of him, though. "So I figured we could end our date out here."

There's a checkered, oversized blanket laid out on the ground, the perimeter of it is covered in delicate fairy lights, and there's a pile of blankets and pillows sitting on top of it. Not only did he cook dinner for me, he also took the time to think about what to do after dinner. A place to sit under the stars together. To be in one another's arms.

"Emerson... this is... *beautiful.*" I look at him, and the joy lining his features is enough to bring so many emotions to the surface. My eyes immediately start to sting. No one has ever put this much thought into a date for me. Well, Dominic did a couple of days ago. And now having two of these experiences back to back almost feels entirely overwhelming. I've tried so hard for so long to keep my heart locked up tight. To keep it safe from anyone wanting to break through its hard exterior. Desperate to find someone worthy enough to drop my defenses. But with them... with Dominic and Emerson, I'm realizing I don't need defenses because I already feel it.

Protected.

They've made me feel that way for a while now, and I don't even think any of us have realized it. I wasn't supposed to be falling for them—none of us were—but when I think about life without either of them, it makes me sick to my stomach. It's apparent that there's no life I want to be in without both of them at my side.

*Well, shit.*

There's not one moment that I can think back on and know for certain that's when I really fell for the both of them, but I can say the falling is done. I'm at the bottom. I've hit the ground from falling, and looking back it's been the slowest descent. They've grown on me, broken down the views and expectations I had on love.

I've slowly fallen for the two men in my life that were never supposed to be more than just a fun fuck.

But they're so much more than that.

I *love* Emerson Baker and Dominic Foster.

The *L word* is bouncing around in my head, and I'm not freaking out. That's progress, right?!

"Sit. I'll be right back." He has no clue about the mental gymnastics I've been performing in the two minutes we've been out here, so I mindlessly do as he says and drop to the blanket in the grass. Allowing myself to get lost in the night sky while he rushes inside the house.

Before I know it, he's dropping onto the blanket next to me with his hands full. "Momma's famous crème brûlée and the wine you brought over."

*The man can bake too… I'm fucking cooked.*

Emerson pours us more wine in each of our glasses that were waiting out here for us and hands me one of the spoons. I scoop up a bite, and the moment it hits my tongue, my eyes roll into the back of my head.

Yeah, I'm going to need this recipe.

Scratch that. This man is making this for me all the time.

Emerson's eyes darken before shaking his head and taking my spoon from me. Biting his lip, he uses his to scoop up another bite and feeds me another spoonful of creamy goodness, and I groan. "Send my thanks over to your mom. This is so fucking good."

"She'll be asking. I had to call her earlier and get the

recipe from her." He huffs a soft laugh. "I ended up having to call Jax because my mom never has her phone on her, and they were curious about whether this was being made for my boyfriend or girlfriend..."

He trails off nervously but I just smile at him. I'm sure he is thinking I will flip a lid at the mention of him officially being mine and Dominic's *boyfriend*. But the more I've been thinking about it, I don't know if I want to call this anything but that. I mean, what else would all of this be? It doesn't feel just for fun anymore. And if I'm being honest with myself, I don't think it's been "just for fun" since the moment we sat down in that cafe. Even when we made up those bullshit rules. Not for me at least. But how do I tell them that? What if I'm the only one? I don't want to risk all of this falling apart.

I have no fucking clue about any of it.

So, I ask, "And what did you tell her?"

"That we were just having fun..." He says it, but it sounds bitter on his tongue. Like even saying the words pained him. "Is that still what you want? To have fun?"

I don't want to ruin what we have. The bliss. The ease. Is this what it'll be like—always wanting more but unsure whether we should reach out and grab it? Always desperate for the next step we're *supposed* to take? I don't want that either. But Emerson and Dominic feel like they're mine. They feel like more than "fun." They feel like so, *so* much more.

Swallowing the lump in my throat, I answer playfully, "I never thought I would say it, but you two are growing on me."

"You've grown on me like a fungus in the rainforest, Lil."

We're both chuckling when I joke, "Why is that gross but equally as cute?"

As we sit in a comfortable silence under the stars for I don't even know how long, I find myself wondering what I've done to deserve not just one gentle and kind-hearted man, but two. It's enough to bring tears to my eyes anytime my mind goes to the thought, and I try to think back to when these emotions started, but it's just been a gradual and steady freefall from the moment I met them. I like to think that Turks and Caicos was always meant to happen.

The three of us were meant to be in one another's arms. We were meant to share looks of lust and longing. I was meant to see the way the two of them love one another, and they were meant to see the way I lo—

*Shit.*

No. Nope. Can't do that now. I can't come to that conclusion now. Not when there's so many uncertainties. So many unsaid words.

But the one thing I do know, the one thing that's safe, is the way we get lost in one another. The way they light me on fire.

Sipping my wine, I murmur to Emerson, "I've come to terms that crème brûlée and wine under the stars is the quickest way to get in my pants, Mr. Baker."

# CHAPTER 32
# THAT FEELING...



*F*uck me running.

She's giving me those fucking eyes.

Her sage-green eyes have the power to bring me to my goddamn knees on a good day, but when she looks at me like *that*.

Well, I feel like I can't breathe.

And as tempted as I am to give in right here and now, I want, no, I *need* her to know this is about more than sex for me.

That I feel *more* now.

That after a life of feeling invisible, she and Dominic make me feel like the most important person in the room. They make me feel like I can be more than carefully put together. They make me feel *seen*.

I know she feels the same.

I saw it in the way she was looking at me. Liliana Campos likes to pretend that nothing can shake her, that she's incapable of letting anyone in, at least fully. But she plays her every thought across her face like my favorite motion picture.

Just like she is right now. Judging by the way her brows are pinched together and her pink lips are parted ever-so-slightly, she's wondering why I'm not jumping her bones. But I have one more thing I want to do first.

[1] Standing up, I pull my phone out of my pants pocket and press play on the song I have queued up. MGK and Julia Wolf's cover of "Iris" starts playing through the portable speaker I have sitting on the patio table as I hold my hand out to her.

She looks up at me, and I see an unexpected gloss cover her eyes. "Emerson…"

I give her a soft smile. "Dance with me, Darlin'."

Wrapping her delicate hand in mine, I pull her from the blanket. As she stands, I take a moment to drink her in. She's wearing a casual summer dress, black with small white flowers all over it. It has a slit on one side that goes up her leg just far enough to get a view of her toned thigh, and the thin spaghetti straps allow me to take in the slope of her shoulders. She's barefoot from coming from inside, and the Florida breeze is blowing her dark, curled strands out of her face, allowing me an uninterrupted view of her pink cheeks and full lips.

*Breathtaking.*

With her hand still in mine, I bring us chest to chest and rest my other hand on her waist. A soft sigh leaves her lips before she places her opposite hand flat on my

---

1. Iris - MGK and Julia Wolf

chest. The two of us start swaying back and forth, dancing beneath the stars in a place neither of us are from, but now call home.

As the chorus sounds through my backyard, my eyes remain glued to hers, silently willing her to understand that this is how I feel. That I want her, I want *them*, to know how I feel. To see me for everything I am despite the world around us.

And it's funny, I've spent my entire life wanting to be heard, wanting my voice to be louder than everyone else around me. But with them, I find myself not needing to speak at all. It's in the silent moments that she and Dominic hear me the loudest. I don't know when it happened or how I realized it, but I'd be the luckiest man alive to sit in silence and watch the two of them be, well, them.

"Emerson…" she sighs my name again. God, the way it sounds leaving her lips.

"Yeah, Lil?"

"Can you kiss me now?" We didn't say the words, but once again, I can read it all over her face.

*Can you kiss me now that I know?*

A huge smile blooms across my face. "Sure can, Darlin'."

Without a second thought, I slant my mouth over hers, and her body immediately melts against mine. Her lips part and I take the invitation to sweep my tongue inside of her mouth. She moans against my lips, and even with the music in the background, I let the sound wash over me.

Dropping her hand, I bring both of mine to her face and tip it further back, allowing me to kiss her deeper. Both her hands are on my chest now as she fists my shirt hard enough that a couple of the buttons on my Henley pop open. She smiles against my lips, but neither of us stop kissing, desperate to get lost in one another. And when one of her hands slips inside of my now-open shirt and her palm connects with the skin of my chest, any semblance of self-control I once had goes out the window.

Letting go of her face, I place both of my hands beneath her ass and lift her off the ground. Her long legs wrap around my waist before I carry her inside the house. As tempted as I am to stay out here and fuck my girl beneath the stars, I don't have a fence to block the view of my backyard. So, while hearing us have sex is one thing, nobody is going to see the way she's about to fall apart for me.

The moment we're inside, I quickly slide the patio door closed, followed by the curtains, all while Lil kisses along my jaw and neck. And when she nips at the skin just below my ear, I decide the dining room is far enough. I kick one of the chairs away with enough force that it goes flying across the room. Her eyes go wide, and she sucks in a breath before I place her on the table in front of me.

Grabbing her face with one hand, I reach up to my neck with the other, rubbing the spot she just bit to check for blood. Because she's definitely done that before and wouldn't hesitate to do it again, even though we both know she likes to act like a brat to see what I'll do next.

I pull my fingers from my neck and inspect them to find no trace of blood. But judging by the mischievous twinkle in her eye I knew that's exactly what she was going for.

*See. Brat.*

"You know—" I lean down so my face is right in front of hers. Her jaw is still in my hold, and if I glance down, I can see the swell of her breasts as her chest rises and falls with each heavy breath. "I was going to take this slow—was going to be gentle—but that's not what you want? Is it, Sweetheart?"

The corners of her lips twitch. "No," she answers breathlessly.

"Yeah. Didn't fucking think so." Her breath hitches and her expression changes from playful to desperate in the blink of an eye. Yeah. My girl may not take shit from anyone but she'll gladly drop to her knees for me. As a matter of fact—

I drop my hand from her face and take half a step back. Looking her dead in the eye, I command, "Take it out, Liliana." She raises her brows in question but doesn't move. So I repeat, "Get on your knees, and take out my cock."

I watch as she clenches her teeth and tightens her thighs together. There's always this moment, a split second after I tell her what to do, where she battles with herself. Her mind wants to argue, wants to give me attitude, and to tell me to go fuck myself. But there's the stronger part of her, the one that loves when I speak to her this way, the one that has her dripping underneath that pretty dress at the thought of doing exactly what I say. And eventually, like it always does, the latter wins out, as she stands from the table and drops to her knees in front of me.

My cock is already painfully hard beneath my pants, so when she undoes the button and zipper and reaches into the front of my briefs, I immediately hiss at the contact. When she opens her pretty mouth, I find myself desperately wanting to sink inside of her, but the dominant side of me wants *more*. "Spit on it," I tell her.

I watch with rapt attention as she purses her lips and lets a bead of spit land on the head. A deep groan builds in my chest at the sensation. Batting her hand away, I fist my cock. Using her spit as lube, I work my fist up and down my length.

Her eyes stay glued on the movement of my hand until a bead of precum leaks from the tip. She moans at the sight of it, and then… she licks her fucking lips. She licks her lips and I almost say, "Fuck it." But I don't. Because there's one thing I want to hear her say first.

"See what you do to me, Lil? Do you see the power you have over me?" She drops back, so her ass is resting on her heels as she looks up at me, her green eyes glowing beneath her dark lashes. "Just looking at you has me wanting to come apart at the seams. There is never a minute of the day where I find myself not wanting you."

More precum leaks from the head of my cock, and I

watch as she squirms in her spot. Likely trying to dull the ache between her legs. It only spurs me on further. Here goes nothing. "I want you. *Always.* Tell me you want this, Sweetheart." Her breathing quickens as she realizes the weight of my words. Because I'm not just talking about this moment, and we both know it. It's not just the sex or the fun we can have together in my head anymore. I need to know she wants this as much as I have come to. I need to know if I'm alone in this feeling or if she's with me. Because if there's any chance of building something with Dominic, she has to be on the same page. I won't risk hurting him if she's not all in.

My hand stills as she contemplates what I'm asking of her. The silence stretches on, and just when I think she's going to get up and tell me she's not ready, she does the exact opposite. She places her hands on both my thighs, letting her thumbs brush against the fabric of my pants before she focuses all of her attention on my face and utters the four words I'm desperate to hear. "I want this, Emerson."

I let out a breath I didn't even know I was holding. Bending over, I pick her up off the floor and spin her around so her back is to my front. She grinds her ass against my dick, and I use that as my opportunity to nip at her neck. She yelps when my teeth make contact with her skin. "Such a fucking brat."

"Hmmmm. But I'm *your* brat."

"And I'll spend the rest of my days making you pay for it." The words sound playful, but we know they're so much more.

"Emerson…" She says my name for the third time tonight. But this time it's different than it was when we were outside. Now there's desperation. Longing.

"Be a good girl and bend over for me, Sweetheart." She does as I say, bending over so her torso is flat against my dining room table, her cheek pressed against the wood as she does her best to look back at me.

Reaching down, I gather up the fabric of her dress and push it up around her waist only to find her bare beneath it. "Fuck, Liliana," I say as I stare at her glistening pussy before me. I run one hand along the inside of her legs until my fingers find what I'm looking for. I let her arousal coat my fingertips as I drag them through her wet folds. "So wet for me. So *perfect*."

"Yes," is the only word she utters.

Wrapping my hand once more around my cock, I work her wetness up and down my length before notching myself at her entrance. This wasn't my plan. I wanted to spend hours worshipping her. I wanted to plant my face between her legs and never come up for air. But this is what she does to me. She fucking unravels me until this is all I have to give. All I can bear.

Fucking her on my table.

But that's okay. I'll spend all night making it up to her.

"Say it again," I tell her. Not pushing any deeper until I hear the words just one more time.

She doesn't hesitate. "I want this, Em. *Please*. I want it so bad."

Music to my ears. In one swift motion. I slam home inside of her and she cries out. Any other day, I might give her a second to adjust, but not today. Pistoning my hips, I thrust in and out of her with such ferocity the table moves across the floor with every movement. "Holy shit. Oh—yes—keep going," she moans. As if I would ever stop.

It doesn't take long before I feel her tighten around me. "That's it, Sweetheart." Tightening my hold on her waist, I keep up my rhythm. "Just like that. You're doing so good."

Her hands grip at the top of the table, trying to find purchase as her orgasm builds inside of her. "The edge —of the—*oh*—the edge of the table… *fuck*. Emerson, it's too much. It—"

My hips don't stop as I fold over her. Putting my face against her, I growl, "It's not too much. You can do it. Come for me, Lil. Come all over this cock."

The edge of the table continues to rub against her clit, and I pound into her harder. My hips hitting her hard enough I'm almost certain they'll be bruised in the morning. But I don't care.

No. The only thing I care about right now is feeling her cunt strangle me.

My teeth clamp down on her earlobe, and it sends her into a free fall. She orgasms so hard that if her body wasn't pressed between me and the table I know she'd be shaking uncontrollably. It doesn't take me more than another five seconds to come buried deep inside of her.

And as the two of us gasp for breath, completely clothed in the middle of my dining room, I realize the rules we made all those weeks ago in that coffee shop couldn't matter less. Because right here, in this moment, I feel for her what I feel for him.

*Wholly and completely.*

But I don't say it. Not yet at least. Instead, I plant a soft kiss on Lil's cheek, scoop her up in my arms, and carry her to my room where I spend the rest of the night sticking to my original plan.

# CHAPTER 33

# BOY AQUARIUM

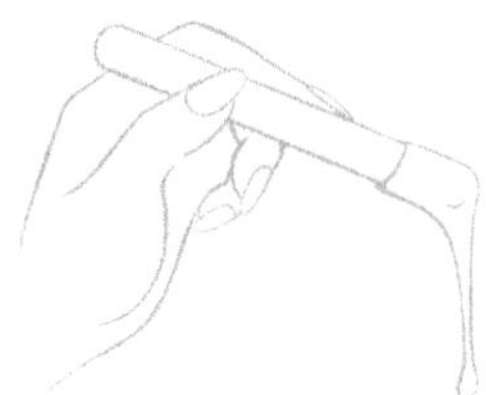

**LILIANA**

I'm in-between clients when I hear two deep voices at the sliding door to my salon. I look up and smile at my two favorite guys, who happen to be loaded with coffee and pastries from the mom-and-pop shop down the road.

"What are you two doing here?" I ask, but I'm up and helping them empty their hands before the full sentence is out of my mouth.

Emerson starts, "Practice released early, so we thought we'd stop by and see you." Then he's gently pressing a kiss to my lips.

Dom follows right behind him, pressing his soft lips to mine. "We had to come and invite our girl to the hockey game on Friday."

"Ohhh, this seems like official business. Am I getting invited since the whole school knows our business now?" I joke, poking fun at both of them for the blabbering in the locker room.

"You're always welcome to come sit that pretty ass in the stands to watch us play, Honey," Dom purrs like he does in his audios, and I'm over here mentally berating my traitorous pussy because now is not the time for her to be purring back at him. "But no, we always just figured you didn't want to watch hockey."

I smile at that. "I may not know much about hockey, but it's a sport. And with the exception of like, well, golf, I can get down with just about any sport. Plus, hockey has practically pornographic stretching and men fighting, so, consider me there."

"Come over to Dom's once you get off if you don't have any plans for tonight," Emerson instructs. I nod, and they both hit me with smiles that take my breath away. They're starkly different from one another, but they each set my soul on fire.

I break my eyes away from both of them, remembering I have one more client left. "Shoo, go on, both of you. My client is about to be here." I shuffle them towards the door right as Ashlee walks to the door with two more iced coffees in her hand.

I truly have the best clients. They bring me coffee and random treats all the time. My heart might explode if I try to drink all of these at once though, so I shove the coffee they brought me into Dom's hands and whisper, "Put that in the fridge at your place for me," before giving him a wink and a slap on the ass out the door.

The two of them leave, and I'm left here waxing a vagina, wondering to myself where I can get a custom jersey made with both of their names on it to wear to the game. I don't know much about hockey, but I know a decent amount about hockey players. For some god forsaken reason they go all caveman about who wears their jersey, and I'm not listening to them fight over it. Pissing matches are cute sometimes, but I think that one would end in best friends fist fighting, and that doesn't sound enjoyable to me.

[1] I've got on a full face of makeup, my hair is curled, and I'm slipping on my custom-made jersey that I got made at the local print shop. I'll be the first to admit that sometimes I'm glad I'm a lot more personable than my older brother. Because when I word-vomited to the sweet old lady on the other side of the counter, she absolutely swooned before telling me not to worry and that she had the perfect idea in mind for a jersey. And when I showed her pictures of Emerson and Dominic she fanned herself and told me she completely understands not being able to pick between the two.

Twenty-four hours later, Barbara had a brand new jersey for me, and I was able to pick it up on my way to their game. When I pull into the parking lot outside of the hockey rink, I find the parking lot absolutely packed.

---

1.  Muse - Isabel LaRosa

Who would've thought college hockey would be so big in Florida?

*Definitely not me.*

Once inside, I stop by the concession stand to grab a pretzel, popcorn, and a beer. My hands are full as I walk down the stairs to find my seat, but as I search, I quickly realize I'm going to be in the front row. Right behind the plexi-glass barrier.

Finally finding my seat, I make myself comfortable before looking out onto the ice, or what I'm now referring to as the *boy aquarium*.

Because that's what this feels like. A glorified fishbowl. I'm like Darla tapping on the fish tank in *Finding Nemo*.

There are pucks everywhere as the teams warm up. Some are doing stretches, some are skating around, hell there's a few of them standing in the middle of the rink shooting the shit with the other team. It all seems very chaotic, but organized. My eyes don't know where to look as I break off a piece of my pretzel, dip it in the cheese, and pop it in my mouth.

*Fuck, there's nothing better than a concession stand pretzel.*

Taking a sip of my beer and setting it back in its cup holder, my eyes dart up to the glass in front of me when I hear a loud bang. It's none other than Dom and Emerson, lit up with smiles, banging on the glass. I can't help it, I smile like a fucking fool.

*This really is a damn boy aquarium.*

I joke between my hysterical laughing, "Don't tap on the glass, it scares them."

They look at me like I've lost every marble, and I'm sure the people sitting beside me are also.

Then I watch in slow motion, as their stares simultaneously land on the front of my jersey. Emerson gets a smug look on his face noticing his name and number on the front. "She's wearing my name," he says loud enough for me to hear too.

*Yep. Smug fuck.*

Standing up, I spin around to show them Dom's name and number on the back of the jersey. "Ha! She's wearing mine too." Dom doesn't sound smug, more so shocked. I watch his face, and for a moment, a look of concern takes over him before he notices me staring and quickly covers it up with a smile.

He places his hand on the glass, and I put mine over his. Emerson's does the same, and we all three sit there for a second, mutual understanding passing between us.

The three of us.

Together.

Always.

# CHAPTER 34
# A NEW MEANING TO PRE-GAME JITTERS

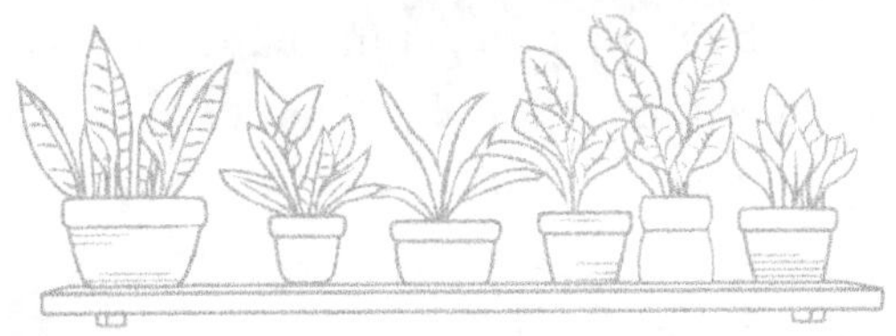

## DOMINIC

She's wearing my jersey.

Liliana Campos is wearing my jersey.

Well, half my jersey.

But it doesn't matter. Because she's here. At my game. At *our* game.

I'm equally mesmerized by the sight of her wearing our numbers as I am turned on by it. I'm not going to lie, there was a moment before she turned around and showed me the back of her jersey that I wanted to straight up punch my best friend in the face. I haven't been jealous of him once for a single second when it comes to our relationship with Lil, but seeing the front of that jersey almost did me the fuck in.

She made it up to me, though.

I don't know where she got that made as fast as she did, but I make a mental note to find out later so I can shout their names from the rooftop.

I'm not sure I've ever seen a woman look so sexy in a hockey jersey in my life.

*Fuck.*

Now I want to know what she looks like wearing it and nothing else.

Goddammit, now I'm hard. I find myself thankful I'm behind all my goalie gear so no one can see.

See, this is becoming another problem. Here I am, daydreaming about my girl, getting hard out on the ice in front of thousands of people, when I'm supposed to be warming up for the game.

*My girl.*

*That's* the other problem.

[1] She's not *my* girl. Or is she? God, I don't even fucking know any more. Ever since our date the other night, my thoughts have been all scrambled inside of my head. Which makes me feel like a complete and total asshole. Because I saw the way she looked at me that night, just like I saw the way she looked at us through the glass, the way I know she's looking at us right now. The way *I know* Emerson's looking at her. She's *our* girl.

Which is absolutely terrifying.

But the way she looked on top of me, the way her head tipped back in pleasure as she rode me and called out my name, in that moment, it didn't feel terrifying at all. But as she drifted off to sleep in my arms, and in the days that followed, all the thoughts crept right back in.

---

1.  WHY - Jon Bellion & Luke Combs

No matter how hard I try to keep my fears at bay, they're always there, ready to bring me back to reality.

But I don't want that to be my reality. I don't want to be scared of wanting. And yet, no matter how desperate I am to let them go, I can't quite seem to. All because of the one singular thought that's haunted me for years.

Why bother loving anything at all when the higher you fly the further you fall?

And yes, I have loved—I *do* love people. I love my mom and my teammates. Hell, I even love Emerson. But now the love I have for him is starting to feel all-consuming. Like he's slowly becoming my reason for breathing. My reason for existing. Both of them are.

And I'm not sure if I can risk *anyone* being my reason. Because once that reason's gone, I'll be left with nothing.

*Fuck, why does it suddenly feel like I can't breathe?*

Stopping my movements in the crease, I pull a mitt off and grab at my goalie mask, trying to get it away from my face even a fraction of an inch—*trying* to breathe.

I don't know how long I stand there like that before I hear the blow of a whistle, signaling for the teams to come in from warmups and get in line for the National Anthem. But I can't move.

I can't fucking breathe.

Suddenly, I feel hands clamp onto my pad-cladded shoulders. It takes me a moment to refocus my vision, but when I do, I see Emerson in front of me. His bright blue eyes bore into mine. He's saying my name, I know he is. I can tell by the movement of his lips. But I can't hear him. The only thing I can hear is the sound of my own heartbeat.

That goes on for a moment, until I finally manage to hear him say, "Dom, Baby, just breathe," barely loud enough for me to hear over the sound of the crowd.

To anyone else, I'm sure it just looks like we're having ourselves our own little huddle, but apparently, I'm just having myself my own little panic attack.

But his words finally get me to suck in a breath.

"That's it. Just like that. Deep breaths, Dom." I do as he says, doing my best to breathe deep. "Good, Baby. Good."

I take a few more breaths before my eyes dart over to the stands. No one is really paying attention to us, but she is. Even from here, I can see the small wrinkle between her brows as she furrows them in concern. Emerson's eyes must follow mine because he grabs my helmet with one hand, bringing my focus back to him. "If it's too much for you right now, just focus on me. Only on me."

*I don't want it to be too much. I want her here.*

But I can't find a way to verbalize it all. At least not right now. It's not the time. So I just shake my head in his hold.

Once he realizes I'm finally present, a soft smile pulls at his lips, and he drops the front of his helmet to mine. "Alright, let's go kick some ass, yeah?"

"Yeah." I nod in agreement. Even though I'm suddenly feeling like the one who just got their ass kicked, and the game hasn't even started yet.

# CHAPTER 35
# SEX ON BLADES

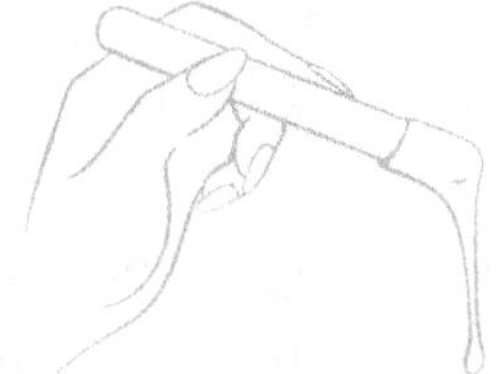

**LILIANA**

Something weird is happening with Dom. And I don't fucking like it. When I saw him there, frozen on the ice, all I wanted to do was break down this plexiglass barrier and go to him. But I couldn't. I'm just thankful he had Emerson.

I can only hope that whatever was going on wasn't because of me, but deep down in my gut, I know it was. Because even though I've never seen him play hockey until tonight, one thing I do know... *nothing* shakes Dominic Foster.

But before I could bring myself to get up and leave, to not be a distraction to him any longer, the center for each team was on whatever that middle line is called, the ref holding the puck between them. It was so quiet in this damn arena you could hear a pin drop. No, I take that back, you could hear the puck drop.

*That should be the saying.*

And from that moment on, my eyes have been glued to the ice.

The second the puck drops, it's pure pandemonium. It takes me a minute to even realize where Emerson is. He's skating around like a wild man, but once I spot him, my eyes don't leave him. That is unless the other team is trying to score, then I find my ass out of my seat screaming, making sure Dom is blocking the puck from getting into the Panthers' net.

*I don't know how they keep up with where the damn puck is.*

I might not know hockey, but most sports have some kind of defense and offense, and my years playing volleyball made me a little more aware of figuring out how other sports work. Emerson seems to stay on the side of the ice where Dom is, protecting him, and to say it doesn't make me hot would be a lie. Since Emerson is a defensive player, he and the other guy, who plays on the opposite side of him, protect Dom at all costs.

Dom is guarding that net like his life depends on it, and it's one of the most attractive things I've ever seen the man do. And that's saying a lot because he's done some hot shit in the time I've known him. I mean he's a damn erotic voice actor for crying out loud. But this... this tops that by *a lot*.

He's so powerful out there.

*Sex on blades.*

The way his body can move at the speed it does is genuinely shocking, especially knowing how big he is. I'll never understand the science behind it. All I know is that he's a fine-tuned machine. Mentally and physically.

Every so often, my eyes will find his through his goalie mask, and even from here, I watch them darken as he stares at me across the ice before refocusing his attention on the game in front of him.

And when I'm not ogling Dominic, I'm staring at Emerson. Like right now. Emerson's more like a blur as he passes, chasing down the other team's offensive man who currently has the puck in front of his stick. They both get to the end of the rink and Em slams the guy into the boards. I grimace because I sure as hell wouldn't want to be on the receiving end of that. But the check works. The opponent isn't able to keep control of the puck and is too stupid to pass it to one of his teammates.

I watch as Emerson gets the puck back to the other side, slamming it to who I think is the center, only for him to quickly pass it to one of Palm's offensive men.

And before I can even blink, the buzzer behind the goal is going off, and everyone's out of their seats screaming.

Holy shit. We scored!

Call it naivety, but I really didn't realize how athletic these two actually are. I guess I underestimated what it took to be a hockey player. Why?

*I have no clue.*

For God's sake, they're on blades, skating on ice, chasing a damn puck around. All while the other opponents are actively trying to get the little rubber disc away from them in any way they can. It could never be me, but I can appreciate the hell out of them and their athletic abilities. There's something so attractive about how passionate they are about the sport and how the two of them dominate the rink around them. Like they own the ice and nobody can tell them otherwise.

*Ugh, maybe I am getting invested in hockey after all.*

I feel like it's similar to baseball—hate watching it on TV, but in person it's an experience you can't put into words. The energy in here is electric. Contagious. You can't not pay attention to what's going on. As the second line hops over to give the first line a break, I meet Emerson's eyes right beside their bench, and the smile he gives me is infectious. I can feel the power of it sink into my chest. I think he's happy I seem to be enjoying myself, and I'm not absolutely miserable sitting here watching them play.

I don't think I could be miserable watching the two men I lo—*fuck.*

*Fuck.*

*Fucckkk.*

It hits me.

It's *been* hitting me.

All of the moments, big and small, hit me in rapid succession. I think I've been brushing it to the side for days now. But watching the two of them have the moment before the game, seeing them out on the ice tonight, the feeling in my chest when Emerson simply winked at me, and the way they care for one another… the thing that hits me the hardest is how they both care so much for *me*. Together, separate, it doesn't matter. They're always there when I need them, and even when I don't think I do… they're there. Both of them. From the lock on my apartment door that Emerson replaced, to ordering me food when I don't schedule enough time between clients for lunch breaks, and dropping anything at the drop of a hat if I call or text them.

I've always looked for a love that was loud. Bold. One like I've seen in some of my favorite couples. A love so loud it outshines me even on my boldest of days. But here they have been, loving me in the quiet moments. The ones that go almost unnoticed unless you're really paying attention.

My god.

I love Emerson Baker and Dominic Foster.

I sit in my epiphany for the remainder of the game. When I thought about this moment, I figured it would send me spiraling into a panic. Commitment used to scare the shit out of me, but with Emerson and Dominic I feel we could take on the world when we're together. I've known for a while now how much I care about these two—I was just heavily in denial.

When Palm University wins 3–0, the seats clear and I wait as everyone leaves the arena. Once the majority of the people are cleared out, I make my way to the locker rooms. The guys wanted me to meet them down here, and I'm not putting up a fight knowing damn well they're about to look good as hell with their post-game suits on.

Right as the thought pops into my head, they seem

to appear out of thin air. They come out of the locker room door, snatching the breath from my lungs. Emerson is wearing a dark, forest-green suit, which is the perfect contrast to Dom's creamy-beige suit.

I let out a low whistle as I eye them up from down the hall. "Lord have mercy, who are these two studs?"

The two of them blush and give me the shyest smiles as they make their way to me. Neither of them hesitate to kiss me deeply. Dom holds my face in his hands as he kisses me. His shaky breath sweeps across my cheeks as his lips ravage me. But regardless of the intensity of his kiss, there's an apprehension there. I can feel it. I can feel it in the way his lips move against mine. Like he's trying not to fully sink into the way we feel against one another. But before I have a moment to analyze it, Emerson rips me from his hold. Wrapping his arm around my waist, he presses my body tight against his before crashing his mouth to mine. The wet strands of his hair brush against my forehead as I let out a whimper. None of us care who sees the three of us in this hallway. And regardless of what's going on with Dom, knowing neither of them are ashamed, only makes me want them more.

I manage to pull my mouth from Emerson's only for him to look at me with that panty-melting grin and say, "Gotta say, Darlin', I could get used to seeing you in my jersey." His voice is deep and raspy, and it sends a rush of heat straight to my core.

"Is that so? How about you, Foster?" I ask, looking over at Dom.

His nostrils flare at the use of his last name, and I

can tell he's trying to downplay his reaction. He pauses a moment before finally answering. "I know one thing's for sure, Honey. It's a miracle the score was 3–0 when I spent half the game staring at you. I pulled that shutout straight out of my ass."

My cheeks heat under his praise, and as I look between the two of them, assessing the way their eyes continuously rake over my body, I already know how we're going to be spending the night.

# CHAPTER 36
# SOMETHING'S GOTTA GIVE, RIGHT?



Dom said he didn't want to drive, so the three of us are in my Jeep heading back to Lil's apartment. Our girl kept herself busy trying to drive me insane as she rubbed her hand up and down my thigh the entire way. But as much as I wanted to sink into her touch, I couldn't, because half of my attention was on Dom in the backseat as he stared mindlessly out of the window.

I know what's going on with him.

I'm his best friend. His person. Some days I know him better than he knows himself. So it took me all of two seconds to decipher what was going on as he stood frozen in the crease. Because I saw the way he looked at her in that jersey. He looked at her the exact same way I did. We looked at her like she belonged there. Like she belonged sitting just behind the plexiglass wearing our numbers. Like she belonged in that chair cheering us on. Because she does. She belongs. At that rink. In our lives. In our minds. In our *hearts*.

So, yeah, I know why Dom's spiraling.

I also know that if he just gives the three of us a chance, he'll realize that this is all worth it. That if he lets it, this could be the start of something great.

But I'm not sure that this situation, especially with the state Dom is in, requires words.

*No.*

Right now, I think we should let our bodies do all of the talking. Which is perfect because, judging by the way Lil's attempting to undo my tie while holding onto Dom's hand for dear life as I key in the code to her apartment, it's safe to say she's on the same page I am. And as chatty as Dominic Foster usually is, when he clams up, I can always count on his body to say the words his mouth won't.

I don't know what planet we've landed on where *I'm* the one trying to get *him* to open up, but if that's what it's going to take, I'll do it.

Finally, I manage to punch in the security code correctly, and I push the door open in front of me. Lil lets go of her feeble attempt to undo my tie and places her hand in the center of my back, ushering me into her apartment.

Once we're all the way inside and the door is shut behind us, I turn to face the two of them. Lil's hand is firmly clasped in Dom's. In one fell swoop, I undo my tie, rip it off from around my neck, and set it on the counter next to me.

"Fuck, why was that so hot?" Lil says on a breath.

Smiling, I shrug my suit jacket off and drape it on the chair at her kitchen counter. My eyes move to Dom as he clenches his jaw at the sight of me undressing before them.

"Ugh, even the way you take off your jacket is sexy," Lil groans. She attempts to step toward me, but, as he always can, Dom silently reads my mind and keeps her in place.

"What if I do this?" I ask before undoing the top two buttons of my dress shirt, followed by the two at my wrist. I roll my sleeves up my forearms stopping once I get to my elbows.

Lil bites her lip and Dom's nostrils flare. "Please," she says. "You know damn well that the way a man's forearms look underneath a dress shirt is basically like pornography. Especially yours."

"You want to talk about pornography?" Dropping the grin I've been wearing since I took my tie off, I look from her to Dominic. "Dominic, come here." Reading my expression and tone of voice, he doesn't waste a second following my instructions. Letting go of Lil's hand, he comes to me. "Stand next to me, and look at our girl."

Dom stands at my left, and the two of us stare at Lil, still standing in the entryway of her apartment. Her eyes are wide, her chest heaving beneath our jersey.

*Fuck me, that jersey.*

"Show us what you have on underneath that jersey, Sweetheart."

[1] A slow smile spreads across Lil's face before she kicks off her shoes, followed by her socks. Reaching underneath the front of her jersey, she undoes the buttons of her skinny jeans before shimmying them over her hips and down her legs. Once she kicks them off to the side, she's left standing before us in nothing but her panties and *our* jersey.

She moves to take it off but I stop her. "Wait."

She immediately drops her hands at her sides as Dom and I drink her in.

"Fuck," Dom says under his breath.

"Now *that,* is fucking pornography," I tell her. "I have half a mind to fuck you with that on. But as much as I'm enjoying this view, I'll save that for another day. Right now… well, I think we deserve to see what's underneath it after our hard fought win. Don't you, Dom?"

I manage to break eye contact with Lil long enough to *finally* see the corners of his lips turn up. He waits a moment before he answers. "Hell yeah we do."

*There he is.*

Lil breathes a sigh of relief, likely thinking the same exact thing I am, before grabbing the hem of the jersey and lifting it over her head. Her dark hair falls free of the fabric, draping over the slope of her shoulders and the swell of her breasts.

And there she stands before us in nothing but a deep-green lace bra and panty set. Looking absolutely—

---

1. REACTION - Xavier Mayne

"Perfect," Dom utters.

"Yeah. Perfect," I repeat.

Dom and I stand before her in our suits, me sans the tie and jacket, and it's taking every ounce of my will power not to fuck her right here on the floor.

Actually, now that I think about it—

Leaning over, I whisper in Dom's ear. Even looking at his profile, I watch as his eyes go wide as he hisses a sharp breath. He turns his head to look at me and nods in Lil's direction. "First can I—"

I nod, knowing exactly what he's asking.

Without a second thought, Dom's in front of Lil in two long strides, kissing her as if his life depends on it, and I have to bite back the groan wanting to spill from my lips as I listen to the two of theirs. Not knowing the instructions I gave him, Lil becomes desperate for the kiss to become more, but Dom pulls away before it can. He runs the pad of his thumb across her bottom lip before giving her one more chaste kiss and walking right past me and into Lil's room.

Looking confused, she asks, "Wait. Where's he—"

Now it's me who crosses the room, pressing my lips to hers before she has a chance to finish her question. Her mouth is open in shock, so I use it to my advantage and sink my tongue in. It only takes her a second to reciprocate and lean into my kiss.

As I kiss her, she starts eagerly trying to unbutton my dress shirt. When she groans in frustration, I smile against her lips. "Just get it off, Lil."

Gripping the front of it, she rips it open. The sound of buttons hitting the floor fills the room, and I can't find it in me to care that she just ruined one of only two white button-ups I own because now my skin is against hers.

Desperate for more, I wrap my hands underneath the swell of her ass and lift her off the ground. On instinct, she wraps her legs around me. I don't go far. Taking a few steps, I slam her back against the wall of her entry way. She grunts at the contact but she doesn't stop kissing me. As a matter of fact, when she attempts to lean forward, and I pin her against the wall again, she moans at the forcefulness of the silent demand.

I'm faintly aware of the sound of Dom rummaging around Lil's room, doing what I asked of him, but I don't focus on that. Right now, my sole focus is on the woman in my arms, as she rubs her wet pussy over my dick, likely leaving a wet spot on my suit pants.

More than capable of holding her with one hand, I move the other to grip her face, pinning her head back against the wall as my mouth makes its way down her neck. And when I bite at the skin along her collar bone, her hold on the hair at the nape of my neck tightens.

*Yeah, my girl likes it rough.*

Lowering my face, I nip along the swell of her breasts, savoring the sound of each moan that falls from her lips. "More," she pleads.

"Put your feet down," I tell her, and she does. Once I'm sure she's stable, I bring my mouth to her nipple, sucking it through the thin lace of her bra.

"More, Em."

"Hmmmm, I love when you say my name like that," I tell her before pulling the cup of her bra down, exposing her breast. My eyes latch on her pointed nipple, and I take it into my mouth yet again. And when my teeth clamp down on the tight bud, I feel a wave of pleasure surge through her body beneath my hands.

"Again."

I move to the other breast, expose it from the cup of the bra, and do the same thing before dropping to my knees. Lil's hands find my hair again as my tongue drags down the center of her stomach. She tastes so fucking good, and I haven't even made it to the best part yet.

When the lace of her underwear meets my tongue, I look up at her. "You look awfully good on your knees, Mr. Baker."

I smile up at her. "Well that's good, Miss Campos. Because I'm quite fond of the view from down here."

A soft moan sounds from her room, and Lil's eyes go wide. She looks down at me in question and my only response is, "He'll get his turn with you, Sweetheart. I just needed him to do something for us first." I place a soft kiss on the wet spot of her underwear. "But right now, I need you to focus on me. Got it?"

"Got it," she replies without hesitation.

"Good girl," I praise. "These gotta go." Wanting to see these again, I decide against ripping them off her body, and slide her underwear down her legs. Once she's free of them and I have an unrestricted view of her glistening pussy, I don't waste another second before burying my face between her legs.

Knowing exactly what she wants, Lil drapes one

toned leg over my shoulder as I run my tongue through her folds. Once I reach her swollen clit, I suck it into my mouth. "*Fuck,* Em. That feels so—oh—"

Her words are cut short when I insert one finger into her pussy, followed by a second. There's often a time for a slow build to orgasm, but right now isn't it. I'm *desperate* to hear her fall apart. To see it. To *feel* it beneath my touch. So I fuck her with my fingers, hard. I don't let up, not even for a second, as I work her clit with my mouth. In mere moments, she's grinding her pussy against my face and helping fuck herself on my fingers—as desperate for her release as I am.

I can feel my cock leaking in my pants as I bring her closer and closer to orgasm. But as much as I want to touch myself, to fall apart with her, I don't. Not yet.

I can feel the walls of her cunt tighten around my fingers, so I curl them toward me, ensuring I brush up against her G-spot with every movement.

"Oh, *yes!*" she shouts. "Just like that, baby. Keep going. Keep—*oh!*"

I quickly pull my mouth from her clit to look up at her, wanting—no, *needing* to see her face. "That's it, Sweetheart. Keep going." Turning my head to the side, I bite down *hard* on the inside of the thigh she has draped over me, and let my thumb take over on her clit. The moment my teeth make contact with her skin I know she's done for. "Come for me," I command as I look back up at her.

And that's exactly what she does.

Lil comes so hard, I can feel her release dripping

down my hand as my fingers continue to pump in and out of her.

Finally, when her screams start to die down, I slowly pull my fingers from her pulsing cunt, place one soft kiss on her clit, and stand in front of her. Raising my soaked forearm in front of her face, I command, "Lick it off. See how fucking delicious you taste."

Still breathless, she picks her head off the wall, sticks out that gorgeous tongue, and runs it up my forearm and over my fingers before sucking them into her mouth.

I can't help myself, I press my throbbing cock against her as she works her tongue over my fingers, moaning as she licks off every drop of her release.

And when she's done, I look her in the eyes and say, "Let's go see what our boy is doing. Shall we?"

# CHAPTER 37
# DOUBLE PENETRATION...

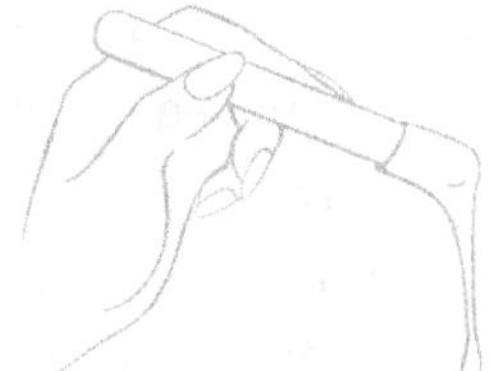

**LILIANA**

Emerson carries me into my bedroom, where I can still hear Dom's deep moans of pleasure. I need to see what the hell he's doing in here, but I know one thing... the noises are going straight to my already soaking cunt.

Emerson sets me on my feet once we're in the room and groans when he spots Dominic. "Baby Boy—*fuck*—you look so good with that pretty hole of yours plugged."

The shameless moan that crawls out of me from Emerson's words alone should have me embarrassed, but as I spin around to witness whatever Dom's doing to pull that kind of reaction from Emerson, I gasp. Dom is on his hands and knees, ass facing us, and is working one of my plugs in and out of his ass.

*Why do I want to peg him right here and now?*

I don't have a harness or I sure as hell would be

breaking that bad boy out. "Fuck do I get to watch you two?" I ask, but it sounds like more of a prayer.

Emerson leans down and whispers in my ear, "No… well, not yet. You're going to ride Dom while he has his plug in. I want him ready for me." He apparently says it loud enough for Dom to hear because he responds with a wanton moan as he flips over to his back.

I waste no time striding over to the bed and climbing up to straddle Dom's waist. As I rub my pussy up and down his rock hard length, he groans. "Fuck, you're soaking, Sweetheart."

"Blame our boy for that," I tease, but don't miss the way he tenses when I say "boy." He thought I was going to say boyfriend.

I want him to want us to be more than whatever the hell we are now.

I don't let that pull me from this moment though, as I start to rub my core up and down his cock as it lies on his stomach. Without any warning, I fist it and slide onto him, not stopping until he's fully seated inside of me.

"*Shit*," he grunts, breathlessly.

[1] Wrapping my hand around his neck, and forcing him to look me in my eyes, I grit out, "That's right, tell me what this pussy does to you."

The look in his eyes says it all; he doesn't even need to say it. I know I'm everything to him, and that scares the hell out of Dominic Foster.

*I just wish I knew why.*

---

1.  Tidal Wave - Chase Atlantic

"Can this pretty cunt take more?" Emerson asks as he crawls up the bed behind me. As I bounce up and down on Dom's cock, Emerson spreads my ass cheeks apart, giving him an uninterrupted view of where Dom and I are connected. He hums. "Lil, Darlin', she's begging to be double stuffed."

*She, as in, my cunt—yes, she is.*

"Yes. Yes, she is *begging*. Please, Emerson…" I plead, and I don't care how pathetic I sound. "I need you both in me at the same time." You could blame it on the fact that I'm ovulating, but the thought of my cunt being stretched by my two hot-as-fuck men has me ready to fall apart at the seams.

*My men.*

Did I ever think I would be fitting two cocks in my vagina at once?

No.

Not even in my wildest, nastiest fantasies. And it very well could not be possible, but I'm up to seeing if it is. For them, I think I'd try just about anything.

I'm not the biggest fan of anal. A finger here and there is about all the fun I enjoy with the back door, but when Emerson mentioned wanting to be in my cunt at the same time as Dom, I didn't even hesitate.

Emerson's lubed finger presses at my vagina as I slow my movements on top of Dominic, allowing his digit to breach me. As I think Emerson's finger isn't going to fit in me alongside Dom's cock, I feel the tip of his finger break past the resistance.

All of us groan in unison as Emerson works in and out of me, stretching and prepping me to take his cock.

Em pushes Dom's cock to the front wall of my vagina, and like the euphoric bliss my body always floats into, my eyes cross from the bliss. Dom reaches between us and starts to work my clit, and I let my head tip against Emerson's shoulder as a wave of pleasure ravages my body. "More, Emerson, please. I can take it."

"You're a greedy whore tonight, aren't you?" he asks as he pushes in what I think is the third finger. It all feels like too much until I hear Dom's deep voice whispering.

"Come for me, Lil. Come on my cock before he's in here with us." I smash my lips to his in a desperate effort to hold off my orgasm, because I'm nothing if not a brat, but I quickly realize the kiss was the wrong thing to do if that was the goal. The motion of leaning over Dom to reach his mouth only pushes his cock further into my G-spot, and right as my lips land on his, I'm screaming out in ecstasy.

As my body starts to come down, I hear the telltale sound of a lube bottle cracking open. Emerson pulls his fingers from my throbbing pussy. "Are you two ready for me?"

Dom and I answer him in unison. "Yessss."

The head of Emerson's cock pushes against my entrance along the underside of Dom's, and the pressure already feels like it's going to be too much, but my breath hitches as his swollen tip finally pushes into me. "Oh my fucking—" My words are cut off from the shear fullness that is already consuming me.

"Breathe, Sweetheart, that was the worst part. Relax

and take us like this beautiful body was meant to." I take a deep breath just as Emerson instructed me, and he slowly works himself in and out of me in what feels like inches at a time. I'm thankful for his patience so I can adjust to the two of them a lot easier than I initially thought was going to be possible. The pain eventually morphs into intense pleasure. It's unlike anything I could have ever imagined.

Dom is the first to almost shatter. "Em, move, or I don't know how much longer I'm going to last. This is all too fucking hot." He takes a deep breath, trying to steady himself, then suddenly blurts out, "Fuck, we should've recorded this one too!"

I laugh, causing them both to groan at what I can only assume is my muscles squeezing them, and I grin. "Move, Em, come on, fuck me."

And fuck me he does.

They both do… pulling in and out of me while I sit, leaning over Dom, a pleading, whimpering mess. And even though this is new for all of us, it feels like we've been doing this for a lifetime. Like the three of our bodies were meant to be one like this.

*This* is bliss.

*We're going to have to do this more often.*

Right as that thought leaves my head, Dom grips my hips, and I feel his movements start to sputter. "I'm going to—" That's all he gets out before his orgasm washes over him and his cock starts twitching inside of me. Fuck, I can feel each movement clear as day when they're both inside of me.

As he comes out of his blissful haze, he whispers,

"Let me taste it, Sweetheart. I'm fucking desperate for it."

If my greedy cunt weren't already dripping, it would sure as hell be now.

Emerson pulls out of me, and I slide my lower half up Dom's body, landing right on his mouth as he requested. I feel Dom's legs push up to the sides of his stomach, and Emerson instructs me, "Spin around, Sweetheart. I know you wanna watch me fuck his tight little hole."

Dom moans from beneath me, and I can't stop myself from panting, knowing this is about to be one of the hottest things I'll ever get to witness.

As I spin around, Dom pulls me back to his lips, licking his release from my cunt like his life depends on it. My eyes land between his legs where Emerson is toying with the plug that been in his ass this whole time. I don't know how Emerson didn't come while they were in me at the same time, but his cock is leaking, hanging heavy between his legs.

Dom is already starting to get hard again, and this sight will be ingrained in my mind for the rest of my life. I feel my clit get sucked in between his lips, and I try to buck away, but his hands are wrapped around my thighs like a vise.

Emerson finally pulls the plug free and tosses it to my floor. Like Emerson has a string pulling him to Dom, the two of them so perfectly in sync, he doesn't waste another moment before notching his cock at Dom's back entrance and pushing inside of him. The humming and vibration that is leaving Dom and traveling to my already sensitive clit, has me screaming out in pleasure.

Emerson begins pounding into him. Using him for exactly what he needs—hitting Dom's prostate at the perfect angle with every thrust. "This ass is everything. You're taking me like such a good little whore."

Dom's mouth pulls away from my clit long enough to get the next couple of words out. "Fill me up, Emerson."

"*Fucckk.*" Emerson groans, and Dom is quick to pull my throbbing clit back between his lips, as Emerson's movements begin to stutter. When I feel his teeth graze against the swollen bundle of nerves, I'm gone.

On another planet.

No… another universe.

Emerson does what Dom wanted. He fills him, his moans of pleasure echoing off every surface of my bedroom as I climb off to lie on the bed. As I stare up at the ceiling, coming down from all of the emotions and bliss, I find myself thinking that absolutely nothing could be better than this.

# CHAPTER 38
# FIRST, COFFEE

**DOMINIC**

I don't want to move.

For the first time in I don't even know how long, the sun has just risen and I don't want to get out of bed. The alarm on my phone never went off—not that I ever really need it—because I never got a chance to plug the thing in last night. It was only at ten percent after the game. Surely it's sitting in my duffle bag completely dead. I should probably get up and charge it. Get a start on breakfast, but…

I can't move.

I want to lie here. Trapped between the two of them, Lil's leg draped over mine with her head on my chest and Emerson's arm over me as his fingers lay splayed across my stomach. The three of us crammed together on Lil's tiny queen-sized bed. There's not a sound to be heard out Lil's apartment window. No birds. No sprinklers. No cars. And the only thing to be heard inside is the sound of their soft snores on either side of me. No sounds of breakfast being made. No music being played. Nothing. Just silence.

I'm uncomfortable. I'm hot. And the silence makes it all even worse.

Yet… I still don't want to move.

I want to remain trapped here. Forever in their hold.

Because despite my freak out last night during our game, I realized something as I sat in Lil's room, listening to the sounds of Emerson making her come from the other room.

I wouldn't be panicking if the deal wasn't already done.

I love Emerson.

I've loved him for years. He's been my person for as long as I can remember. The two of us are so connected we breathe in sync. But now… now I need his breath as if it were my own. I need him, to be *me*.

And Lil.

*Fuck.*

I didn't want to love her. But I've never been with someone so capable of making me feel complete.

If Emerson is the breath in my lungs, Liliana is the heart that beats in my chest.

I'm panicked because, without me even realizing, they have slowly become the best parts of me.

And as I laid here in this room last night, listening to the two of them, alone, I started to think that was the last place I wanted to be.

*Alone.*

On the outside.

But knowing that I'm in love with them, and admitting it out loud, are two entirely different things. If my feelings become words then they become real. Every impulse to run, every instinct to keep people at arms length goes right out the window. And it's hard to rewire your brain when you've spent so many years making it that way.

Lil starts wiggling against me before a dramatic groan spills from between her closed lips. I can't help the smile that takes over my face. Every worry that was running through my head seems wholly insignificant.

And when she blindly slaps Emerson's arm, he lets out an equally dramatic groan. If mornings weren't already my favorite part of the day, watching the two of these crabasses groan about would make it so. It's never not funny.

"Emmmm," Lil groans. "Tell Dom to make us some coffee."

A string of literal gibberish leaves Emerson's mouth, and I chuckle even louder this time.

"Good morning, Honey," I say before kissing her on the top of her head. "You know you could just ask me to make you coffee."

"Mmmmm. I'm afraid if I speak to you you're going to want to have an actual conversation with me, and I can't handle that right now."

Eyes still closed, Emerson moves his hand up my torso until he finds Lil's face. He places his large hand over the entire thing. "Shhhhhhh."

She grabs his wrist and throws his arm back to his side of the bed, and I continue to laugh as I slide down the bed, untangling myself from the two of them. "I'll go make copious amounts of coffee, then what do the two of you say about having ourselves a day? We have no classes. No games. No practices. And Lil doesn't have to work."

*Honestly, this literally never happens, so I'll be damned if I don't take advantage of the opportunity and my new found look on life.*

Lil mumbles into the pillow. "Ten more minutes."

"I will go anywhere with you as long as you leave me alone right now," Emerson adds.

Smiling ear to ear, I pat both their legs before heading to Lil's kitchen to make them their coffee.

If I'm going to be spending more mornings with them, I should probably look into the possibility of injecting coffee directly into one's bloodstream.

# CHAPTER 39

# DATES ARE IMPORTANT

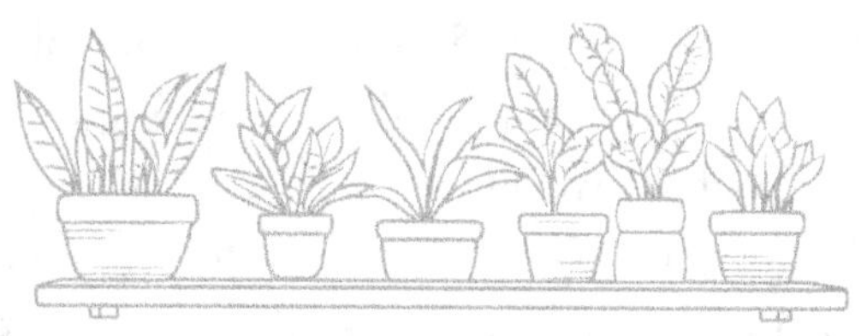

## DOMINIC

"You cannot have the chocolate one, Dominic! It's mine!" Lil attempts to take the cupcake from my hand, but I stretch my arm over my head, well out of her reach. She crosses her arms, raises her brow, and purses her lips at me, doing her best to silently intimidate me. But it won't work. I've had too good of a day to be deterred by her glares.

"I know chocolate is your favorite, Honey, but you picked the cookies and cream one."

She looks genuinely offended that I would say something so proposterous. "I absolutely did not. You give me that cupcake right this second or I'll—"

I can't help it. My grin is so wide it's starting to hurt my cheeks. "You'll what? Hmmm?"

"I'll-I'll—"

Emerson reaches over and taps my dick with the back of his hand. I fold over and he snatches the cupcake right out of my hand. "Here you go, Darlin'," he says as he hands it to her, followed by a wet kiss on her cheek.

"My hero," she replies before sticking her tongue out at me.

I'd argue some more, but when she swipes at the frosting on top of the cupcake with her tongue, she lets out a satisfied moan. The sound goes straight to my dick, and I look over at Emerson to see if it's having the same effect on him, but he's just looking at me with a smartass look on his face that screams "I knew that would happen you moron."

"A smack to the stomach would have sufficed," I say as I stand up straight. I subtly adjust myself to make sure the tip of my dick is still intact.

Emerson shrugs. "Yeah, but that wouldn't have been as satisfying. Here"—he hands me the cookies and cream cupcake before taking a bite of his vanilla bean one—"eat your damn cupcake."

Only Emerson Baker would order a basic vanilla bean cupcake at a gourmet bakery because why, and I quote, "ruin a good thing."

I quickly kiss a spot of chocolate frosting off the corner of Lil's lips before the three of us walk down the boardwalk for a while, each of us taking turns talking about our favorite parts of the day. I think today was just what we needed. What *I* needed.

I couldn't pick a favorite part of today if I tried.

I got to wake up between them. Made them coffee and breakfast, and watched them with a satisfied smile on my face as they ate it. Their morning scowls slowly faded into satisfied smiles with each bite they took. Once we got ready, after having a slow midmorning fuck in the shower where Emerson and I pinned Lil up against the wall and had ourselves a second breakfast, we spent all day down at the boardwalk. We went in shop after shop, relaxed on the beach, listened to street music, and had some of the best pasta I've ever had for dinner. The three of us have kissed and held hands, despite how we each initially felt about PDA, every chance we could get. Not once caring how anyone might have looked at us strangely. There was a feeling of pride in my chest every time one of them showed affection toward me or toward each other, despite there being people around. Like none of us could give a damn what the outside world thinks about us. Today, we're just happy being happy. Now the sun is setting with the most stunning shades of vibrant oranges and golds, creating the perfect backdrop to end a perfect day.

Lil stops along the edge of the boardwalk once she's finished her cupcake and rests her arms along the wood fence separating the walkway from the beach. Her black hair, styled in beachy waves, blows in the breeze, allowing me to see the profile of her face in all its beauty. Her tan skin glows as the sunset lowers to meet the ocean, her cheeks the most flawless shade of pink from being out in the sun all day.

I couldn't think of anything more perfect if I tried.

When I look to my right, I find Emerson staring at her with the same awe. And as I watch him watch her, I think the same thing all over again.

Finally, he notices me staring at him and smiles softly up at me. The two of us stare at one another for a moment before looking back at Lil. "Take a picture of her like that," I tell him.

My phone has been dead all day. I haven't had a second to charge it, and honestly, it's been nice not having any interruptions. But I've also had to steal Emerson's phone every five minutes for pictures. He sighs at me half-heartedly before pulling out his phone and snapping a picture of our girl. He shows it to me, and I instantly know that it's going to be printed and put somewhere in my apartment. Without me having to ask he says, "I'll text it to you. It'll be on your phone once you finally charge it."

The two of us stand there staring at her for what feels like hours, but in reality it can't be more than five minutes. It's only once the sun dips below the water that Lil looks over at us, a knowing smirk on her face. "The two of you going to stand there and eye-fuck me all night, or can we go back to my place now?"

Emerson and I both huff a laugh. He reaches up and rubs a hand down the back of my head before moving toward her. He grabs her hand in his as he looks back at me. "You coming with us?"

I reach for Lil's outstretched hand. "Not even a question."

The three of us make it back to Lil's apartment, satisfied smiles covering each of our faces. When we get inside I set my phone on the counter. "Hey, Honey. You got a phone charger I can borrow?"

"In the junk drawer," she answers before throwing herself down onto her couch with a groan. "Oh my god. I'm so full I think I might explode. Sex might have to wait a couple of hours."

I bark out a laugh as I open the junk drawer. It takes me a few moments of rummaging around to find what I'm looking for. Once I do, I plug in my phone and wait a few moments for it to power up. It's been dead for almost twenty-four hours. I probably should make sure I'm not missing anything serious. However, if I was, I'm sure someone would probably just call Emerson.

I find a few random social media notifications, followed by a string of texts from the team asking if Emerson and I wanted to go to a party tonight. When neither one of us answered, Flowers was quick to call out the fact we were probably busy "banging Campos' sister."

"You didn't feel like telling me they were shit talking to us in the group chat?" I ask Em as he digs for a bottle of water out of Lil's fridge.

He cracks it open and takes a swig before answering. "That would have required me to read the group chat."

[1] Smiling, I roll my eyes to find two more unread texts from my mom. It takes all of three seconds for me

---

1.  Glass House - Sad Version - mgk, Naomi Wild

to read them, and when I do, my heart falls from my chest.

MOM

I'm here if you need me today, Sweetie. Let me know if you want to go visit Dad this morning.

I didn't hear from you, so I'm going to go spend the day with some girlfriends. Try to put a smile on my face. I love you, Sweetie. I hope that whatever you're doing today puts a smile on yours too.

*I forgot.*

Today is the day my dad died. And for the first time since he's been gone—I forgot.

I forgot him.

I forgot my dad.

All because I let myself slip. I let myself push aside the panic and lean into the fact that I love them.

*Fuck.*

Tears sting at my eyes. My phone remains frozen in my hand as I reread Mom's messages. Emerson must finally notice because there's a slight panic in his voice when he asks, "Dom. What's wrong?"

I don't answer.

I fucking forgot my dad.

I missed it. The entire day. One I usually spend with Mom.

Oh my god. *Mom.*

I left her alone. Today of all days.

"Dominic," Emerson says, his tone harsher now. I

faintly hear Lil walk across the room behind me just as Emerson grabs the phone from my hand. It takes him a moment to read the texts and make sense of their meaning. But when he does he hisses, "Oh shit."

"What? What's wrong?" Lil asks.

Emerson doesn't answer her, his focus remains solely on me. Lil doesn't know the significance of today. How could she? I've never even told her. But Emerson does. He knows, and he let me forget too.

The rational part of my brain knows that's not fair. It's *my* dad and I forgot, so how could I expect him to remember. But the other part of my brain, the one that wants to blame this on them, the part of me that *knew* this wasn't a good idea, the part that fought against my feelings for so long only to give into them for *one day,* and this be the consequence... well that part wants to blame the two people standing next to me.

Emerson locks my phone and sets it on the counter in front of me. "Dominic, look at me."

I don't. I can't.

"Will someone tell me what's going on?" Lil's tone now sounds just as panicked as Emerson's.

"Not right now, Liliana!" he snaps. I don't have to look directly at her to know she's taken aback by his tone. But he doesn't console her. Instead, he reaches out to hold my face between his hands. "Dominic. *Look* at me."

He strokes his thumb along my cheekbone, and I finally manage to lock eyes with him. There's sadness there. Guilt. Like he's taking just as much responsibility for forgetting this day as I am. "It's okay," he soothes.

But his words don't strike their intended cord. Because it's *not* fucking okay.

With a shaky breath, I grip his wrist tightly with both of my hands. Emerson's eyes widen at the forcefulness of my hold. "I told you I couldn't do this. I fucking *told you.* And now look. Look what happened, Emerson!" My volume rises with every word I say. Out of my periphery I watch as Lil takes a step back.

"Dom. Baby. It's—"

"No!" I shout before throwing his arms down to his sides. "It's not okay! Don't you get it? *It's not okay.*" My voice cracks as those last three words leave my mouth. I let Mom down. I let Dad down. This can't fucking happen again. Shaking my head, I take two steps backward toward the door as tears sting my eyes. Emerson's face morphs from concern to panic. I don't dare look over at Lil. I know when I do I'll want to drop to my knees to let her comfort me. But I can't. I can't stay here. "I have to go. I can't do this. It's–it's too much," I say, my words barely audible. Yet, regardless of how quiet I speak, the next two words that leave my lips feel as if someone sets off a bomb in the otherwise quiet apartment. "I'm done."

Without another word, I spin on my heels, rip open the door, and sprint down the stairwell of Lil's apartment building, not wanting to risk them catching me as I wait for an elevator. I faintly hear Emerson shouting after me, but I don't stop.

*I can't stop.*

# CHAPTER 40
# ONE'S OUT, EVERYONE'S OUT

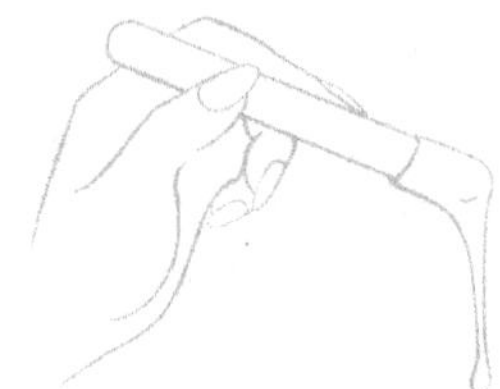

**LILIANA**

"Fill me in now, or I'll call his fucking mother. What the fuck was all of that?!" I practically scream at Emerson once he gets back into my apartment.

Emerson's pacing back and forth in my little entryway, and I swear to all things holy, I want to shake the answers out of him. What in the hell could have been texted to Dominic to cause a reaction like that? And for *both* of them to be this upset. Nope. I don't like the feeling of this one bit. My stomach rolls at the thought of someone hurting them.

Finally, Emerson heaves a heavy sigh and looks in my direction. "How much do you know about Dom's dad?"

I think back to the one time Dom opened up about his dad passing. "I know he passed away when Dom was twelve, and his mom raised him as a single mom, but that's all he's told me." My brows pull together as I try to read Emerson's face. I feel a moment of regret at the fact that I didn't push Dom for more information about his dad, but I could tell how bad it was hurting Dom to even tell me that much. So I dropped it. More than willing to let him discuss it at his own pace

I watch as Emerson wages an internal war with himself. Silently deciding if he wants to tell me whatever he's about to tell me. If it's his place. Eventually, he explains, "He died in his sleep. A heart attack. His Mom woke up to his dead body the next morning. Dom heard her scream. He says the sound of her crying out for help is what he remembers most from that day." Emerson's eyes gloss over. "His dad was *everything* to him. He's never really gotten over it. It's why, with the exception of me, and well, now you, he's always kept everyone at arm's length. It's why he's been so adamant on keeping everything *casual*. He's afraid, Lil."

"Em…" The tears are already welling in my eyes, as I choke out, "Why wouldn't either of you tell me this?"

"We figured *Miss No Commitment* herself would've never fallen for either of us. Let alone both. And not many people know, and he prefers it that way. It's never been my story to tell." The hurt that rips through me at Dom not trusting me with this information when I easily could've comforted him if he ever needed it is like a dagger to the chest. But I also know that's not necessarily logical.

It's not that he doesn't trust me, I remind myself. It's that he doesn't know how to trust that the universe won't rip me away from him in the blink of an eye. I can't even imagine. The *thought* of even losing one of my parents in such a horrific way makes me want to crawl out of my skin. I don't blame Dom for being so reluctant to let us in.

My poor, sweet Dominic. The one who constantly wears this happy facade. The one who will drop anything he's doing to comfort you in a time of need. He's the one who's needed our love the most this whole time.

"But what about today set him off? We had a great day yesterday, and this morning—"

"Today was the anniversary of his death…" He lets that float through the air, and I'm still confused about why that sent him spiraling, when Emerson clarifies, "His phone was dead the whole day… He forgot his dad's death anniversary, Lil. His mom texted him to make sure he was okay, and to ask if he wanted to go visit his grave."

I finish the rest of what he's thinking, "But he was too busy hanging out with us to remember…"

*Shit.*

I hate that his first instinct is to run instead of leaning on us to help him through the rough times, but I don't think he's used to having anyone in his corner besides his mom and Emerson. But Emerson, his best friend, is now a package deal with me, and I think that has a lot to do with how this whole thing has blown up.

"He said he was done… Lil, I can't lose him." The pain lacing Emerson's face is enough to bring me to my knees, because, neither can I. But, I stand tall, I'm not the one the attention needs to be on at the moment. I want to get all of us through this in one piece, as the throuple we are, and for us to thrive together.

*We're not* us *without* him.

Moving to him, I hold Emerson's face in my hands, stroking his cheeks with the pad of my thumbs. "We aren't going to lose him, Em."

"I think we already have…" I can hear the defeat in his voice, and I don't like it one bit.

All my mind keeps floating back to is a little pre-teen Dom, scared, having just lost his dad—his role-model—now having to be the man of the house, all while entering one of the hardest times of a child's life. Without his father there to guide him through it. His mom sure as hell stepped up and raised a hell of a man, but that man, to his core, is still that wounded twelve-year-old deep down. Who is so scared to open his heart and let anyone in to see his true colors.

I want to drown in those colors… the colors that make up the beautiful person that Dom is—but he won't let us. Not fully. You would never know by Dom's personality, and how well he hides all this pain, that he's been through what he's been through. I wish so deeply that he would've let me crack him open and help, but it seems a little too late to be wishing the past didn't happen.

Mine and Emerson's phones both ding with an incoming text message. It doesn't take a genius to figure out who it is. I pull mine out of my back pocket, and Emerson and I read the message in unison.

DOM THE DON 🎙

I'm sorry.

***Dom the Don 🎙 has left the group chat.**

We both stare down at my phone screen, not knowing what to say, and when our gazes meet, that's when the floodgates open. The rest of the day goes by in a blur, and of course, it's the end of the weekend, and everyday life is on the other side of daybreak. The two of us move about my apartment in silence. Neither one of us speaking, but too afraid to part. Only the soft sounds of the occasional sob fill my apartment. I get my groceries for the week delivered, force Emerson to shower with me, and we both crawl into my bed.

When our heads hit the pillow, and the smell of Dom surrounds us, the silent tears run down my face once more. I meet Em's eyes, and he has matching tears falling from the corners of his eyes as well.

*What the fuck are we going to do?*

But as I stare at Emerson as he lies next to me, the two of us share a silent conversation, because we already know the answer. So, for one last night, I wrap my arm and leg around his body, crawling into his skin.

How am I going to live with out this? Without them?

*Both of them.*

I need them like I need my next breath, but without Dom, we can't.

We made the rules. It was the one thing that we agreed to.

If one's out, everyone's out.

# CHAPTER 41
# WHO NEEDS RULES?



I didn't sleep a fucking wink. I couldn't.

All I did was lay in bed all night, with Lil wrapped around me, tears falling down my cheeks as hers landed on my chest. Eventually, exhaustion won out and she fell asleep in my arms. But I stayed awake. Staring at the ceiling wondering how in the hell I was going to fix this.

First I was understanding. I get why Dominic is so upset. I really do. He's pissed at himself for forgetting his dad, for not being there for his mom, and for disappointing himself. I think that has more to do with his running away than being afraid of *us*, at this point. He was all in yesterday. I could feel it. He was letting go of his fears of loving and losing. He was willing to take the risk. But forgetting his dad... that's not a risk he's willing to take. He thinks of us as a distraction.

A fucking distraction.

The more that word rolled around in my head, I slowly went from understanding, to sad, to actually pretty fucking pissed off. And now as I rummage around Lil's room getting dressed for our Monday morning practice as she does her best to get herself ready for work, while muffeling her sobs behind the bathroom door, the more angry I become.

Sitting at the end of her bed, I wait for her to be ready. I'm not leaving without kissing her. But this isn't going to be goodbye. It's a see you later.

Because I'm *going to* fix this.

Fuck the rules.

We literally haven't followed a single one, so why this one?

He loves us, and I'm not going to let him run away from it. I'm just not.

Finally, the door to the bathroom opens, and I drink her in. She's wearing a pair of pale-pink scrubs with her hair pulled into a low bun. Her red-rimmed eyes are swollen and puffy from spending the last eight hours crying, and her cheeks are pink from our day spent in the sun yesterday. Our perfect fucking day.

I want more of those days.

I'm getting more of those days.

"Come here, baby." Even at her lowest, she takes my breath away. I have to stop myself from rubbing at my sternum to dull the ache in my chest as her sad form makes her way over to me.

Standing between my legs, she threads her fingers through the hair at the nape of my neck. I close my eyes and lean into the feeling. *Fuck,* I love when she does this. Eventually, I open them and look up at her. "I'm going to fix this. I promise."

"What-what if there's nothing to fix?" Her voice is so soft, so reluctant. It fucking kills me. "I don't want to give both of you up. I-I don't want to be alone anymore."

Goddammit, Dominic. "You won't be, Sweetheart. We're not giving anything up."

"But the rules?"

"Fuck the rules. We're so far past those stupid fucking rules it's not even funny." My hands move up and down the backs of her thighs. I know right now might not be the right time to say what I'm about to say but I can't take it anymore. "I love you, Liliana Campos." She inhales a sharp breath, but I don't stop. "I love the way that even on your darkest days, your light shines brighter than mine. I love that you hate mornings as much as I do. I love that you let me take care of you. I love the way you make me feel like the most important person in the room. But most of all. I love that, even in the silence you make me feel heard. You make me feel like I matter."

[1] A single, small tear falls down her cheeks. "Emerson, I—"

"No. Don't say it now. Not yet. I just needed you to know how I feel. I need you to know so you can trust that I'll fix this. I *will* fix this, Lil."

She runs one hand down the side of my face. "I trust

---

1.  Nothing Without You - The Weeknd

you," she replies softly before bending over and giving me one last kiss.

After Lil heads into work, I realize I have a little bit of extra time to kill before practice, so I run into town to grab her a coffee and drop it off at her suite before I head to the rink. If she's as tired as I am she's going to need it.

But when I finally walk into the locker room twenty minutes later, he's not there. "Hey, anyone know where Dom is?"

Patty looks up from lacing up one of his skates. "Heard coach say he's out sick for the day."

My anger from earlier resurfaces all over again. Is he fucking serious right now? Digging my phone out of my duffle bag I pull up his contact and call him. It rings twice then goes to voicemail. *This motherfucker just denied my call.* I try one more time and it doesn't even ring. Just goes straight to voicemail. *Dick.* I do the only other thing I can think of. I call Mary Foster.

She picks up after just a couple of rings, because of course she does. She's a saint. "Good morning, Honey. Is everything okay?"

"Have you talked to Dominic today?" I try to keep my tone level so as not to panic her.

A heavy sigh sounds through the phone. "No. I'm assuming this is about yesterday? I was wondering when this was going to happen."

"When what was going to happen?"

"When he'd have something more important in his life."

Her words hit me hard in the chest. "Mary… there's nothing more important than you and his dad."

"There should be. That's what any mother wants for their son. To build a life for himself. The most impactful thing in his life shouldn't be the day his dad died. At least not anymore."

"He was happy," I say softly.

I can practically hear her smile through the phone. "Then go remind him of that, will you?"

We say our goodbyes, and I run this week's schedule through my head. We don't have a game until Thursday, so if I miss practice today it won't be the end of the world. Coach will understand if I have a family emergency. Because that's what Dom is. He's my family. I'm not letting this go.

"Hey, Patty," I say, grabbing my duffle and heading toward the door. "Can you tell Coach I have a family emergency? I'll be at practice tomorrow."

He gives me a knowing smile before nodding. "Sure thing."

Once I'm in my jeep, I peel out of the parking lot and head straight for Dominic's apartment. I try his cell one more time, anticipating it to go straight to voicemail. But to my surprise, he picks up after one ring. "Leave me alone, Emerson." Then he hangs up.

My grip tightens on the wheel, because now I'm not just pissed at him. I'm fucking livid.

I pound my fist against his door and, little to my surprise, he doesn't answer it. So I use the spare key I have on my key ring and unlock it. Throwing it open, I spot him sprawled out on his couch, wearing nothing but a pair of black sweatpants, staring up at Sports Center as it plays on his TV. I don't waste time greeting him. "What the fuck is wrong with you?" I shout as I make my way over to him. As I stand in front of him he has the nerve to look up at me in confusion. "You have the fucking nerve to make me fall in love with you. To make *her* fall in love with you, and then you have the balls to tell me to leave you alone?! What the fuck is that, Dominic?"

He says nothing, so I say the one thing I know will get a reaction out of him. "And for what? Because you forgot the day your daddy died? Boo hoo. Grow the fuck up."

He's off the couch and fisting the front of my sweatshirt before I can even blink. "What the fuck did you just say?"

His shirtless torso heaves with each angry breath as he tries to stare me down.

*Good. I got a reaction out of him. It's something.*

"You fucking heard me," I seethe. "You're going to give up everything we have because you can't get over the fact that your dad died when you were twelve? You think this is what he'd want for you? To be some asshole who makes people fall in love with you just for you to leave them high and dry."

"Watch it," he snarls.

"Or what?"

His dark eyes narrow. "You don't know what you're talking about. She doesn't love me. Neither do you."

I bark a sarcastic laugh. "Oh get the fuck over yourself. I've loved you for years you giant fucking moron. And that woman." I point in the direction of the door. "If she didn't love you, why did she spend all last night crying in my arms at the thought of never being able to hold you again, huh?"

"I can't do it, Emerson."

I narrow my eyes back at him. "You're being a fucking coward. He would be ashamed of you."

Dominics eyes flare with anger before he throws me across the room. I land on the floor on my back with a thud. It knocks the wind out of me, but it's nothing I'm not used to. I've taken hits on the rink harder than that. But what I'm not used to is the sight of Dominic's fist heading toward my face as he straddles me on the floor. Before I have a chance to stop it, his fist makes contact with my mouth. I feel my lip split instantly. And when I run my tongue along my teeth to make sure I didn't lose any, I feel the familiar taste of copper hit my tongue.

Dominic's eyes zero in on the sight of the blood as it rolls down my chin, and his eyes grow wide. His fist remains paused in the air, and he doesn't climb off of me. He's frozen.

Any other day of the week, I'd be sorry for what I said. I'd say I didn't mean it and that he had every right to punch me.

But not today.

Because that's exactly what he needed. He needed to feel something other than self-loathing. And if the person he has to loathe is me, then fine. I'll take it.

Bracing my palms on his thighs I ask, "Have you even called your mom yet?" He shakes his head. "Well you fucking should. You should hear what she has to say, Dom."

He lowers his fist. "Y-you talked to her?"

"Yeah. I talked to her. I called her when you weren't answering the phone. I wanted to make sure you were okay. Did you notice it's still practice time and I'm not there?" Dom looks at the clock on his microwave. "I'm here, Dom. I'll always be here. Because I love you."

He doesn't say anything. Instead, he falls backward so his butt is now sitting on the floor between my legs. He wraps his arms around his legs as I move to stand in front of him.

"I fucking love you, Dominic. And I love Lil. I love what we have together. And I refuse to let you ruin it. It's not an option." He looks up at me. His eyes filled with so much emotional turmoil that all I want to do is get back on the ground and hold him in my arms. But I can't. He needs to figure this out on his own. He knows how we feel about him. He knows how far gone we are or he wouldn't have ran. "You should call your mom, Dom."

Turning on my heels I open his door, but before I leave I look over my shoulder at him. His eyes still on me. "We will give you some space, but just so you know —we are so not done."

# CHAPTER 42
# WHEN IN DOUBT, GO TO MOM'S HOUSE

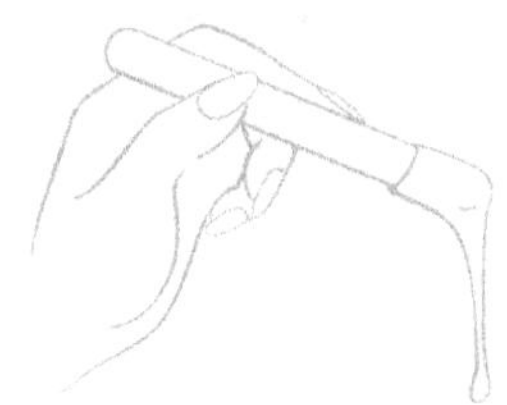

## LILIANA

It's been three days.

Three miserable, hopeless, fucking days, since Dom dropped the bomb in the middle of our perfect—or what was perfect—relationship.

After he disappeared I had two full days in the salon, so full that I was able to turn my mind off and work on autopilot. I know most of my clients could tell I wasn't being myself, but I knew if I were to open up to any of them, the tears would've never stopped.

So, instead of continuing the cycle of crying, then talking myself down, and doing it all over again, I decided to go to my parents' house. I need out of my apartment, away from the very place that reminds me of the three of us together, and so many *good* memories that keep playing in my head like my favorite movie.

*This movie just has me sobbing.*

I've even missed, or more so ignored, all of Gigi's

texts and calls. She just so happened to be in the hallway when Dominic stormed out, so she definitely knows that something is going on. I'm honestly surprised she hasn't stormed through my front door. But she's giving me space, and I'm thankful for that. Wallowing in self-pity is what I needed, but I also need to pull myself out of it. So, before I leave for my parents I shoot my best friend a message.

ME

Hey so sorry I've missed all of these...

GIGI

I know you're sugar coating all of this, Liliana Campos. I'll give you until the end of the week, then I'll be barging in there to make sure you're okay.

I sit here, in my quiet apartment on the couch, trying not to break down again. I'm beyond thankful for the people I have in my life. My friends, my family, and—

*Emerson and Dominic.*

But they're not here surrounding me, drowning me with everything that makes them, *them.* I've been desperate to be in their company. But after Emerson went to see Dominic, of which he only told me after the fact, he said it might be best to take a breather for the week. He didn't want to risk Dominic seeing us and thinking we were moving on without him. Because there is no *without him.* Emerson said he would make things better, and I'm trying to give Dominic the space that he clearly needs, but I don't like any of this one bit.

Because what if he can't fix it?

What if we all have to go our separate ways, like we originally set the rules to? Would Emerson survive that? Because I know I wouldn't. The resentment toward Dom for calling this off would eat me alive if I were Em. But I'm not. And neither is Dominic. So, no matter how much I want to force his hand, I'm not going to make him love me.

Not wanting to go down this spiral for what feels like the hundredth time, I decide to finally get dressed in whatever I have lying on my bed—clean or not—and head out my door.

The only people who can pull me out of this funk are my parents.

After a drive across town, I pull into their driveway and I sit in my car for a moment, staring at my parents as they sit on their front porch swing. Laughing and thoroughly enjoying each other.

Once I climb out of the car, Mom's up and off the porch, speed walking toward me. The moment she wraps her arms around me and asks, "What's wrong, Liliana?" I feel myself break.

Well, I've been broken, but this is the sledgehammer to the already cracked glass that has been holding back the emotions. Horrible sobs are wracking my body, and my mom places her hands on my shoulders to pull me away from her, asking in a panicked tone, "Liliana, are you okay? What's happened? Are you hurt? Do we need to take you to the hospital?"

I shake my head, and between sobs, squeak out, "They can't fix a broken heart, so there's no point."

"Oh, sweetie..." She wraps me back up in a hug,

and my dad steps up and is at our sides, squeezing both of us in his arms too.

And I sit there and sob. I sob until I'm to the point of dry heaving, and my head has more of a heartbeat than my heart does.

Eventually, Mom manages to walk me over to the swing, and we both sit down. As she rubs my back, comforting me like she has my whole life, she whispers, "I'm here, honey. I'm here." She pauses a beat, then asks, "Who broke your heart, Liliana?" She has heat behind the question, and it brings a smile to my face. I clearly got the fire in my personality from her, and if anyone ever hurt us, well, she would be right there ready to go to bat for me, no matter what.

I've been so wrapped up in Dom and Emerson and my job that I haven't had the time to explain our whole situation to my mom, which is rare for me. She's my best friend, and it makes me feel even worse knowing I've kept this from her. But in that same breath, I didn't realize we were going to take whatever fun we were having to the next step.

Finally being able to get words out, I explain, "We—Dominic, Emerson, and I aren't together anymore..." I brace myself, waiting for a shocked expression to take over her face at the mention of the fact that the three of us are together. But it doesn't come. Instead, her eyes soften, and she nods in understanding.

"Is-is this a new thing?" she asks, and I nod my head, not wanting to speak because I know I'll just start crying again. "Well, I don't know what happened, and I know it's fresh right now, but I will say if your person is truly *yours*, they'll find their way back to you." She gives me a sad smile. "Even if that's two people."

[1] With my hands in my lap, picking my nails, I start to explain a little of the situation. "Emerson said something similar… and I still don't know if I believe him, but he's trying to get through to Dom."

"They've been friends for a long time, whatever it is, Emerson will get it through his head." I haven't said much, but somehow she knows it would be Emerson fixing the situation. That's who Emerson is—he fixes whatever needs to be fixed. And right now, that is Dominic Foster and that wounded heart of his.

My dad takes a seat beside my mom, placing his hand on her shoulder. "I'm just an old man at this point, but if those two boys have any sense about them, they wouldn't let someone as amazing as you go." His brows raise when my eyes meet his. "If they don't, daddy-o can still whoop some ass when I need to," he says as he flexes his biceps dramatically. I can't help it, a soft smile crawls across my face at my dad's antics.

I really start to laugh when my mom smacks his chest and rolls her eyes. I'm quick to add, "No ass beatings are needed—I promise." Unsurprisingly, I'm already feeling better. Just being here, with them, seems to have lifted some of the weight off of my chest just enough that it feels like I can breathe for the first time in three days. I knew my family was just what I needed.

But it only lasts another moment, as I watch my mom and dad look at one another. Tears gather in my

---

1.  Gunpowder & Lead - Miranda Lambert

eyes yet again, and I think to myself how badly I want the love that they have. I want to experience the love that shines through their eyes when they look at one another. I want the love that you don't have to question whether it will be there, even on your worst days. I want a lover who's a built-in best friend.

I don't just want it, I *need* it.

*And I fucking had it.*

I had it twice over. Until it blew up in my face. But what's love without some trials? Especially this early on. I know we can get through all of this at the end; Dom just needs to learn that it's okay to be afraid. It's okay to lean on the ones you love. To let them be part of the hard times. I'll give him a few more days, and after that it's going to be me annoying the shit out of him until he gets it through his thick skull that we love him, and that you can't hold love back because you're scared of losing people.

I decide right here and now that it's settled. Three days is enough. Enough time to wallow and drown myself in sorrows. Now it's time to pull myself up. Because when he does come back to us, *which he will*, he needs to see that I understand. I might be beyond pissed at him, but I understand. I understand *why* he's afraid. But I also need him to understand that courage is not defined by the lack of fear. But rather by the ability to act *despite* fear.

And that's what I tell myself, over and over again while I help my mom cook dinner for the three of us, like the old days. I leave their house that night feeling a lot lighter and a little more optimistic.

# CHAPTER 43
# IT'S OKAY TO BE AFRAID

**DOMINIC**

I've spent the better part of three days going over every single thing that's happened between Lil, Emerson, and I since Turks and Caicos. Hell, my train of thought has gone all the way back to the day I met Lil a little over a year ago, and Emerson freshman year. I've done my best to analyze every moment. Every laugh. Every argument. Every kiss. Every conversation had. And each time being around them has made me think of my dad.

Because he would have loved both of them.

And the fact that being with them, *falling* for them, made me think of the man I lost, made me terrified of losing them both, should have been sign enough that there was no turning back. But when the two people that have consumed my every thought and desire, made me forget the man I was positive I never would, well, it was the equivalent of every feeling I have pushed to the side slamming into me like a brick wall. Because I do love them. I love them with everything inside of me.

I love them so much that my dad dying is no longer the most important thing that's happened to me.

It's falling for them.

Emerson was right. Dad would be ashamed of the way I behaved.

Don't get me wrong, Em still deserved to get decked in the fucking mouth, but I honestly think that was his goal. He would never say anything like that to me unless he felt like he needed to. I know that much for certain.

I also know that Dad would have punched me in the face himself if he knew that I've been avoiding Mom for the past three days. She knows I'm not dead because I've sent her the occasional "I can't right now, Mom," but that's all I've given her. And she deserves more than that. Especially after I left her all alone the other day.

Which is exactly why I'm currently sitting on the edge of my bed, my thumb hovering over the call button on her contact information. Because I know if I have any chance of fixing all of this, she's where I need to start. There would be no me without her. She's been my constant through the storm, and I know that I won't be okay until I know she is.

"Jesus Christ, Dominic. It's just your mother. Get a grip," I mutter to myself before taking a deep breath and finally pressing the call button.

It rings and rings, and just when I think she's not going to pick up, the voice that's gotten me through my darkest days greets me. "Dominic?" There's what sounds like music playing in the background along with countless people talking around her. "Hold on, Sweetie. Let me get somewhere quiet."

She's out? Having fun? This week of all weeks. Now that I think about it, she did mention she was hanging out with her friends when I didn't answer her text the other day. I was too consumed with myself to think anything of it. But now that I have, it's… strange.

For years, all she did during this week every year was sit around the house and look at pictures of him. She'd tell endless stories about him. She'd let herself sit in the memory of him as long as she could. Then after a week, she'd pull herself together and move on with her life.

But now, she's going out with friends? When did that happen?

"Okay," she huffs. "Can you hear me okay?"

I can still faintly hear the music and the dull sounds of conversation, but it's not nearly as loud as before. "Yeah-yeah, Mom, I can hear you."

She doesn't waste time getting to what we both know is the point of this phone call. "Well, it's about time you called me."

I hang my head. "I know, Mom. I don't even know where to start. I'm sorry I've been avoiding you. It just —I—It all felt like too much. Everything with Emerson. With Liliana. With Dad." My voice cracks at the mention of him. "With *you*. God, Mom. I'm so so sorry. I can't believe I forgot. It will never happen—"

"Don't you dare apologize, Dominic Foster," she

scolds, and it catches me completely off guard. "I mean, yes, you can apologize for ignoring me. I'm your mother. You should never ignore me unless you're planning on surprising me with something. Preferably in the form of flowers. Ooo or a grandchild!" Her wild jump from flowers to a grandchild makes me huff a laugh. "But don't you apologize for one moment about the other day."

"But-but I forgot, Mom. I *forgot him.*" A small, single tear rolls down my cheek.

She's silent for a moment before she lets out a heavy sigh. "Dominic, my sweet boy. There was a time when your father's death consumed us. When the grief of his loss felt so big that neither of us were sure we would ever feel anything stronger. I lost my husband, my person. And you... you lost your father, the man who was a part of you. I don't blame either of us for feeling that way." *Well, fuck. So much for a single tear.* "But that feeling... that all-consuming feeling of grief and loss, it shouldn't be the strongest thing we feel in this life. He would want us to be happy. To be brave. To be bold. To be *loved*. There is nothing stronger than that, Sweetie. To be loved, to *love* with everything you have... *that's* the peak, Dom.

"Your dad would want that for us. He would want there to be more important things in your life than the fact that you lost a parent. I know I do." She sniffles softly on the other end of the line.

"I'm-I'm so afraid, Mom."

"And that's okay. It's okay to be afraid. But you wanna know what?"

The way she asks that reminds me of when I was a child. When she'd say, *"It's okay to be afraid, but you wanna know what? You are so, so brave, Dom."* The memory eases some of the pain in my chest. "What, Mom?"

"You have already gone through one of the hardest things you're ever going to face. And sure, loving someone, or *someones*," she mutters, "means there's a chance you will lose them, but think of the life you could have in the meantime. Think of the happiness, the smiles, the memories made. You could have a lifetime of memories, Dominic. Don't rob yourself of that just because you're afraid."

*You could have a lifetime of memories, Dominic. Don't rob yourself of that just because you're afraid.*

The words hit me so hard they may as well be branded on my skin. Because I know, from this moment on, I will never forget what she just said.

*Don't rob yourself of that just because you're afraid.*

"Is that what you've been doing? Creating memories?" I ask her.

I don't have to see her to know a slow smile is spreading across her face. "He wouldn't want us to be alone, Dominic. And I'm not. I have you. I have friends that love me. I'm rebuilding the life he would have wanted for me."

For the first time in three days, a true and genuine smile spreads across my face at the thought of my mother moving on from something so horrific. "We don't have to forget about what happened to us, Dominic. We can share him and his story with new loved ones. We don't have to forget about him. But we do have to feel *more*."

"I know, Mom. I know," I answer softly.

"Listen, I have to go, it's almost my turn for karaoke, but can you do me a favor?" A deep laugh rumbles in my chest. I should have known that's what she was doing. I gotta get my performance skills from somewhere.

"Anything, Mom."

"I was supposed to have a therapy session this afternoon with Dr. Miller. I won't be able to make it because, well, if I'm being honest the sangria has gotten away from me and I have about five more songs I'd like to sing. But the time is already booked. So, I want you to go."

I curl my face up at the thought. It's been years since I stopped going to therapy. I never felt like it was the right fit for me. "I dunno, Mom…"

"Just try. Go once, and see how you feel. You never know, it might make everything you're feeling a little bit more digestible."

She's right. I'm a different person now than I was five years ago. It couldn't hurt. Right? "Alright, Mom. I'll go."

"Perfect! I'll shoot Dr. Miller a text and let him know to expect you."

I smile to myself. "Alright, Mom. I love you. And… thank you. For *everything*."

"I'm always here, Sweetie. I love you."

Knowing she won't be the first to do so, I hang up, letting her get back to her day. Mom texts me the time and address of Dr. Miller's, and two hours later, I'm sitting on his couch, ready to word-vomit a lifetime's worth of bottled-up emotions in the span of sixty minutes.

But if this is what I need to do to prove to myself that I can be with them, that I can be worthy of everything they want to give me. Well, so be it.

# CHAPTER 44
# DEEPLY & IRREVOCABLY



As I'm walking out of my Friday afternoon broadcast journalism class my phone chimes in my pocket. I expect it to be another text from Lil asking if I've heard from Dominic, but when I pull it out I find a message from the man himself.

DOM

Can I see you?

Holy shit. This is the first time he's reached out to me since I left him sitting on the floor of his apartment Monday afternoon. We've seen one another all week at practice, and during our home game last night, but the exchanges have been brief and in no way personal.

I know he hasn't reached out to Lil either, considering she texts me twice a day asking about him. But she and I agreed to give him some time. He needs space to come to terms with whatever he's dealing with. We can't fix this for him. Regardless of how much we want to. He has to do it himself, before he can open that heart and soul of his up to anyone.

However, his time to come to terms with this was coming to an end, because I know both Lil and I are starting to feel beyond impatient about this entire thing.

Knowing that I'm right around the corner from the music building, which is where a decent amount of his sound engineering classes are held, including Friday afternoons, I message him back.

ME

I just got out of class. I'm around the corner from the music building. Can be there in 5

DOM

I think we should talk about this in private. Can I meet you at your house? It's closer to campus.

*Don't read into it, Emerson. Just because he wants to talk in private doesn't mean it's bad.*

ME

Meet you there in 15

I'm about to put my phone back in my pocket when I decide to say one more thing.

ME

I've really missed you, Dom

Three dots appear and reappear for what feels like forever before he finally replies.

DOM

I've really missed you too, baby.


*Baby.*

That one word is enough to jump start my heart and send me high-tailing across campus. More eager than ever to make it back to the house I've spent so much time missing him in.

I make it back to my house in record time, only as I approach my house I find Dominic's red F-150 parked in my driveway where he leans against the closed driver's side door, his arms folded over his broad chest, wearing a pair of black athletic shorts and a fitted white tee. The closer I get the more clearly I can make out his stoic expression. His dark brown eyes look as if he has a million and one things rolling around in his brain, and his jaw, covered in more stubble than it usually is, is clenched tight. He looks nothing like the Dominic Foster I've fallen in love with, and yet, I couldn't be more relieved to see him than I am now.

Pulling up to the curb, I don't waste any time shutting off my Jeep and climbing out. Making my way over to him, I give him a soft smile and say, "Didn't feel like letting me park in my own driveway?"

[1] The corners of his mouth lift, barely, and he drops his arms and pushes off his truck. "Been here a while," is his only response.

I stop in front of him, not sure what to do and wanting him to take the lead of whatever it is that's happening here. "I figured."

He nods to my door. "Come on. Let's go inside."

Dom follows behind me as I nervously unlock my front door and usher us inside. As soon as we're both standing in my living room I turn to him. "So?"

His eyes dance between mine as he takes a deep breath, running his hand over his cropped dark hair. Taking a deep breath he says, "I called Mom the other day."

I nod in understanding. "Okay."

"And I went to her standing therapy appointment on Wednesday."

My eyes momentarily widen in shock, but I try to school my expression. "Okay," I repeat.

"And then again yesterday. And this morning."

"Okay," I say for the third time.

Realizing I'm not going to say much until he does, he continues. "And between Mom and Dr. Miller, I-I learned a few things."

"And what did you learn?"

He takes in a deep breath. I watch as he clasps his shaky hands in front of him to nervously rub his palms together. I so badly want to reach out and grab them, but I stop myself, giving him the space to do this. "I

______________

1.  Kerosene - Vanish

learned that my dad dying shouldn't be the most important thing that happens in my life. I learned that he would want me to fill my life with love, and happiness, and laughter. I learned that pretending to be happy all the time, while I'm terrified on the inside, isn't healthy. I learned that there are better ways to deal with his loss, and I'm learning how to do that. All of this you probably already knew." He looks to me for confirmation.

"I did."

"Right. Well, there's one thing you may not know. Actually, you probably do, but I've definitely never said it to you."

He takes a large step toward me, and I swallow the ball in my throat. "And—" I clear my throat. "And what's that?"

"I figured this one out all on my own actually." His voice is softer now. Gentler. "I learned that I wouldn't have ran away if I didn't already know the truth."

Tears sting my eyes as I ask, "The truth?"

He takes two more steps forward so he's now standing toe-to-toe with me. I can feel his chest brush against mine each time one of us takes a breath. Tilting my head up ever so slightly, I look him in the eye as he says, "The truth is that I am so deeply and irrevocably in love with you, Emerson Baker." I can't help it. A broken sob spills from my lips, because I was starting to worry I'd never hear those words from him. "I have loved you for years," he continues. "You have become my person in every sense of the word. But now… now you are part of me. Forever embedded in my soul. And

I'm so sorry I ran out on you. I'm so sorry I tried to throw this all away because I was afraid." He raises his hands and holds my face between them, brushing away the stray tears that have fallen. *Fuck, I've turned into such a softy.* "I'm still afraid, if I'm being honest. But how fucking lucky am I to be afraid of loving and losing. But I won't be the reason I lose you, Emerson. I fucking love you, baby."

I don't lecture him. I don't scold him for leaving me. I don't force him to drag his apology out for any longer. Because I don't fucking care. Speaking those words doesn't interest me. The only thing I want to say to this man is, "I love you, Dominic. I love you with every part of me." He releases a deep breath and drops his forehead to mine. "Don't ever leave me again," I say softly.

He gently shakes his head. "Never again." The moment those two words come out of his mouth his lips are on mine. Dominic kisses me as if I'm breathing life back into him for the first time in days. I'm part of his soul now, and it's a place I always want to be.

We kiss one another in the middle of my living room for what feels like an eternity until he finally pulls his mouth from mine. "I'm so proud of you," I tell him.

"I'm proud of myself too," he answers. "Can we go get my girl back now?"

I smile ear to ear. "*Our* girl?"

"Our girl," he repeats

I place one more quick kiss on his lips. "Let's go."

Twenty minutes later we're standing in Lil's hallway, pounding on her front door. I'm about to yell her name again when the door next to us opens. "If the two of you don't shut the fuck up, I swear to god. Charlie is *sleeping.*"

"Shit. Sorry, G," Dom says quietly.

"Hey, do you know where Lil is?" I ask her.

She rolls her eyes dramatically and looks at Dom. "She left for *your* apartment ten minutes ago. Probably to rip you a new asshole if I have to guess."

Dom and I both smile.

*That's our girl.*

Gigi narrows her eyes in our direction. "Now go fix whatever you broke or her yelling at you is going to be the least of your worries."

She mocks a fist at us, but I have the sneaking suspicion that, even at all of five-foot-two, she won't hesitate to hold up her end of the bargain.

In no time at all, Dom and I are racing up the stairwell to his apartment, only to find his front door thrown open with Lil standing in the middle of his living room, spinning in small circles. Sadness marring her features.

The two of us walk in, Dom slightly in front of me. It takes her a minute to notice us, but when she does she turns to fully face us, tears in her eyes. "I-I totally came here to yell at you for taking so long. But I got here and you weren't here. So, I used my key to let myself in so I could wait for you, and I found… Dom, your plants."

I take a second to look around. She's right. In the week he's been away, it looks like his plants haven't seen an ounce of sunlight or water. His pride and joys now hang limp, void of the things they need to survive. As if they were mimicking that of their owner.

Staying in my spot, I watch as Dom takes a few cautious steps in her direction. "What can I say, Honey. Didn't have much energy to give them life when I felt like I was barely surviving myself." She sniffles and wipes her nose but doesn't say anything. "You wanna yell at me now?"

She shakes her head vigorously.

"Then can I go first?" he asks.

Lil takes a deep breath, and I watch with pride as she stands a little taller. "Yeah. You can go first."

# CHAPTER 45
# NEVER CAN HAPPEN AGAIN

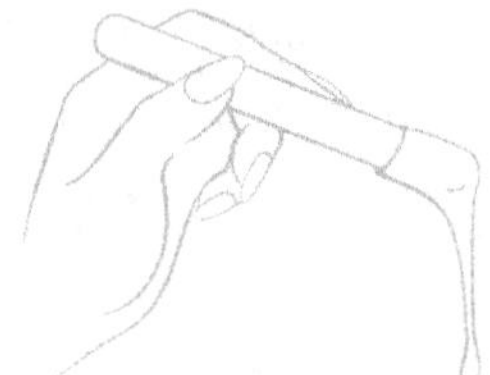

**LILIANA**

The shock of walking into Dom's apartment and seeing his plants in the state that they are in was... scary. I think I was spinning in circles, gasping every time my eyes landed on a new plant that was wilted and holding on for dear life. My hand covers my mouth, and tears are lining my eyes, even as Dom takes a couple more cautious steps toward me. He's looking at me like I'm a rabid animal, but I feel I should be looking at *him* that way. I'm so afraid he's going to take off again, leaving me with this broken, torn-up heart, all alone with a panicked Emerson trying to fix everything.

As our eyes lock, I'm still waiting for him to tell me what's been going on. But all I can imagine is how bad off he must have been this past week to let things get this bad.

*This isn't the Dominic Foster I know.*

[1] Then, Dom finally speaks, and I suddenly feel like I can't breathe all over again. "I love you, Liliana Campos." A smile spreads across his whole face, and my eyes glance to Emerson to find him wearing a similar one. "I've loved you for longer than I think I even knew. There's no loving you quietly. I want to shout it from the rooftops, and from here on out, that's exactly what I'm going to do."

*Shouting it from the rooftops.*

That's exactly what I wanted. But, why do I want him to keep loving me the way he has been? How they *both* have been. Nothing they do is over the top when it comes to showing love. But it's what I've grown to love about them. The little things that keep me going every day, the things that make my life so much easier.

Emerson and Dominic make my life easier.

*It's just easy to love them.*

I can't help it. I stand, momentarily frozen. The feeling of shock rendering me incapable of moving. I feel bad not immediately saying it back to him, but I also need him to know what he did this past week hurt me. It hurt me bad. "If we agree to this, Dominic"—I motion my hands in a circle to all of us—"you *cannot* do this again. You cannot leave us *again*... I will not survive it." I told myself I wasn't going to break down in front of him, and I've held it together, but my voice is starting to crack.

He takes a couple of steps to reach me finally and holds his arms out to me. I step into his embrace and

---

1.  No Friendship - Daniel Di Angelo

inhale the woodsy scent that is Dominic Foster. His strong arms hold me to him, and I wrap mine around his waist.

There's no way I won't cry if I say this to his face, so I murmur the words I've been keeping to myself for so long, "I love you, Dominic." I feel him suck in a sharp breath before the two of us fully relax into one another's hold. We stand there holding one another before I pull away, and we both hold out our arms closest to Emerson, inviting him into the hug. "Come on, Em," Dom jokes, but Emerson looks at him with a seriously scary look that I'm very glad I'm not on the receiving end of.

"That ass is mine tonight after all the shit you pulled the past week. We almost lost Lil, Dominic. I don't ever want to see her like that again. If it had fixed things, I would've handed her my heart to stomp on, I would have, but the only thing she wanted was you... And I couldn't give her that."

I grab both of Emerson's hands to try to break a little bit of the tension between Dom and him. I know they made up before they got here, but I think seeing me upset all over again got Emerson back into his feelings.

So I say the one thing I know will ease his pain. "Emerson, I wouldn't have made it through this if it wasn't for you... Or my parents." I don't miss the slight wince from both of them at the mention of my parents, knowing they're going to have to face them both sooner rather than later. But I won't mention the fact that they seem to be completely at ease with the fact that their daughter is dating two men. For now, I'll enjoy watching them squirm. "You make everything seem so simple. Loving you is simple. *Easy*. Like I should have been doing it from the first moment I met you. I love you, Emerson." I place a soft kiss on his lips and take a second to breathe him in.

"I love you too, Darlin'. More than you'll ever know." Emerson gives me a panty-melting smirk and places another quick kiss on my lips.

"I'm sorry… to both of you," Dom says apprehensively. "I had to work through that on my own. And Lil, I told Emerson this earlier, but I've started therapy. I should've done this a long time ago; fixing myself should've been what I was focusing on, but it wasn't. I was hiding behind what I thought was normal behavior after losing a parent. But then again, I don't know if my younger self would have been open to fixing himself. I was in a tunnel with blinders on when it came to my father and how I handled his death. But I now know that was still no excuse. I hurt both of you with how I reacted, and for that, I truly am sorry. I'm going to do better. I'm going to *be* better—for both of you."

I spot the tear running down Emerson's cheek and tell Dom, "I'm proud of you for recognizing your wrongs and not just living in the self-pity. We want what's best for you, Dom. We will show you what it feels like to love."

Em adds, "We'll love you so hard, and fly so high… *together*."

Reaching for him, I hold his face in my hand and swipe away a tear as it escapes his eye. A slow smile spreads across his face as his eyes dance between

Emerson and I. A look of peace settles over his features before he says, "Our very own *hat trick*."

THE END.

**Want a little more of Lil, Dom, & Emerson two years later?**

**Scan the QR code below or click here, and it will take you to the extended epilogue.**

# ACKNOWLEDGMENTS

## SIERRA

When we created Lil as a side character in Strong Side, it was almost immediately a no-brainer that she needed her own book. Then came Jackson's little brother Emerson, who was destined to be at her side. And then… well, if there was an Emerson, there had to be a Dominic. These three were the reason we decided to make this into an entire series and not just one book.

They quite literally stole the show.

I have fallen in love with the three of them, and I can say without a shadow of a doubt that this trio has changed who I am as a writer. And now here we are… at the end of book three, ready to start the fourth and final book. It's actually insane.

To Tilly… as always, thank you for running the show. This book, and my life, would be nowhere without you. I'll be forever grateful that I get to take part in all of your wild ideas. You continue to push me out of my comfort zone, make me laugh endlessly, and are the best partner I could have asked for.

Sadie. Sarge. Our saving grace. I've said it before, and I'll say it again. This entire series wouldn't have happened without you. You're why we're here. And you're a big part of the reason we've even made it this far. Not just in this series, but as authors. I am so thankful to have met you and that I can call you, not only my editor, but my friend.

Nicole! You didn't have to help us with this book, but you did purely out of the kindness of your heart. And my god, are we thankful. This book is polished and shined to perfection, and you are a huge part of the reason why (just ask Sadie)!

To our ARC readers, there are not enough words to express how much we appreciate each and every one of you.

Lemmy... Luna Literary Management is making waves and going places, I just know it! So, on your rise to stardom, thank you for being there for us.

To the rest of our readers, I hope you are as obsessed with our new character, Gigi, as we are. Because boy oh boy, do we have a real tear-jerker in store for you.

*Love you all x a million, Sierra*


## TILLY

Book three of Palm University is in the books, and this one was truly a fever dream to write. These three have been in our heads for so long, and Lil was actually the one who made both of us think "damn, I want this to be a series..." and here we are about to head into the fourth and last book of Palm University.

Sierra, I don't know how you've stuck out writing

with me this long, but you've got one more in ya, right?! The chapter titles of Lil's POV, I thought would send you into stroke territory, but you took 'em in stride lol. ILYSM, and I'm so thankful for you and the friendship we've grown over the past year!

To you, the readers, we truly can't thank you enough. These books are so far out from what we both originally were writing, but we're starting to dive further into the contemporary worlds. We wouldn't be here without every one of you!

Sarge, Sarge, Sarge, where would we be without you? (I know where, actually, and it's my personal hell having to use any other editor besides you) so there's no escaping me at this point. Thank you for all you do for us, and I know you don't think so, but you're truly a life-changing editor (the best out there imo), and I'm so thankful we crossed paths when we did. ILYSM my little boomer (she's not actually a boomer, just hates technology lol)

Lemmy at Luna Literary Management, thank you for taking on book three so last minute yet again lol. This time, we at least had it pretty much done and weren't running around like chickens with our heads cut off. You're an angel and truly are out to help us indie authors.

ARC readers, thank you so much for taking the chance on us and our third co-written book babe! Releases would be horrible if it weren't for you all!

Book four, I'm sure you can guess it…
*Drum roll, please!*

Gigi and the baseball man from the bar that one night—Ford!

Volleyball player single mom x Baseball player that'll win over everyone's hearts.

*XOXO, Tilly <3*

# ALSO BY S.R. CLARK AND TILLY RIDGE

**Triple Threat: A Reverse Harem Halloween**

**Short Story**

Triple Threat is my newsletter freebie! This follows the triplets at the end of Strong Side! It's skull face painted triplets with one lucky gal, making all her fantasies come to life! Triple Threat can only be found in S.R. Clark's newsletter or Tilly's newsletter.

**Tropes you'll find in Triple Threat:**

MFMM

Triplets

Bringing her fantasy to life

Primal play

Cuck boyfirend

College romance

**Strong Side: An MM College Sand Volleyball Romance-
Book One in Palm University**

## <u>Available on Kindle Unlimited!</u>

Clayton Aldrich is everything I'm not, and everything I despise. He's rich, never had to work for anything a day in his perfect life, is the pretty boy on campus, and is always doing everything he can to get under my skin. But when we're forced to become partners, I have no choice but to set my predisposed feelings for him aside. However, as the season progresses, two things become abundantly clear. There's more to Clay than meets the eye, and my feelings for him don't appear to be so black and white.

My entire life has been mapped out for me since the day I was born. Major in business, dedicate every moment of spare time to volleyball, win the Olympics, and when the time comes, take over my father's company. And the only part of that plan that didn't make my skin crawl was playing the sport I loved. Rockwell Campos, the infuriatingly cynical man I feel an inexplicable draw toward whenever he's near, thinks he has me all figured out. But, when we unexpectedly become partners our senior year, Rocky shows me there's more to life than sacrificing who you are and who you want to be in order to be part of a family. Sometimes the families we find are stronger than the ones born in blood.

The two of us may share the same goal, but the question remains… is our strong side, strong enough?

Dive into book two of Palm University!

**Side Out: An MM College Sand Volleyball Romance- Book Two in Palm University**

### <u>Available on Kindle Unlimited!</u>

I knew from the moment I saw him moving into the house down the street. I knew that a man like Jackson Baker was going to be the one to turn my world upside down. I saw it coming a mile away. But what I didn't see coming was finding out he is one of my patients at my brand new job. I know it's wrong. I know it's against the rules. I know it could destroy the white picket fence that's being thrust upon me, and yet... chasing Jackson Baker is a high I can't seem to quit.

Theodore Young. My neighbor. My Athletic Trainer. My every waking thought. My addiction. I should be spending my fifth year at Palm University--my second chance at the perfect senior year-- making memories with friends, being the team captain everyone is counting on, and setting myself up for a career after college, and yet, the only thing I can think about is him. Watching him. Touching him. Kissing him. He's everywhere and nowhere all at once. But it's not enough. Because he's not mine and I know I can't have him. And yet, whenever I look into his eyes I know...

**THE GAME HAS ONLY JUST BEGUN.**

****Side Out is an MM forbidden lovers, college romance. It will be book two in the Palm University Series.****

**Triple Threat: A Reverse Harem Halloween**

**Short Story**

**Triple Threat is free** when you sign up for our newsletters. It's triplets and one lucky gal on Halloween night that is in this world of Palm University.

**Dangerously Safe: A McDermott Empire Novel (Book One)**

### <u>Available now on Kindle Unlimited and Amazon.</u>

### <u>Listen to the audiobook here.</u>

Harper Hayes is an introverted, curvy, curly-haired, coffee-loving bookstore owner. And now, she's officially all alone. She has no family, friends, or life outside her parent's bookstore. She's made it her mission to live the rest of her life alone, not willing to take the risk of loving and losing. Again. That is until the three giant men, cloaked in danger, came to steal her in the night.

Ronan, Mac, and Finn, leaders of the Irish Mafia in New York City, have been given the impossible task of keeping her safe. Little did they know that their lives would be changed forever the night they walked into the bookstore. They quickly realize they'd give anything to keep her safe. But from whom, and at what cost?

**Dangerously Kept: A McDermott Empire Novel (Book Two)**

**<u>Available now on Kindle Unlimited and Amazon.</u>**

**<u>Listen to the audiobook here.</u>**

After finally allowing herself to love again, Harper wakes up miles away from the men that have kept her safe, and in the hands of those determined to destroy her from the inside out. Unsure of whether or not she can rely on Ronan, Mac, and Finn to save her, Harper must find the strength to free herself. But if she does, how is she meant to face what comes next?

With a world of unknowns hanging in the balance, Ronan, Mac, and Finn know two things for certain. They are willing to burn the world down around them to get her back, and just as they own her heart, she owns theirs. They just need to figure out how to keep her.

**The Prices We Pay: A Vittori Enterprises Novel (Book One)**

As CEO of Vittori Enterprises, Luca Vittori has made his fair share of enemies both in the corporate world and in less . . . legal business. But with the help of his teammates, best friends, and family—Enzo, Dante, and Sebastian—no one has been a worthy opponent. That is, until they're forced to hire a new employee in the tempting form of Josephine Jenkins. The four of them rapidly have to decide whether or not their feelings for Josephine and one another are worth the risk.

**Will love destroy everything they've built, or will it make it stronger?**

Josephine Jenkins is a woman who truly marches to the beat of her own drum. After running from memories better left buried, Joe made a life for herself in New York City. She finally had the life she always wanted for herself. Everything was perfect . . . until she took a job at Vittori Enterprises. Upon her arrival, she quickly learns the four men who captured her attention have more going on behind closed doors than they lead on, and if she isn't careful, they could be the end of the life she so carefully crafted.

**Masked & Mine: Jump right into book two here! I know that cliffhanger is brutal**

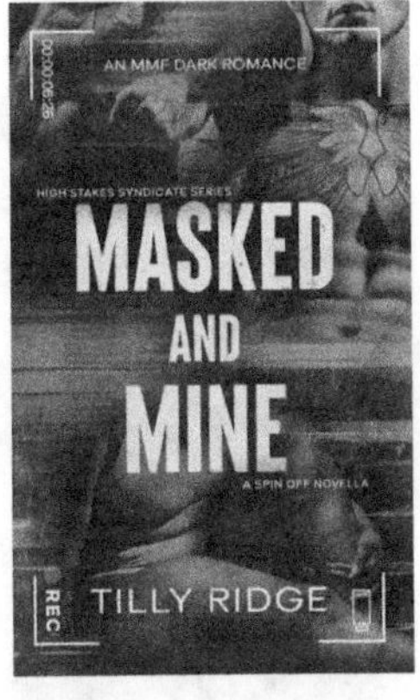

Available on Kindle Unlimited!

**Tropes you'll find in Masked & Mine:**

MMF

Masked COD cosplayers

Cam performers

Fast burn

Collaboration turned obsession

Plus-size d0mme

Somnophïïia

C ň C / Dũb-Con

Breeding w/out pregnancy

Pegging

<u>Playing for the Dark & Taking Over the Dark</u>: **A Completed Duet: A Why Choose Mafia Sports Romance**

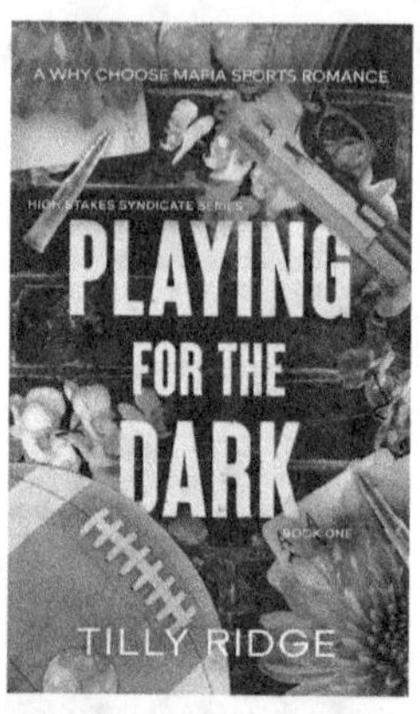

Available on Kindle Unlimited!

**Tropes you'll find in the duet:**

MMFM

Mafia

football

She falls in love with her Stalker

Degradation

PCOS rep

Bi awakenings

Strong heroine

Organ harvesting but for good

Somnophilia

**Contentment: A MMF Rockstar Romance**

Available on Kindle Unlimited!

**Tropes you'll find in Contentment:**

What you'll find in here:

MMF

Rockstars X Hairdresser

"We shouldn't be doing this"

Pansexual awakening X 2

Forbidden relationship

Only one bed

A wiener dog along for the ride

Fast burn

**Play the Game: A Dark Why Choose Romance**

Available on Kindle Unlimited!

Available on audio

**Tropes you'll find in Play the Game:**

Gaming Buddies turned COD Masked fantasy

COD Orgy Party

MMMFF

Sharing his wife with their friends

Hotwifing

comes in his pants

Breath Play

Knife + Blood Play

All the praise + degradation

Size kink

Age gap

# ABOUT S.R. CLARK

S.R. Clark is an indie author who lives in West Virginia with her husband, toddler, and hound dog. She has a soft spot for characters who live unapologetically for themselves and who will lay down their lives for the ones they love. When she's not writing, she loves getting lost in a good book, cooking/baking, and exploring with her family.

Be the first to hear about updates, sneak peeks, and much more with my newsletter!

# ABOUT TILLY RIDGE

Tilly Ridge is a romance author who resides in the middle of nowhere, Kentucky, with her husband, two kiddos, and two dogs. She loves to dabble in a variety of romance topics, themes, and subgenres, but you'll typically find her writing in the dark and polyamory sections of the shelves. Tilly can be easily identified by the pink slush clutched in one hand while her laptop is in the other, ready to write whenever the mood—or the character—strikes! In her free time, she enjoys playing sand volleyball in her local rec league. But what she finds most exciting is her podcast, Releasing Romance, where she shares her knowledge and experience about indie publishing, often bringing on guests to discuss the ins and outs of indie publishing from different professional points of view! This podcast is a passion project of Tilly's as she finds true joy in helping and educating others in a way that is easy to understand.

Join Tilly's readers group for exclusive BTS, art drops, first looks at pretty much anything, and even chapter-by-chapter releases of her ongoing projects at: Tilly's Thots

The newsletter is where the fun is, and maybe even a free ebook will hit your inbox after—along with a first look at the big news.

Find everything you'll need to stay connected at https://www.tillyridgeauthor.com/links